STARS

ISBN 978-1-909122-68-0

"There are thousands of non-Jews who saved Jews, risking their lives with boundless self-sacrifice in Warsaw Their names will forever remain engraved in our memories - heroes who saved thousands of humans from destruction in the fight against the greatest enemy of the human race."

Emanuel Ringelblum, Warsaw, Poland 1942

For the countless silent heroes whose courageous deeds are absent from the pages of history and in loving memory of my grandfather

Mark Lishak
1901 - 1986

STARS

ANTONY LISHAK

A story of friendship, courage
and small, precious victories.

Acorn Digital Press

MAP OF WARSAW

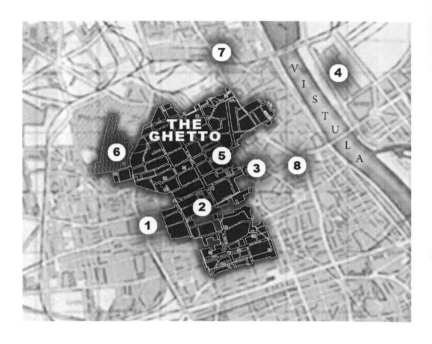

1. Korczak's first orphanage

2. The site of Korczak's second orphanage

3. The Great Synagogue

4. The Zoo

5. The Sztuka Café

6. The Jewish Cemetery

7. Tragutta Park

8. Pilsudski Square

SOME HISTORICAL BACKGROUND

After Adolf Hitler became leader of Germany in 1933, his Nazi party passed hundreds of anti-Jewish laws. As a result Jews were not allowed to vote, own property, become doctors, enter parks, possess bicycles, attend cinemas, and much more. Non-Jews were discouraged from using Jewish shops and school children were taught that Jews were an inferior species. Physical attacks on Jews were commonplace; their synagogues were destroyed, businesses were boycotted and property routinely confiscated.

Fuelled by the desire to rule all of Europe, Hitler's army invaded neighbouring countries, and by the summer of 1939 had occupied Austria and Czechoslovakia. On September 1st they attacked Poland, provoking World War II. Hitler's anti-Jewish laws were enforced in every country he invaded. As a result millions of Europe's Jews, from communities that had been established for many hundreds of years, were moved into small, heavily guarded areas cut off from the rest of the population. The largest of these ghettos was in Warsaw where over 400,000 Jews were crammed into an area of 3.5 square miles – practically all of them perished. By the end of the war, six million Jews had been killed in the ghettos and death camps created by the Nazis.

Sadly, many other people in Europe shared Hitler's anti-Jewish views. The climate of fear created by the Nazis' ruthless brutality prevented those who opposed his policies from doing anything to save Jewish lives, which makes the courage and bravery of non-Jews such as Jan and Antonina Zabinski all the more remarkable.

CONTENTS

Part One

July 1939

ONE

Suddenly Mr Rokus tore the Polish flag off the wall and wrapped it round his neck like a cape. He was a huge walrus of a man with a crazy grey moustache that seemed to dissect his face. He clumsily stepped onto his chair, lumbered up onto the desk and, glaring down at his pupils, wielded a long wooden ruler high above his head like a sword.

The man was a lunatic – it was the one thing that practically everyone in the class agreed on.

Then he threw his head back and bellowed out the Polish National Anthem at the top of his voice – *"Poland is still alive! As long as we still breathe, whatever our enemies have stolen from us, we will recapture with our sabres!"*. By the time he'd completed all six verses, a handful of patriotic students had joined him, dutifully standing to attention behind their desks – a suitably strange way to end a maths lesson in such peculiar times.

It was the last week of the summer term, when even the strictest of teachers would traditionally let their hair down. Last year Mr Rokus had even brought in sets of playing cards and taught the class how to play poker. All the end-of-year exams had been taken and classroom chat should have been dominated by the approaching holidays. But there was no sense of excitement in the school, only dread. Instead of looking forward to long lazy days by the beach, the class just felt fear and uncertainty. No one even knew for sure if there would still be a school waiting for them when they returned after the holidays.

"I lost my brother, twenty years ago, in the war against the Bolsheviks," proclaimed Mr Rokus, still standing on his desk. "The waters of The Vistula ran red with the blood of brave Poles who sacrificed their lives for the freedom we now enjoy. And no one is going to take it from us – not even that trumped-up little maniac in Berlin!"

The lunchtime bell eased the tension in the room and they watched their teacher slowly climb down from his desk and slump back into his seat. Eventually Mr Rokus lifted his head up from his hands and mumbled "class dismissed".

As the boys filed past, one of them stopped and rested a hand on the man's shoulder. "Don't worry, Uncle Kurt, our army is ready for anything Hitler might be planning."

Marcus Tenenbaum's powerful build made him look much older than his twelve years. It also ensured that none of the senior boys bullied him, which was the usual fate of children whose parents taught in the school – his father, Simon, was the head of science. Mr Rokus had known Marcus since he was a toddler. He had worked alongside Simon Tenenbaum for many years and was a frequent guest at his dinner table. He looked up and forced a smile at the boy, "you're right, of course".

"Is he OK?" asked Stefan Zabinski, Marcus' best friend, who had been waiting for him in the corridor.

"Yes, he's fine," Marcus replied. "He gets like that sometimes. My father said he even burst into song in the staffroom, once."

"Did anyone else join in?"

"Most people left the room in embarrassment," said Marcus as they joined the stream of fellow pupils that flowed towards the playground. "Apparently he had just downed half a bottle of vodka, and my father had to use the remaining half to calm him down."

Poland's summers weren't particularly long but they were invariably hot and in recent weeks the skies over Warsaw had been an unbroken expanse of blue. For a moment, the warmth of the afternoon threatened to dampen the tensions that had become a regular feature of playground life – but only for a moment.

"It's Jews versus Poles," declared Pawel thrusting the battered leather football into Marcus' face. "And what about you?" he snapped, turning to Stefan. "What side will you play on, Jew-lover? Are you one of us or one of them?"

As the smallest boy in his year, whose best friend happened to be a Jew, Stefan was used to being picked on – especially by Pawel, but he stood his ground. Having the strongest boy in the school as an ally had its advantages – nobody risked a one-on-one fight with Marcus, not even Pawel.

"You'd better play on their side, Stef," said Marcus. "If they're going to have any chance of beating us, they'll need at least one player who knows what he's doing!"

Recently football had become hugely important in Poland. The fabulous Hungarian team were about to play in Warsaw; it was the only topic that overshadowed talk of invasion.

Marcus gathered his team of fellow Jews together in a huddle. "Take my advice and forget the ball," he warned. "War is about to break out in this playground!" He'd swapped his mother tongue for Yiddish, the language that was known to Jews across Europe; half of the group were Germans, recently forced to flee their homeland, who barely knew a word of Polish. He had no idea how good their football skills were, although if his instincts were correct, right now the ability to kick a ball properly was the last thing they'd need.

TWO

Zamenhof High School blended seamlessly into its surroundings – most people walked past without noticing it. Only the wave of children that ebbed and flowed through the entrance made it any different from the other buildings on the street. The tight, square courtyard that doubled as a playground was set so far back that even when it was full, no significant sound reached the outside world. But today a large crowd of lunchtime office workers had gathered by the school gate, curiously peeping through the wrought iron bars. There appeared to be some sort of riot going on…

It was Shlomo who struck the first blow, which surprised no one (apart from the owner of the nose that cracked under the force of his fist). Marcus had made him goalkeeper, but it took barely a minute for him to join the attack. From then on the ball became a bystander. Pawel grabbed Shlomo's neck and grappled him to the ground, rolling onto the cobbles. Within seconds they were ringed by baying teammates, urging them both to go in for the kill. Suddenly a heavy boot crashed into one of the fighters' backs. Nobody cared whether the foot inside was Polish, Jewish or German; it was the spark that lit the touch paper and the whole place exploded.

Playground brawls regularly flared up; with so much fury in the world outside it was inevitable that some would seep into the school. But these were normally brief affairs, easily quelled by merely prising the scuffling combatants apart, leaving nothing more than damaged pride. But this was no regular punch-up; it was all-out battle.

Shocked teachers looked down from the staffroom window at the raging sea of fists and feet below.

"It's bedlam."

"There's nothing we can do – let them sort it out themselves."

"But someone's going to get seriously hurt down there!"

Marcus' father couldn't afford to be a spectator. He bolted out of the staffroom and ran downstairs, followed by a handful of equally worried colleagues. He had no doubt that his son would be in the centre of all the chaos.

Close up, the fury of the battle was all the more shocking – you could smell the anger. The air was thick with screams of pain and cries of abuse. Fallen fighters from both sides groaned helplessly on the ground, many being ruthlessly kicked further into submission. All around were the scarred, snarling faces of demented children mercilessly pulling at each other's mouths, eyes and ears.

For a few dreadful seconds Simon Tenenbaum and his fellow teachers froze. Where should they go? The battle had no centre; violence was everywhere. But they couldn't just stand there, it was carnage. Something had to be done or a child could be killed.

"Stop this right now!" yelled a teacher as he snatched at the collar of the nearest boy.

"Back off at once!" cried a second, trying to restrain the arms of another child.

"That's quite enough," screamed Simon, forcing his hand between two bodies locked together in a fearsome crush.

Even though the boys were aware there were teachers in the thick of the fray, the momentum of hatred was unstoppable.

Suddenly a loud crack split the air. Someone had a gun – this was going to get even worse. Then another shot echoed around the courtyard. Gradually fists were lowered and grips loosened.

Instinctively teachers and pupils alike glanced around to see who had been killed.

"Everyone against the wall now!" barked an angry voice from the corner of the courtyard. It was a police officer – the uprising had clearly caused the alarm to be raised outside. As Simon Tenenbaum watched the students of his beloved school retreat to the perimeter of the playground, he was torn between relief and despair. Although calm had returned to this corner of Warsaw, if friends and classmates could turn on each other so savagely, what hope was there for the rest of Poland?

THREE

The most seriously injured boys were shepherded away by the school nurse while everyone else was herded into the main hall to await their fate. They were tightly corralled in the middle of the room, ringed by a few strategically placed teachers to prevent the fight from reigniting. To Marcus' relief, his father was not one of these guards – the longer he could put off that confrontation the better.

"Did you get hurt?" Marcus whispered to Stefan.

"Not really. I managed to back away when everything kicked off? What about you?"

"Just this," he said showing off his swollen knuckles. "That's what happens if you hit people too hard with bare fists!"

"Did you get Pawel?" asked Stefan.

"I didn't need to," he replied. "Shlomo-the-Bull practically killed him!"

"Will you two stop mumbling?" barked a nearby teacher striding towards them. "You've been told to remain silent... Oh look who it is!"

Marcus froze and stared straight ahead.

"Young Mr Tenenbaum; the son of one our most esteemed teachers." It was Mr Richter – or 'the rat' as he was known amongst students. He was practically blind. Although a pair of glasses hung on a chain around his neck, he rarely wore them. He preferred to thrust himself into the face of anyone he spoke to. Marcus could smell the stale pipe tobacco on his grey moustache. "A fine example you're setting to the other boys, I must say!" Then he turned his attention to Stefan. "And here we have little Zabinski, the loyal sidekick – how predictable!" He placed himself between the two boys, leaning forward so that they could feel his breath on their ears. "You two represent all that is wrong with this country," he whispered. "Oil and water, dogs and cats, Poles and Jews – they don't belong together."

"Gangway!"

All eyes quickly turned towards the heavy oak doors at the rear of the hall. A procession of stern-looking men swept towards the stage, led by the vast familiar figure of Principal Bartel.

"Your attention please!" His deep voice boomed out from behind the dense forest of a beard that masked half of his face – no child had ever seen his lips move. He was wearing the shiny top hat that only accompanied bad news. Beside him stood one of the Polish policemen who had restored peace to the playground, and behind them was a line of senior teachers, including Marcus' father.

The Principal cast his steely gaze over the hall, which was heaving as the entire school population had been summoned to hear his pronouncement. "This is a devastating day in our history. Never before has there been cause for outside agencies to enter the premises to restore order." Then he turned his glare towards the cluster of culprits. "You have brought shame and dishonour upon this place." The raw emotion in his words sent a chill through the room; this was no routine speech about upholding the good name of the school – he clearly meant what he was saying. "And it pains me to inform you that the punishment for such an offence has been taken out of my hands. As I am unable to guarantee that such a disturbance will not reoccur, the police have taken it upon themselves to pass sentence on us all." His voice started to falter; to the boys it was as if their own father was up there, struggling to maintain his composure. "To ensure that public order is maintained, the end of term has been brought forward three days and the school is to be closed forthwith." Slowly removing his monocle, he dabbed his eye with a handkerchief and forced himself to carry on. "I beseech you to convey my regrets to your families for the inevitable inconvenience this will cause. I fear that we live in dark times where everyone is forced to suffer for the deeds of the minority – I pray that the world comes to its senses before it is too late." Then he abruptly stepped down from the stage and passed through the silent throng, his head bowed low, a broken man.

Nobody knew how to react. While it was certainly distressing to watch their principal crumble so dramatically, they had just been given an early summer holiday – surely that was good.

The vice principal stepped forward. "You are required to gather all your possessions and leave the premises immediately," he announced. "Please do this as calmly as possible. I look forward to seeing you all when we reconvene at the start of the next school year."

It was obvious that the school staff were just as surprised as the students. A few stared at each other in shock while most joined the steady stream of stunned children flowing out of the hall. Even the teachers who had been guarding the guilty children abandoned their posts.

"What do we do now?" Stefan asked Marcus. But his friend didn't have an answer.

"Go to the zoo." Both boys turned to see the severe face of Marcus' father glaring down at them. "I will collect you from there," he said to his son. "Now get your things and leave."

FOUR

Stefan and Marcus weren't the only boys crossing the huge iron bridge that spanned the Vistula (the river that dissected Warsaw) and led to the zoo. Ever since the monkey house had been renovated, it had become the most popular attraction in the city and was the obvious place to spend an unexpectedly free afternoon.

"My mum'll kill me," said Shlomo. "She hates it when I fight at school."

"Stop complaining," replied Marcus. "At least you can pretend you had nothing to do with it. You can't do that when your father's a teacher!"

"Oh yeah," he snapped, pointing to his swollen eye. "Then how am I going to explain this – say I fell down the stairs?"

"Convince her that you punched yourself on purpose," joked Stefan. "Say that you wanted to be the first panda to appear in a zoo outside China!"

"Very funny," replied Shlomo, waving his fist in mock anger. "And how would you like to be the second?"

"Well at least neither of you will be facing your parents till later," Stefan added. Marcus and Shlomo couldn't dispute that – while for every other boy the zoo was the ideal place to avoid the inevitable barrage of questions that awaited them at home, it was anything but that for Stefan. This was the last place in Warsaw he would have chosen to hide from his parents – he lived there.

As they approached the main entrance they noticed a group of Zamenhof boys clustered in front of the gate.

"Hi Stef…"

"We're here, Stefan, just like you told us…"

"Yeah, we've been waiting for ages. What kept you?"

None of them were Stefan's friends; most wouldn't have even acknowledge him if their paths crossed in the school corridor. But merely telling the staff at the ticket kiosk that they were "guests of Stefan Zabinski" wasn't enough to gain free entrance to the zoo.

"Are all these boys with you, Stefan?" asked the woman at the arched window.

How Stefan longed to say he'd never seen them before in his life, waltz past with Marcus and Shlomo and then turn to see their shocked faces through the bars of the gate. "Yes, Magdala, they're all my friends," he called out. "School finished early today, so I invited them here for the afternoon."

A heavy arm wrapped itself round Stefan's shoulders, pulling him close in. "You see – we said we were with Stef!" It was Pawel, being his most arrogant. "Come on, Stef, show us that giraffe you've been talking about all morning," he announced, striding forward with his human free-pass clasped firmly to his side.

The fixed grin on Stefan's face masked his embarrassment – he felt as if he'd bought the approval of the school's biggest bully for a few zlotys and the whole world was laughing at him.

"You're scum," growled Shlomo when they'd entered the zoo. "If there weren't so many people here I'd knock the rest of your teeth out right now!"

"Shut your big Jewish mouth," Pawel snarled, as his tongue explored the gap that Shlomo's fist had created earlier on. "It'll be feeding time at the monkey house soon, why don't you run along and get some lunch?"

As Pawel led his gang of loyal followers into the body of the zoo, Marcus and Stefan had to restrain their enraged friend, who was clearly prepared to resume his attack no matter how many people were watching.

"Let's go to the seals," said Stefan, walking towards the path that led to the corner of the zoo furthest away from the zoo director's official residence – his home. "If we get there in time the keepers will let us feed them..."

"You're home early, young man." Stefan froze – so much for remaining invisible all afternoon. "I trust there is a perfectly good reason why half of Zamenhof High School has descended upon the zoo today?" It was his mother.

"Good afternoon, Mrs Zabinski," said Shlomo.

"Hello Auntie Antonina," added Marcus. "How are you?"

"Well?" Stefan's mother persisted, determinedly ignoring all attempts to distract her attention. "What do you have to say for yourself?"

Stefan knew that hiding the truth from his mother was a very risky business – she rarely asked questions that she didn't already know the answer to. Besides, Marcus' father was bound to have phoned the zoo by now. She'd probably been waiting by the entrance ever since.

"There was a disturbance at the school and..."

"Riot, I heard," she interrupted. "Apparently the army had to break it up."

"No," said Shlomo. "It was only the police with guns..."

"Oh, that's alright then!" Stefan flinched at his mother's harsh tone. "What a silly woman I am – I must be over reacting. How foolish to be concerned when I hear that bullets were fired in my son's school playground. And there I was thinking that school was for learning... how naïve of me! I should have realised that lessons are only there to keep children occupied until it's their turn to go outside to be shot at!"

"Really, Mum, it wasn't that bad..."

"Wasn't that bad?!" she snapped. "The police close your school because its students can't be prevented from trying to murder each other and you say 'it wasn't that bad'? Tell me, how much worse can it get?"

"Stefan didn't really have anything to do with it, Auntie," said Marcus. "He tried to get out of the way."

"It was basically a fight between Jews and Poles that hate us," added Shlomo. "Stefan would never get involved in that."

Antonina Zabinski folded her arms, finding it hard to maintain her stern look of disapproval. Her son was the last person to start a fight, that's for sure – there wasn't a violent bone in his body. And there was something very heartening about the sight of him wedged between these two Jewish giants. Slowly her anger began to fade. "You'd better come up to the villa," she said. "That eye of yours could do with a good soaking!"

As the boys followed Stefan's mother towards the private part of the zoo grounds, Bonnie and Clyde, the peacocks that nested by the nearby pond, approached them. Shlomo immediately stopped in his tracks. "Don't worry," Stefan reassured his friend. "They only attack if you go near their nest."

"And anyone who did that would deserve what they'd get!" added his mother, holding the front door open for the boys to walk through.

"I've just had a brilliant idea," whispered Stefan to his friends as his mother went into the kitchen.

FIVE

The boys re-emerged from the villa patched up like soldiers returning from battle. Shlomo's head was half-covered in tightly wrapped bandages to protect his wounded eye and Marcus' knuckles were so heavily strapped that it looked like he was wearing a boxing glove. Mrs Zabinski's homemade biscuits had revived their spirits, and they were eager to hear what Stefan was planning. He might be the last person you'd want to defend you in a fight, but he was the world's best schemer.

"Right," he said, "we're off to the lion house."

"Why?" asked Shlomo.

"It's the highest part of the zoo – you can see everything from there."

"Again, why?" Shlomo repeated, but Stefan didn't want to waste any more time and started to lead the way.

"Trust him, he knows what he's doing" said Marcus.

The zoo had been Stefan's home since he was a baby, and he treated it like his own back garden. None of the grounds were out-of-bounds for him and he happily stepped over the low walls designed to keep the general public at bay. Marcus, who had grown up with Stefan, was used to walking through the behind-the-scenes areas where keepers prepared food and sick animals were tended to, but Shlomo felt like an intruder; everyone treated Stefan like one of their own and most of them knew Marcus' name.

Stefan led them into a huge dingy workshop where a line of vehicles stood in various states of disrepair. He paused by a table, grabbed a rectangular black box that had a long black strap and slung it over his shoulder. "What's that for Stef?" asked Marcus, but his friend was too deep in his own world to reply.

Next they cut through a barn that housed a mountain of straw and along a corridor that was lined with cages. Each area had its own distinct smell that occasionally made Shlomo gag; he was amazed at how much went on at the zoo beyond the public gaze.

Eventually they arrived at the foot of a steep staircase.

"Nearly there," Stefan called, bolting up the steps two at a time. "Hardly anyone ever comes up here; it's my favourite part of the whole zoo." By the time the others had joined him, Stefan was peering through the binoculars that hung from a hook on the wall, gazing out at the zoo through a small square opening. "I told you that you could see everything from up here," he said. Stefan handed the binoculars to his friends. "There he is. Can you spot him – right next to the seals?"

"Who?" asked Marcus.

"Pawel, of course!"

"Don't tell me we came all this way just to get a bird's eye view of the biggest wally in Warsaw!" said Shlomo.

"How else were we going to locate him?" said Stefan. "It would have taken ages to find him down there and he'd probably have seen us coming anyway."

"What is the point of all this, Stef?" asked Marcus. "It's not as if we've got a giant pea-shooter or something up here..."

"Where are the lions?" asked Shlomo.

"Pardon?"

"The lions – you said we were going to the lion house."

"Where do you think they are?" said Stefan, pointing downwards out of the hole in the wall. "We're inside the very top of their mountain, see?"

"Wow!" Shlomo's eyes nearly popped out of their sockets as he looked at the creatures that seemed to be just an arm's length away.

"What's the plan Stef?" Marcus persisted.

Stefan smiled at his friend and slid the strap of the black box off his shoulder. "My dad brought this back from New York when he was a guest at the opening of the Central Park Zoo."

"What does it do?"

"Just watch this!" He flicked a switch on the top of the box, turned a dial on its side and held it to his ear. "Otto, Otto, are you there? This is Grumpy – come in please, do you read me?"

"Why Grumpy?" asked Shlomo.

"It's a nickname," said Marcus. "Long story… don't bother asking…"

"And who's Otto?"

"The head keeper… the guy who looks after the elephants… everyone knows him!"

"Oh yeah, I remember."

"Otto, is that you?" continued Stefan. "Great! I have a favour to ask!" He quickly sketched the outline of his plan into the mouthpiece – "Group of boys, Zamenhof High School uniforms, next to the seals, Bonnie, Clyde, eggs… thanks, over and out." He threw the strap back over his shoulder and thrust his head through the hole in the wall. "Right, guys, now watch this!"

You didn't need a pair of binoculars to spot Otto – even from the lookout post at the top of the lion mountain, the sight of his massive frame bustling through the crowd was unmistakeable. The boys watched as he made his way around the seal pond and approached the cluster of Zamenhof blazers. They were clearly stunned when Otto wrapped his arms around some shoulders and leant into the centre of the group. He was a great performer; Stefan was sure that he could convince Pawel and his gang of anything.

In fact, things happened much faster than Stefan expected. "Quick, we've got to run – now!" he announced, charging towards the stairs. "We've got to get there before Pawel!"

"Where?" asked Shlomo.

"The pond, of course, you dummy," said Marcus following close behind his friend. "What have you got in that head of yours, a brain or a bowl of chicken soup?"

The three boys retraced the route that had led them to the lion house and re-emerged from the workshop in no time. Stefan signalled his friends to be quiet and motioned them to follow him to a hiding place behind some nearby bushes that provided a perfect view of the pond while still being far enough away not to alarm Clyde.

"What did Otto tell them?" whispered Marcus.

"Probably the old 'count-the-eggs-for-me?' trick. He's done it before to kids who misbehave in the zoo – he says that he needs to check on the peacock eggs, but he's very busy right now, and that if they go and count them for him he'll pay them 5 zlotys."

"And people fall for that?" said Shlomo.

"Well you would for sure!" replied Marcus. "You'd swim across the Vistula completely naked if someone paid you for it!"

"True," conceded his friend.

"Shush, they're coming," snapped Stefan, urging his friends to crouch even lower as the gang of Zamenhof boys came into view. "Not a noise from now on."

"You lot wait here," Pawel ordered his companions. "That fat bloke asked me to do this."

"But what about that money?"

"If you're lucky I'll share it out when he gives it to me – meanwhile just shut up and stay there!"

There was a rustling sound from the side of the pond – Clyde's head appeared above the reeds and he let out a short piercing scream. This seemed to please Pawel, obviously unaware of the danger he was in, as he didn't have to waste any time searching for the nest. Certain that he was about to earn the easiest zlotys in his life, he marched confidently towards his target.

"Look out, Pav, he looks mean!"

"Don't be stupid. That guy warned us they'd kick up a fuss but they'd be far too scared to do anything else!"

At first Clyde seemed to be shocked that any human would be bold enough to get so close and by the time his defensive instincts kicked in, Pawel was practically next to him. There was a sudden flash of blue and in an instant the intruder was thrown to the ground. He struggled to get to his feet, frantically trying to pull the bird from his throat. His screams alerted Stefan's mother, who came charging out of the villa. Pawel managed to get to his feet and stumble away from his attacker, but he'd lost his bearings and in his confusion, staggered towards the pond. Before Mrs Zabinski could get anywhere near, Clyde had resumed his onslaught, sending his petrified victim flying backwards into the water.

Eventually she managed to shoo the peacock away. "What were you trying to do?" she said reaching out to pull Pawel onto dry land.

"Count the eggs," he replied.

"What?!" exclaimed Mrs Zabinski, letting go of her grip and sending him back in the pond for his second dipping. "Fools like you don't deserve to be helped!" and she stormed back to the villa.

"Stop laughing, you morons!" barked Pawel as he trudged past his friends towards the exit. But it was impossible for either them, or the three onlookers behind the hedge, to do anything else.

"It couldn't have worked out any better," said Stefan breathlessly.

"You're mother's a legend!" gasped Shlomo.

"Here, take my hand..." Marcus lifted Stefan from the ground, "...er, no, think I'll let you swim some more!" and dropped him back down again.

They felt like they'd be laughing forever...

"I hope none of you had anything to do with that!"

...they were wrong. Suddenly the two stern faces of Stefan and Marcus' fathers glared down at them over the hedge.

"I think I'd better get going," said Shlomo, briskly getting to his feet. "My mum will probably be wondering where I am..." Then he turned and charged down the driveway leaving his friends to whatever fate lay in store for them.

SIX

"You two just wait here in the hall. Don't dare move from this spot!" snapped Stefan's father, opening the door that led to his office.

"We'll deal with you both later," added Marcus' father, following his friend into the room.

Their mothers always said the boys were merely younger versions of their fathers. Jan Zabinski was a thin, bespectacled figure whose receding hairline made him appear much older than his forty years. Simon Tenenbaum was only a few months younger than Jan, but could easily have been mistaken for someone half that age. He had been a keen amateur boxer in his youth, and although he had hung up his competitive gloves when Marcus was born, he still looked capable of stepping into the ring. Both of them were Zamenhof boys as well – they'd met on their very first day, became the firmest of friends and went on to study science together at Warsaw University. Although there were many friendships that bridged Poland's Jewish and non-Jewish communities, few were as close as Jan and Simon's.

"His going to kill me," whispered Stefan to his friend. "I've never seen him so angry!"

"Well at least you'll only get a tongue lashing," Marcus replied. "Have you seen the size of my father's fists?!"

"Oh do stop being so dramatic, you two," said Stefan's mother, emerging from the kitchen doorway with some more biscuits.

"Both of you know that your fathers would never so much as harm a hair on your heads. Now take one of these and stop talking such nonsense."

The Zabinski villa was more than just a family home. Although Jan and his parents were the only people who actually lived there, it was a constant hive of activity. Sick animals were often brought there to be examined. Antonina possessed as wide a range of veterinary skills as her husband – Jan always said that his wife could genuinely sense what the animals were feeling. Vast amounts of medical equipment were stored in the spacious villa basement. And at the centre of all this was Helda, the housekeeper. She had worked at the zoo for as long as anyone could recall, but no one could remember the last time she smiled. It wasn't even clear whether she actually liked animals. But despite her grouchy disposition she was an efficient organiser and fiercely loyal to the Zabinskis.

The boys had been standing in the hallway for so long that they were genuinely startled when the office door eventually swung open.

"Come," commanded Stefan's father.

Whenever Marcus entered this room he was reminded of his own father's study with its shelves lined with books and glass jars of dead animals. The only difference between the rooms was the contents of the jars; instead of Mr Zabinski's birds, snakes and rodents, at his home there were only insects, mostly beetles – hundreds of them.

"I have heard the whole story," announced Stefan's father, "the fight, the police, the guns and Principal Bartel's sad announcement. Is there anything else either of you wish to add?"

Stefan and Marcus looked at each other – they could have tried shifting the blame onto Pawel and his friends, but there was little point; their punishment had probably already been decided.

"Fair enough," said Stefan's father. "You both have the right to remain silent. But I have one question to ask you, young man," he leant forward and stared coldly into his son's eyes. "Pray tell me, since when have you been able to use one of these?" He suddenly produced the two-way radio from behind his back and held it up by its strap; it must have fallen on the ground when they were discovered behind the hedge.

Marcus and Stefan dared to relax and shared a cautious smile. But the stern looks on their fathers' faces indicated that it was dangerous to celebrate too much.

"And you're going to have to think of a convincing explanation for that new white glove you're wearing by the time you get home," said Marcus' father pointing to his son's hand. "And don't try the falling-down-the-stairs routine; your mother would never swallow that one!"

"Happily both your hands seem to still be in perfect working order," said Stefan's father to his son, placing the radio on his desk. "It means you can put in an hour's extra piano practice before supper."

"Yes father."

No further words were exchanged. The boys knew that the day's events had neither been forgiven or forgotten; just that there were clearly far more important matters on their fathers' minds.

SEVEN

It didn't feel like the start of the holidays. Although the weather was perfect for swimming, the banks of the Vistula, where Warsaw's children traditionally met on warm summer days, remained empty. Like most of their friends, Stefan and Marcus had been forbidden from leaving their homes. This was more out of shame than as a punishment; as none of the other schools in the city had broken up yet, any child of their age would be easily identified as a Zamenhof boy, bringing disgrace upon their families.

Stefan's curfew was lifted on Saturday morning. "You've got ten minutes to get ready," called his father. "Then we'll be off!"

"Where are we going?"

"Where do you think?"

Stefan hoped that the correct answer to that question was "to the Tenenbaums", but after three days confined in the house he didn't want to tempt fate. Apart from the kitchen and his bedroom, the only other room he'd been allowed in was the lounge, to practice the piano. Even the courtyard, where his pet pig, Hercules, lived, was deemed out of bounds in case he was spotted by a member of the public.

As Stefan skipped down the stairs he could smell the fumes from the car idling outside on the drive. Although he knew that his parents were waiting for him, he couldn't resist dashing through the lounge and out into the yard, to say hello to Hercules and pay a quick visit to his pet rat, Apollo, who lived in a network of wire cages and tunnels beside the sty.

"Hurry up," called his father as Stefan finally climbed into the car. "They'll be closing the roads soon!"

"Why?"

"Think about what's happening in Warsaw today."

Stefan finished buttoning up his jacket and gasped – how could he have forgotten? "The Hungarians!"

"Yes the Hungarians!" repeated his mother. "One football match brings the entire city to a standstill – craziness! And why are you wearing that jacket? It's a boiling hot day."

"I'm a bit cold," replied her son.

"You must be ill," she responded.

"Maybe."

It was obvious from the moment they left the zoo grounds that the journey was going to take much longer than normal. The steady stream of excited pedestrians overflowed onto the road on the bridge that spanned The Vistula. Only a few were lucky enough to have tickets for the match, but the stadium was next to a favourite picnic spot and everyone wanted to be as close to the action as possible.

The colours of the national flag were everywhere. Red and white ribbons were wrapped round lampposts and woven into plaits on little girls' heads – Stefan even saw a dog whose collar had been similarly decorated.

"All this, just for a football match!" exclaimed Stefan's mother disapprovingly.

"It's got very little to do with football," insisted her husband. "We've played Hungary many times before…"

"Nine, to be precise," Stefan interrupted. "And we've lost every one!"

"…thank you for that, Mr Statistician! As I was saying, this is more to do with timing than football. It's probably the last game that will be played by a free Poland."

"You shouldn't talk like that, Jan," scolded his wife. "It's not right to be so pessimistic."

Stefan's father drove on in silence – he didn't have the heart for yet another discussion about the impending war; and why should he let Hitler spoil such a perfect Polish summer's day?

By the time the car had crawled across the bridge, the traffic was practically at a standstill. "You can drive the rest of the way, Antonina. We'll walk from here – come on Stefan."

"But aren't we going to Marcus' house?" asked his son.

"Eventually, yes."

"What do you mean, 'eventually'?" Antonina was clearly as surprised as Stefan by this sudden announcement.

"We're meeting Simon at The Sztuka first. We've got a few matters to discuss."

"Why can't you discuss them in their house?" asked his wife. But Jan had already got out and was opening the door for his son to join him.

"We'll see you later," he said, walking away from the car.

Gripping tightly to his jacket collar, Stefan had to chase to keep up with his father. "Is Marcus going to be there as well?"

"What do you think?" replied his father.

EIGHT

Leszno Street, where The Café Sztuka was situated, ran through the heart of what was known as Warsaw's Jewish District; an area of the city where Jews had lived for over five hundred years. Most of non-Jewish Warsaw looked upon the place with bewilderment. Although there were no physical boundaries to this area, its borders were widely known and clearly defined. Just like every other Jewish area in Europe, day to day life in this part of Warsaw was mainly conducted in Yiddish, a unique Jewish language. It was so widely used that many Jews struggled to hold a conversation in their country's mother tongue.

Jews made up about a third of Warsaw's one million inhabitants. Some had moved across the river to Praga, the suburb that housed the zoo, but most still lived in "The Old Town", as its residents liked to call it. Lonia Tenenbaum, Marcus' mother, had tried to persuade her husband to swap the hectic lifestyle of the Jewish District for Praga's more tranquil atmosphere, but Simon couldn't break the emotional bonds that tied him to the area. His grandfather had been a master watchmaker who, like many of Warsaw's Jews, had arrived with nothing and succeeded in growing a thriving business that had helped gain wide respect for the family name. Although he had eventually agreed to move a few streets to the north into a house that his grandfather would have referred to as a "palace", that was as far as Marcus's father was willing to go.

Jan Zabinski was unusual amongst Warsaw's non-Jews in that he had grown up in this part of the city and understood what made its community so vibrant. He was even familiar with the frequently heated debates between religious and non-religious Jews, and was comfortable with the outspoken way that people expressed their opinions here; where many saw this as coarse and unsophisticated, he considered it to be refreshingly direct and honest.

As it was Saturday, the day that Jews didn't work, the streets were much quieter than usual. Although as Jan and Stefan approached the café, they could tell from the clamour of raised voices leaking onto the street, it was going to be as difficult as ever to find an empty table. By the time Marcus and his father had joined them in the café, Jan had already had to fend off two stern requests for the chairs they'd been reserving. It seemed that they had arrived just in time as the place was starting to get very crowded.

"Are you cold, Stefan?" asked Marcus' father as he ordered some tea from a passing waiter. "You're the only person here wearing a winter coat!"

"He's a *mashugana!*" said Jan, which made Simon smile. It always amused him to hear his friend sprinkle some Yiddish into the conversation – and the word for "crazy person" was one of his favourites.

As the drinks arrived the two fathers slipped quickly into what clearly was a resumed conversation, most likely the one they had started in the zoo three days earlier. Within seconds they were muttering animatedly to each other, completely ignoring the boys.

To begin with Stefan and Marcus tried to follow their fathers' discussion, but after a while they lost interest and soon had no idea what they were talking about. Every now and then a familiar word like beetle, millipede or scorpion would leap out at them, but on the whole the adult chatter swept over them like a swarm of locust.

Boredom descended and their milkshakes drained dry. Soon they were reduced to sucking hard and loud through their straws in an attempt to finish off the dregs at the bottom of their glasses.

"Do you have to do that?" snapped Marcus' father. "It's really rather rude."

"Sorry father."

For a moment Marcus thought that now he had won his fathers' attention their glasses would be refilled, but he was wrong. The two men quickly resumed their conversation, as if their sons were invisible. That's rather rude, thought Marcus – although he dare not say it.

The café was brimming with people now, and Marcus and Stefan seemed to be the only children there. Surly, stone-faced waiters bustled between the tables, coldly depositing drinks as if their customers were unwelcome guests. The smoke-filled atmosphere was heavy with barked orders for extra coffee or more cake. The cacophony of sound had spiralled so high that only those who shouted could be heard – so everybody did.

An ever-growing huddle of people stood at the counter sipping their drinks while elbowing themselves an extra inch of space. There was an edge to the atmosphere, reminiscent of the tension in the boys' playground, a few days earlier. An outsider would have thought that violence and chaos was threatening to engulf this popular Warsaw café, and that a seething mass of people, each jealously guarding their own selfish world, was condemning themselves to a hell built on misery and discomfort. But they would be wrong. The truth was that the entire room was united by a single purpose and it was the vacant piano in the corner of the room that bound them together.

Suddenly the boys' empty glasses were whipped away. "More drinks?" snarled the waiter. He was quite an old man; much greyer than either of the boys' fathers.

"Not just now, thank you," Stefan's father replied.

"Not just now?" mimicked the waiter. "I have paying customers standing up who would kill to have your table, and you say 'not just now'? You have been staring at your empty cups for too long, my friends. If you want to stay – pay! If not, there is a bench in the park outside where you can sit and chat."

Stefan froze. He noticed the cold stone stare in his father's eyes that preceded an outburst of anger that usually started with "do you know who I am…?" Luckily so did Marcus' father.

"It's ok, Jan, I'll get this. Two more teas, please."

"Poppa…" pleaded Marcus.

"Oh very well, and one more vanilla milkshake… with two straws." The boys shrugged; well it was better than nothing. The old waiter mumbled to himself and turned away.

"What do you say to Mr Tenenbaum?" asked Stefan's father.

"Thank you, sir."

"You're very welcome. And make sure that greedy son of mine doesn't drink more than his fair share."

"And no slurping sounds," added Marcus' father raising his finger to his lips. Clearly their conversation had been put on hold once more. "The maestro has just arrived."

NINE

A hush had descended on the café, and the sound of scraping chairs peppered the air as everyone turned to face the corner of the room where the piano stood. Tense faces that had been locked in fierce debate were now calm and expectant. The thin familiar figure of Wladyslaw Szpilman edged his way towards the piano and meekly smiled at his waiting audience. He slowly folded his jacket and neatly stored it on the floor under the stool.

Without a word of introduction his fingers started to stroke the keys and, within a heartbeat, the magic began. The music, like an enchanted potion, wafted over the room, gently soothing the troubled souls of all who inhaled it.

Recently Jewish refugees desperate to escape the terror that had been unleashed upon them by Hitler in neighbouring Germany had swelled the population of Warsaw, in the broken heart of Europe. Marcus and Stefan had heard about the German synagogues that had been destroyed by angry mobs and of sacred Torah scrolls being burnt in the streets. They knew about that terrible night, the previous November, when a wave of violent attacks had destroyed practically every Jewish-owned shop in Germany, leaving barely a single pane of glass unbroken. A boy from Berlin, who had recently joined their school, had even told them about a huge bonfire of "un-German" Jewish books that their teachers had lit in the middle of their playground. They were also aware of how flimsy the frequently heard adult promise that "it would never happen in Poland" was – no matter how hard you force a smile, it's impossible to hide fear from your eyes.

In a world that was being starved of beauty, the people in the café eagerly gorged themselves on Szpilman's music. They were entranced. Some had come to escape – knowing the sound would lighten the burden of anguish they carried with them each day. Others came to remember, letting the notes transport them back to more carefree days. To some the music allowed them to feel happy again, without the shadow of guilt, and to others it was the only place they could find peace.

But to Stefan it was suddenly the perfect opportunity to let Marcus see something truly amazing; the plan had been to show it to him in the privacy of his own home, but this was even better.

The bedlam that had ruled a little earlier had now been replaced by an eerie stillness – the entire room appeared to be hypnotised. Stefan took a sip of the milkshake, which seemed to have appeared in front of them from nowhere, and nodded at his friend, beckoning him to follow. Their fathers were totally focused on the music. It was now perfectly safe to make his move.

Clutching the top of his jacket, he slid off his chair and slowly edged towards the corner of the room where Szpilman was playing. Intrigued, Marcus shadowed him as they carved a route between the tables. Eventually they got to the performance area, silently sat on the floor and leant lightly against the back of the piano. Deftly, Stefan slid his hand inside his coat. After a moment's fumbling a white furry nose poked out, enquiringly sniffing the air – then a head. Marcus quickly caught on to what his friend was doing and leant forward to help and together the boys coaxed out Apollo, Stefan's pet white rat.

The café erupted into an explosion of applause; Szpilman had finished his first piece. By now the audience were so wrapped up in the music that the boys could have been handling a giant cobra and they still wouldn't have been discovered. They were experts in invisibility amongst adults, and having spent so much of their lives in each other's company, a twin-like telepathy had grown between them.

The applause dwindled and the room was filled again with the expectant silence that always preceded Szpilman's playing. By now Stefan had placed Apollo on a tiny wooden ridge at the back of the piano.

When the music started the boys instinctively smiled at each other. It was Beethoven's *Moonlight Sonata* – the party-piece that Stefan was often urged to perform at the musical gatherings his parents regularly hosted at the zoo.

"Just watch this," whispered Stefan. "It won't take long."

Marcus had no doubt that he was about to witness something incredible. As well as being a brilliant pianist, his friend's rapport with animals was legendary.

"Look – it's started!" whispered Stefan.

Szpilman's magic slowly began to work on Apollo. Gradually the rat stood up onto its hind legs and began to gently sway to the music, as if it was dancing. When it was practically vertical Stefan held the tip of his finger above its nose. Soon the rat was mimicking Stefan's movements exactly – he was playing the animal like a puppeteer. Finally, transfixed on his master's finger, Apollo spun round – Warsaw's very first rodent ballerina.

"How did you teach it to do that?" asked Marcus as they made their way back to their table.

"I didn't really have to," replied Stefan. "A few weeks ago I just placed it on top of my piano while I was practicing and it suddenly started to do this all by itself. I reckon the vibration of the sound goes straight through its body and sends him into a trance." The boys climbed back onto their chairs in the certain knowledge that their absence had not even been noticed.

TEN

Instead of taking the tram back to the Tenenbaums' house the boys' fathers decided to walk through Traugutta Park – the park where the big match stadium was. They had never seen the place so crowded before. The normally empty lawns, with their criss-cross pattern of formal paths, were covered with picnicking families. There was still an hour before the match kicked off and the sound of singing and cheering could be heard from the stadium, which was shielded from view by the Forest of Fire, a dense wooded area that dominated the centre of the park, famous for the vivid kaleidoscope of oranges and reds it became in the autumn. It also had the best climbing trees in Warsaw.

"How long are we staying?" Marcus asked his father.

"Not too long, your mother will be preparing tea."

"Have we got time to go to the forest?"

"Please!" added Stefan.

Their fathers knew what the boys really wanted to do; the stadium would be visible from the tops of the tallest trees in the forest, how could they deny their sons at least a peek?

"I can't see why not," said Marcus' father. "Unless you have any objections, Jan?"

Stefan's father nodded his approval. "We'll be waiting on this bench," he said. "But make sure you're back within half an hour." The boys turned to make their way to the forest. "And please take your jacket off, Stefan. That rat must be gasping for air by now!"

Stefan stopped in his tracks. "How did you know?"

"The smell, of course," replied his father, who was clearly not at all cross with his son. "A zookeeper's sense of smell is almost as keen as his animals' – your mother and I both knew you had it from the moment you got in the car this morning," he said taking the jacket from his son and laying it beside him on the bench. "And mind you don't lose him," he added. "A tame creature like that wouldn't survive a single night in the wild."

As the boys zigzagged their way between the picnickers, Stefan held Apollo up to his friend's nose. "Can you smell anything?"

"No," Marcus assured him. "I can't smell a thing."

Then he pressed it hard against his own nose. "Nor can I," he confirmed.

Apollo was soon alert and immediately clambered up onto Stefan's shoulder, his favourite place to view the world from. "He's like Bruno."

"Who?" asked Marcus.

"My father," Stefan replied.

"You're father's not called Bruno…"

"No, dunderhead, Bruno – the oldest brown bear in the zoo. My father says bears have the best sense of smell in the world, hundreds of thousands times better than humans."

"Really?"

"Oh yes," Stefan insisted with the authority that only someone who lives amongst animals could muster. "In the wild they can sniff out a dead carcass from over 20 miles away. Next time you visit, I'll show you how huge his nose is – apparently in every second of every day it knows exactly where every other creature in the zoo is."

"Wow," Marcus had no idea if this was correct but he knew better than to question the son of Jan Zabinski, the world famous zoologist.

The bright afternoon light struggled to filter through the forest's leafy awning. The air was much cooler under its shade, and the sound of the excited picnickers on the lawn suddenly dampened into to a low dull hum. It was practically silent as the boys made their way further into the forest, and they revelled in the shared thrill of nervous apprehension. Stefan could feel Apollo nestling closer into his neck.

"Do you know why there are so many types of tree in here?" asked Stefan.

"No," replied his friend, "but I'm sure you're going to tell me."

Stefan ignored the hint of sarcasm in Marcus' voice. "It's because this is not a natural forest. It was built by hand, out of samples of trees taken from all over Poland. My father told me that…"

"Come on, brain-box!" interrupted Marcus, dashing ahead towards a particularly high tree with large low-lying branches. "I reckon this one will give us a view of the pitch."

"It's an oak," called Stefan. "It's one of the oldest trees in here."

"I don't care if it's been grown from the hairs of Hitler's moustache," he said as he hauled himself onto the first branch, "Let's climb it."

Stefan gently lifted Apollo off his shoulder. "You'll be safer in here," he whispered as he slipped him inside his shirt pocket.

Marcus fearlessly treated the branches like a giant staircase, reminding Stefan of the monkeys in the zoo, who were as sure-footed in a tree as they were on ground. "You took your time!" he joked as Stefan finally reached the huge round branch he had chosen to stop at. "You can just about see the stadium from here. It looks like a giant bagel with a green hole in the middle!"

Stefan turned his head gingerly to take a look, but was far too shaky to appreciate the view. They'd climbed so high that the markings on the pitch were indistinguishable, and the crowd was just a blur. He crouched down, slowly straddling the branch, lent back against the trunk of the tree and started to breathe more easily. Marcus joined him and they stared out over the sparkling Vistula that lay below them like a giant blue snake basking in the sun. "I can see the zoo!" called Marcus. Stefan fixed his gaze across the shimmering river, careful not to look down – he was still rather nervous, even though the leaves on the branches below masked his view of the ground. "Isn't that your house over there?"

The tree they had chosen to climb turned out to be the perfect vantage point from which to view the zoo. Stefan could clearly identify the elephant house, the polar bear enclosure, the seal pond and the giraffe barn. And, sure enough, at the eastern edge of the complex, was their villa. "Yes," said Stefan.

"What's that beam of light coming out of the roof?" asked Marcus. "It looks like some sort of spot light."

"It's probably the star – it must be reflecting the sun," replied Stefan.

"What star?"

"The one that's embedded in the wall of our villa. Haven't you ever seen it before? It's just like the stars you Jews put on your synagogues."

"A Star of David – how did it get there?"

"Mother says it's a sort of 'thank you' to the people who gave money for the building of the zoo many years ago. I think a lot of it was donated by Jews."

"It's probably the only Jewish star in Warsaw on a non-Jewish building," said Marcus.

"Well it's definitely the only star in Warsaw that shines when the sun's out," added Stefan.

"You dirty Jewish pig!"

The boys froze.

"You filthy, rotten, evil Jew!" It was coming from the ground below them. "You are responsible for all this! You and your fellow Christ-killers! You have brought this on yourselves and now we're all going to suffer because of it!"

Through the branches the boys could see a crouching figure, wearing the heavy dark clothing of a religious Jew, cowering at the foot of the tree surrounded by three men. His *kippah* had been knocked to the ground as he desperately tried to fend off a barrage of kicks and punches.

"We all hate you! The whole world hates you! The sooner Hitler finishes you off the better!"

The boys looked at each other, utterly helpless. They were well used to hearing such anti-Jewish comments in their school playground, but this was the first time they had heard adults use such language.

"Stop it – stop it! You're crazy! Leave me alone!" The old Jewish man pleaded with his attackers but there was nobody around to help. "May The Almighty punish you for this!"

"Don't waste your breath, old man," snapped one of the attackers as he kicked out. "Your God is not going to save you. Not now, not ever!"

ELEVEN

"What shall we do?" murmured Stefan, Marcus was too angry to answer.

"What's he doing now?" barked a voice from below. "What is he saying?"

The old man was coiled up into a ball on the ground, holding his recovered *kippah* on top of his head with one hand and clinging tightly onto his bent knees with the other. His three attackers had momentarily stepped back and looked on aghast.

"He is praying," whispered Marcus. "It's the Shema – the most important prayer there is – every Jew knows it."

"It's some sort of spell!" said one of the men.

"Careful, he might turn us into stone!" quipped another.

"Or send a bolt of lightning to strike us down…"

"Maybe the earth will open up and swallow us…"

"Come on, old man. Do your worst…"

"You'll have to speak up if you want your God to hear you!"

Stefan heard a sharp snap coming from where Marcus was sitting. Before he could say anything a chunk of branch hurtled to the ground. Then a whisper from Marcus, "Stay close to the trunk, don't move."

"What was that?" The three men instinctively looked up.

"His magic is working," said one of the men with genuine dread in his voice.

As if fuelled by fear, the attackers resumed their assault with even more vigour.

Certain now that the leaves and branches of the oak tree were masking them, both boys started to send a volley of broken branches onto the heads of the thugs below. The bewildered men looked up – straight to where the boys were lying. "Don't even twitch," whispered Marcus.

Stefan felt like a giant stick insect merging into the bark of the tree. He knew that as long as they didn't move there was no way they could been seen– especially as the last thing these men would expect to see above them were two twelve year old boys. The old man's prayers were louder now and infused with energy.

"This is madness!" said one of the men in panic.

"He must be some sort of witch…"

Suddenly Stefan felt his friend slide away from him, moving further out along the branch. "Grab my knees," he whispered. "Hold them tight – I'm going for the big one!"

"I'm off…" said one of the attackers.

"Don't be mad," yelled his companion. "You're not going to let a little old Jew frighten you…"

Then an almighty crack above their heads made them look up just in time to see the clump of branches before it crashed down on top of them. It was the final straw – the three men charged out of the forest as if they were being chased by a ghost.

The old man didn't move.

"Is he still alive?" asked Stefan.

"I think so," Marcus replied, although he had never seen a dead person before.

They waited until they were sure that the attackers had gone for good and started to climb down the tree. As they descended, to their relief, they could hear the little Jewish man still mumbling to himself, although he remained curled up like a hedgehog.

The boys tentatively approached the whimpering figure.

"Sir," whispered Marcus lightly touching his shoulder. He

flinched as if it was another blow from his assailants. "It is okay, sir. They have gone now," Marcus was speaking in Yiddish, rather than Polish, to put the man at ease. Slowly he turned to look up at them. One of his eyes was swollen shut and blood dripped from his mouth. "I'll stay here with him – you run and get our fathers," instructed Marcus.

Stefan followed his friend's orders and ran out of the forest, relieved that the attackers had charged off in the other direction. He sprinted as fast as he could across the lawn, leaving a string of disgruntled picnickers in his wake. By the time he arrived at the bench where the two men were sitting he was totally exhausted.

"What's wrong?" said his father lurching forward to hold his son. "What's happened?"

"Where's Marcus?" asked Mr Tenenbaum.

Stefan was desperate to calm their panic but he struggled to regain his breath. "It's ok…" he managed to gasp. "We're fine… Nothing happened to us… But you have to come…"

"Where?" asked his father.

"Follow me." And although there was hardly an ounce of energy left in his body, he managed to trot back towards the Forest of Fire with the two men in tow.

By the time they reached the scene of the attack the old man was sitting up holding his face in his hands, swaying gently backwards and forwards, quietly praying to himself. Marcus was crouching next to him with a comforting arm across his shoulder.

"What has happened?" asked Stefan's father. Then, as if the sudden sound of a friendly adult voice was the sign the old man had been waiting for to confirm he was safe, he stood up and wrapped his arms around Stefan's father and wept uncontrollably. A surge of relief swept over the two boys and they stepped away, in the knowledge that they had done all they could.

Their fathers were too eager to ensure that the old man was okay to quiz their sons on exactly what had happened. They gradually helped him to his feet and delicately used their handkerchiefs to clean the blood from his face. Gingerly they helped him to walk – thankfully it appeared that no serious injuries had been inflicted on him. Marcus' father was conversing with him now – like his son, he instinctively knew that he would gain comfort from speaking Yiddish.

Slowly they made their way towards the open part of the park.

"Where's Apollo?" Stefan frantically patted his empty shirt pocket. "He has gone! Father, Apollo has gone!" Cold blind panic spread through him and the anguish of the afternoon's events dramatically magnified his distress. He realised how pathetic it was to bawl his eyes out over a missing rat when a man could have easily just been killed, but he was unable to control himself. He fell to his knees and for a few dreadful seconds the grief of losing his pet was the most painful thing in the world.

"Found him, Stef!" everyone looked up to see Marcus standing on the highest branch with Apollo in his hand. "He must have crawled out when we were up here!"

Everyone laughed – even the little old man, who had no idea what he was laughing at. And as Marcus handed Apollo over to his grateful owner, Stefan knew that there was nothing in the world that he wouldn't do for his friend – absolutely nothing.

TWELVE

It took the whole afternoon for the boys and their fathers to get the old man home safely to his top floor apartment in the heart of the Jewish District. They'd had to walk all the way, as observant Jews such as him would never travel on a tram on a Saturday. By the time they turned into Marcus' street it was dark.

"Why did no one else help when we came out of the forest?" asked Stefan. "Surely some of those picnickers must have seen us."

"What they saw were four people and a religious Jew," replied his father. "Which means they only saw four people; the old man was invisible to them."

"I don't understand."

"It's why Hitler can get away with what he is doing in Germany," he carried on. "For every thug who beats up a Jew in the street, there are ten others who blindly walk past. It's always easier to do nothing. This evil is spreading across Europe because most people choose to take the easy option and look the other way."

As they approached Marcus' house, the boys were deep in thought. The trauma of the day's events had brought all those stories the new boys from Germany had told them to life. Until now they'd dismissed them as harmless playground banter – it was soul destroying to suddenly realise that they were all true. Even seeing the hordes of jubilant Polish football supporters celebrating their country's surprise victory over Hungary hadn't lifted the boys' spirits.

"Where have you been?" demanded Marcus' mother. "The food's practically ruined – Antonina and I expected you ages ago."

It took so long to answer that question that by the time everyone had finally finished eating it was past the children's bedtime. Stefan and Marcus could barely keep their eyes open.

"Look how tired they are," said Marcus' mother. "Why doesn't Stefan stay here tonight? You know there is a spare bed in Marcus' room."

The Zabinskis looked at each other and then at their son, whose head was now in his arms resting on the table.

"Well I suppose it will be fine. Just as long as you don't mind putting up with Apollo!" said Jan, glancing down at his son's devoted pet, asleep on his shoulder.

"How could I possibly object?" exclaimed Lonia. "From the sound of what happened earlier on in the park, he appears to have been as much a hero as the boys!"

"That's settled then," said Marcus' father. "I'll bring him over to the zoo tomorrow, when the special consignment is delivered…"

Jan Zabinski gagged on his food and shot a glance towards his friend.

"What special consignment is that?" asked his wife, picking up on the sudden tension in the room. "What have you two been planning?"

Jan and Simon looked at each other. They'd been dreading this moment, but there was no escaping now.

For most people "the troubles" was a constant topic of conversation, but for Lonia Tenenbaum it was strictly forbidden. As far as she was concerned, the news was hard enough to listen to on the radio or read about in the papers; to discuss it openly was too awful to bear. The implications were so painful that she simply blocked it from her mind.

"Jan and I have been discussing things and…"

"Thank you… that's quite enough," snapped Lonia, standing up. "Come, Antonina, help me clear up these plates—"

"No!" insisted her husband. "There is nothing to be gained by sticking your head in the sand. These things have to be discussed."

"That's what you say…" said his wife scraping the leftovers into a bowl. "I am quite happy to keep my head in the sand. If it is good enough for one of Jan's ostriches, it's good enough for me!"

"Even my ostriches know something dreadful is about to happen," said Jan. "It is only humans like us that find it difficult to face the truth!" As usual it was the calm wisdom of their friend that won the argument. Reluctantly she sat down and resigned herself for whatever she was going to be forced to hear.

"We have to face the facts; it's only a matter of time before the Germans invade," said Marcus' father.

"Hush – not so loud," his wife scolded, pointing at the two slumbering boys at the far end of the table.

"And what if they do?" whispered Antonina. "The Polish army is ready to defend our borders."

"Alas bravery alone will not defeat Germany's massive war machine," replied her husband.

"But what about the British promise to defend us? Surely that will stop them…" said Lonia.

"You forget who we are talking about. If Hitler was a rational man then yes, I think you could be right. But then if he were a rational man, we would not be in the situation we find ourselves in now. You have to look at what he has done in the last six years. There is no stopping him – he wants it all," said Simon.

"But surely this is different," Antonina interjected. "No one lifted a finger when he marched through the Rhineland and entered Austria. In Czechoslovakia he was equally unopposed. But this time he knows that he will have to fight…"

"And he is ready to do so," added Jan. "Do you think he has been building up his army for fun?"

"Calm down please," interrupted Lonia. "Lower your voices or you will wake the boys."

"You're right," said her husband. "Come, Jan, let's carry these brave little soldiers up to bed."

The two men picked up their sleeping sons (and Apollo) and made their way upstairs.

"I think you should open that bottle of cognac your uncle brought us from France last year," whispered Marcus' father to his wife. "There's a lot to discuss before the Zabinskis go home tonight."

The two fathers gently placed the boys in their beds, carefully covered their sleeping bodies with blankets and delicately placed Apollo in one of Stefan's discarded shoes. Then they tip-toed out of the room, closing the door without a sound. Only on their way downstairs did they permit themselves to breathe normally.

"Are you still awake?" said Marcus.

"Of course I am," replied Stefan.

"Were you awake downstairs too?"

"What do you think?"

The boys decided to wait a while before they made their move. By the time they had reached the top of the stairs their parents had gone from the dining room to the lounge – which made eavesdropping on their conversation even easier, especially because the door had been conveniently left ajar.

"So," said Marcus' mother to her husband. "What are you planning on delivering to the zoo when you take Stefan home tomorrow?"

"Let me say, at the outset, that I hope this is an overreaction. I pray that our worst fears are not realised…"

"Just come out with it, Simon," said his wife.

"…and with any luck it will only be for a short while."

"Will you stop dithering and spit it out, man."

"It's Marcus."

"What are you talking about?"

"What your husband is trying to say," interrupted Stefan's father. "Is that it's going to be much safer for him to stay in our villa at the zoo than to remain here in the centre of Warsaw, until the troubles are over."

Silent shockwaves rippled through the house. It was a while before anyone spoke.

"It's only a precaution, my love," said Marcus' father, clearly concerned at his wife's reaction. "But if the Germans invade it's going to be so dangerous..."

"No!" Marcus' mother's voice was brimming with anguish. "Stop being so ridiculous!"

"We are Jewish," said Simon Tenenbaum. "Do you know what the Nazis do to people like us? I have spoken to many Jews who have fled from Germany and some say that Hitler will not stop until he has enslaved us all or worse. Do you want our son exposed to all that?"

"Stop – stop – stop!" screamed his wife, clearly sobbing. "I don't want to hear another word." Then she burst into tears and stormed out of the lounge, pushing the door wide open. The boys, who had edged as close to the top of the stairs as they could, quickly darted back into their room and dived into their beds.

"You can stay in my room," whispered Stefan. "We can live like brothers!" But Marcus was too shocked to respond – he had never heard his parents fight before.

Soon Stefan was snoring, but Marcus couldn't settle. His parents continued to argue long after the Zabinskis had left and, try as he might, he couldn't block their anger out with his pillow. "I forbid it...you're crazy... not over my dead body!" It was such a restless night that at times he couldn't tell if he was awake or asleep. "Where are you going? It's the middle of the night!" So he couldn't be sure whether the sound of his mother storming out of the house was a dream. "To the zoo, of course," she said. "You can take him there, if you wish. But I'll be waiting to bring him back!"

THIRTEEN

"Come on boys. Breakfast is ready!" Marcus' father called up the stairs. "We've got a busy morning ahead of us!"

Marcus led the race downstairs, desperate to see his mother waiting to greet them, but to his dismay he saw his father standing timidly by the stove. Last night's unwashed dishes were piled up in the sink behind him and there were still some leftovers on the table. "Where's mother?" he asked, trying to sound as casual as possible.

"She had to visit your grandma," his father replied. "Bit of an emergency, I think."

Marcus heart sunk even further.

"Why is our morning going to be so busy, Uncle Simon?" asked Stefan, taking a plate of soggy scrambled eggs from Marcus' father.

"There are lots of things to pack before we leave," he replied. "And you know what they say – many hands make light work…"

Marcus took his breakfast, unable to look his father in the eye. "So what happened to Grandma?" he asked.

"Oh, I'm not really sure," he replied untying his apron and laying it across the back of a chair. "I think it was something to do with her drains – you know how easily they get blocked?" With that he turned and left the kitchen.

Marcus didn't feel like eating. He slid his plate towards Apollo, who gratefully scurried across the table.

"Come on, you two," called a cheery voice from the hall. "In the study at the double!"

The boys left the kitchen and walked across the hall to Mr Tenenbaum's study. Marcus always found this room magical. Although his father was a science teacher, his life-long passion was insects and the shelves were crammed with boxes and glass jars full of the samples he had categorised over the years. The collection was so well known that complete strangers would frequently visit just to look at them, sometimes even from other countries. Marcus loved helping his father. He relished measuring the wing span of a new butterfly sample or using a microscope to count the legs on a giant millipede. "Even the ugliest beetle becomes a thing of beauty when it's magnified," his father would say.

Stefan strode into the room. "So what do you want us to do, sir?" he asked.

But Marcus halted at the doorway in shock. Everything had been turned upside down. How could his father tolerate such a mess? Why weren't the jars in their usual places with their labels all facing in the same direction? And why was his father acting as if everything was normal? His life's work was in chaos, scattered all over the room, and he was behaving like the happiest man in the world.

"Okay, boys, your job is to pack the jars on these shelves into the wooden trunk in the middle of the room. Use the newspaper on the floor to wrap them as tightly as you can."

"Why?" was all Marcus could say. He didn't even say it in an angry way. It was practically a whisper. But his father reacted as if the vilest curse imaginable had just left his lips.

"I don't want to hear any of your back chat, young man. Do you understand? Just do what you're told. I simply don't have the time to hold a debate about it. Here's the paper, here are the jars and there is the trunk. What more do you need to know? Why can't you just get on with things like your friend here? Don't just stand there gawping, we need to leave in two hours." With that he stormed out of the room, barging past Marcus, apparently oblivious to the tears that were now streaming down his son's face

FOURTEEN

Stefan had never seen his friend like this before. Marcus was the brave one – last winter he ventured out on a frozen lake to rescue a stranded child. He never cried, no matter how much he'd been hurt. And calm unflappable Mr Tenenbaum – who would spend hours making sand castles when the two families went on holiday together. The man whose laugh was as loud as a donkey's bray and who Stefan's father described as someone he would trust with his life. Exploding with rage for no good reason...

He wanted to comfort his friend, but was rooted to the spot by fear.

Gradually Marcus regained his composure, but with each snatched breath the room grew more tense. Neither friend could look the other in the eye. They'd been dragged to a bitter place that couldn't easily be sweetened with words or a smile. If only Marcus' father would come bounding back into the room right now, laughing out loud at the joke he'd just played. Then everything would be well again and the world would be able to carry on spinning. But he didn't return.

It was Marcus who made the first move. "We'd better get on, then," he said, slowly drifting past his friend towards the waiting glass jars. "There isn't much time."

"Ok," Stefan answered, joining him on the floor by the pile of newspapers.

So Stefan and Marcus began to wrap newspaper around glass jars containing dead insects – they were together again. But behind their smiles they knew that their world was now a much darker place.

"This is disgusting," said Stefan, holding up a jar with a particularly gruesome beetle. "It's as big as my hand!"

"It's a rhinoceros," said Marcus.

"It's not – it's a cockroach. I know what a rhino is; we've got two in the zoo!"

"It's a rhino cockroach – the biggest cockroach on earth," Marcus liked talking about insects to Stefan – it was the only subject he knew more about than his friend. "Someone from Australia sent it to my father."

"Well I still think it's disgusting. Look at its ugly head…"

"Well it's not as ugly as this," said Marcus holding up a newspaper. "This is what I call disgusting!" He was pointing at a picture of the all-too-familiar face of Adolf Hitler. He picked up another sheet and there it was again – that stern stare and small shadowy moustache haunted practically every page. Stefan snatched the paper from his friend's hand and ripped out the face. Then he picked up the nearby roll of sticky tape and stuck Hitler's face to one of the jars. "Look another insect for your collection!"

Marcus laughed and did the same to another photo. "Look," he said. "I think we already have one!"

Stefan stuck a third face onto a jar, "yes and here's another…"

There followed a frenzy of tearing and sticking until a line of Hitler-insect-jars stretched across the carpet.

"You have a visitor, boys." The sound of Marcus' father's voice startled the two friends to their feet. They stood to attention expecting to be reprimanded for wasting time, but to their relief Mr Tenenbaum's earlier anger seemed to have evaporated. "And you might want to hide your parade of mini-fuehrers before he comes in…"

The two boys quickly covered the jars with newspaper.

"Ah, my little heroes…"

At first they didn't recognise the hunched, bearded figure

walking towards them holding a small cardboard box. "This is Mr Berkowicz," announced Marcus' father.

"Abram, call me Abram!" said the little man. "We are all friends, here! After all, these brave little men saved my life!" Then he stopped in horror and pointed at Stefan. "Argh – what is that creature on your shoulder?"

"It is my pet rat, Apollo."

"Ah yes, I remember now!" said the old man turning towards Marcus' father with a shrug. "The youth of today… what can you do?"

Mr Tenenbaum returned a knowing nod.

Then the boys realised that this was the man from the park; his eye was still swollen and there was a cut on his lip.

"How are you now, sir?" asked Marcus.

"I am still alive!" the man cried out. "I live, I breathe… I am here. And it is because of you, and The Almighty, of course!" Then the little old man placed the cardboard box he was carrying on the nearby desk and proceeded to do a jig around the room.

The boys were far too embarrassed to respond. They had no idea if this craziness was due to yesterday's blows to the head or if he was always like this.

"We live in troubled times," Marcus' father pitched in. "The future is uncertain…"

"Nonsense!" proclaimed Abram Berkowicz. "Yes, life can be difficult at times, but the future is always certain! Never lose faith – the Messiah is coming!" Mr Tenenbaum nodded, although purely out of politeness. The firm belief that, one day, a great spiritual leader would be sent by God to redeem the world and bring peace to all, was one of the many things that separated non-religious Jews like the Tenenbaums from people such as Abram Berkowicz. "And if you want proof that God is taking care of us, then look at these two boys!" He stopped dancing and rested his hands on Stefan and Marcus' heads. "Who do you think placed them in that very tree at the very moment I was confronted by those madmen?

And who do you think helped these two fine young men here to frighten those devils away? The Almighty, of course!" Then he resumed his jig, picking up the box from the desk and holding it high above his head.

"Well we are very glad to see you looking so well," said Mr Tenenbaum. "We were very worried…"

"Worry!" interrupted the old man. "What is there to worry about?"

"Well, quite a lot, if you read the news," he replied.

"Ah, the news!" repeated the Mr Berkowicz. "I too read the news – but then I read the Torah to cheer myself up!"

Marcus was reminded of the Rabbi he visited every Wednesday evening to prepare for his Bar Mitzvah – the ceremony all Jewish boys of his age celebrated. To commemorate "becoming a man" Marcus had to recite a large section of Jewish Law in synagogue. The event was over a year away but it felt as if he'd been preparing for it for ages. Although his teacher had a much bigger beard than the quirky little man dancing around the room, like Mr Berkowicz he often spoke about the importance of studying Torah. "To stay alive you need food, drink and air," he would say, "but if you really want a life, my boy, you must study Torah!"

Marcus' father couldn't help but be a little envious of how such a firm belief in heaven shielded men such as Abram Berkowicz from the horrors of the world down here. Even the traumatic events of yesterday, where he was so brutally attacked purely for being Jewish, hadn't dented his faith.

"And now," announced the old man, bringing his dance to a sudden stop. "The reason I came to see you!" He slowly lifted the lid of the box. "My wife, she bakes the best chocolate *babka* cake in Warsaw. She wants you to have this with her thanks and best wishes!" The circular brown cake floating before the boys' eyes gave off the sweetest chocolatiest smell imaginable.

"There was no need to…" said Mr Tenenbaum.

"Thank you so much…" mumbled Marcus.

"And thank your wife as well..." added Stefan.

"Enjoy!" Mr Berkowicz announced, placing the cake on the desk and turning to leave.

Marcus' father followed behind to let the old man out and the boys just stared at the cake eager to know if it tasted as good as it smelt. Apollo leapt off Stefan's shoulder and had to be restrained from taking the first nibble there and then – he was as devoted to chocolate as Abram Berkowicz was to God.

FIFTEEN

"It's time to leave now," announced Mr Tenenbaum when he returned to the room. "Let's start loading the truck."

We haven't got a truck, thought Marcus.

The boys followed Mr Tenenbaum as he carried one of the wooden trunks into the hall and were surprised to see a familiar huge figure filling the open doorway. "Otto!" Stefan gasped. "What are you doing here?" A question that was answered by the presence of a zoo truck on the driveway outside.

"Well if it isn't Grumpy and Dopey!" he bellowed using the nicknames he'd given the boys ever since the American film *Snow White and the Seven Dwarfs* was screened in Warsaw.

Otto had been a keeper at the zoo for so long that Stefan saw him more as family. He was a mountain of a man – as wide as he was tall. When he was put in charge of the elephant enclosure everyone joked that he was built for the job.

"Don't just stand there like a pair of pillars," said Marcus' father carrying another trunk. "Are you two going to help or not?"

"Hi-ho-hi-ho it's off to work we go!" sung Otto as he followed close behind vigorously swinging his arms. The two boys burst out laughing and shuffled into line behind the jolly giant, joining in with the song. The whole world loved Otto; laughter seemed to follow him everywhere.

Soon all the insect specimens had been loaded onto the truck. "Don't forget that cake!" called Marcus as he pulled a thick canvas cover over the trunks.

"Cake!" exclaimed Otto. "I didn't know we were having a party!"

"Can we ride in the back?" asked Stefan.

Otto stared down at the boys sternly, a look that seemed to double the size of his already double chin. He rested his folded arms high on top of his circular stomach and tutted loud and long. "There's hardly any room left," he said. "You're bound to fall out!"

"But you're always driving children around the zoo in the back of the truck, why is it so different here?" pleaded Stefan.

"I don't think your father would approve! What will he say when he asks where you are and I tell him you've fallen in the Vistula?"

"That's not going to happen, I promise," said Stefan.

"We'll let you have the cake," chipped in Marcus holding out the box.

Otto laughed so loudly that the boys felt its force before they heard it. "It's a deal!" he said snatching the cake. "Now hop in and hold on tight!"

Marcus felt very pleased with himself and climbed up first, offering a helping hand to his friend. But Stefan wasn't smiling back. "Why did you do that?" he said, placing Apollo on the canvas cover.

"You wanted to sit up here, didn't you?"

"But he would have let us," said Stefan. "Couldn't you see that he was only joking? This is Otto – he is *never* serious! And now you've given away our cake!"

"Sorry," said Marcus.

The engine roared into life and the truck slowly edged along the driveway towards the road.

"Where are your clothes?" called Stefan, straining to be heard over the noise of the engine.

"I'm wearing them!" replied Marcus confused.

"No, I mean the ones you're going to need at the zoo when you come to live with us. All we've packed are dead insects – you can't wear them!"

Marcus suddenly thought of his mother and his heart sunk. Unable to speak, he shrugged and turned away from his friend to watch the trams, busses and horse-drawn carriages competing for space on the bumpy Warsaw roads. They sat in silence as the truck drove past tight clusters of armed Polish soldiers on street corners. Fear seemed to be etched on each face in the crowd and practically every shop window was heavily taped, in anticipation of a possible air attack.

Eventually they approached the Kierbedzia Bridge.

"There it is again!" called Marcus, pointing across the river.

"What?" asked his friend.

"That Jewish star, on your house. I can see it from here. And it's shining in the sun just like yesterday."

SIXTEEN

The bridge that spanned the Vistula connected two entirely different worlds. In the few minutes it took to drive across, from west to east, the hectic hum of The Old Town was gradually replaced by gentle birdsong – most of which came from the aviary in the zoo nearby.

"I wonder how long you'll be staying with us," said Stefan as they turned into the road that led to the main entrance.

"I've no idea," Marcus replied, as the knot in his stomach caused by his father's earlier anger started to tighten again.

Although it was mid-afternoon and the zoo was due to close in two hours, the queue outside still snaked past the heavy iron gates and along the road. Always the showman, Otto slowed the truck to wave at the waiting children as if he was their friend – which to regular visitors he was. Ever since his beloved Kasia became the first elephant to give birth in a European zoo he had become quite a celebrity. His face often appeared in the local newspaper when updates on little baby Tuzinka were printed. This used to amuse his fellow keepers, who would often joke that Otto spent more time standing and smiling than he did cleaning and feeding. But it was something that Stefan's father positively encouraged – the publicity it generated had helped to make his zoo the most popular tourist attraction in Warsaw.

Familiar smells slowly roused Apollo; he quickly crawled up onto his master's shoulder, glad to be home.

The Zabinski's villa was situated on a hill in a secluded corner of the zoo grounds. It provided a good view of the whole compound, but was far enough away for the family to maintain a degree of privacy. Although that did not stop the occasional member of the public strolling aimlessly up to their front door and enquiring what animals were exhibited there.

Otto stopped the truck at the foot of the hill. "You two can get off here," Marcus' father called out from the cabin at the front. "We'll unload the truck ourselves."

Stefan was confused, "but won't my parents be waiting for me…"

"It was your father who instructed me to drop you off here," Mr Tenenbaum interrupted. "He wants you to make your way back to the villa when the zoo closes."

The two boys climbed out of the truck and watched it speed on up the hill. Then, to their surprise, it stopped and reversed back to where they were standing. Otto wound down his window and held out the cake box. "You can have this back, boys," he said with a smile. "I think I'll start a diet! Besides, I met the old man who gave it to you on his way out of Marcus' house earlier on. He hooked his arm in mine and danced me round like a spinning top. Then he told me he'd just delivered some cake to the heroes who saved his life – how could I steal such a well-deserved prize?" His booming laugh could be heard as the truck wound its way up to the villa.

"You must come and see the monkeys," said Stefan, sensing that his unusually quiet friend needed cheering up. "Last week the keepers hung an old tyre in their enclosure and they've gone mad for it!"

Marcus followed Stefan through the crowds of visitors until they came to the Monkey House at the far end of the zoo. As usual there was a group of humans making whooping noises and scratching themselves under their armpits while every monkey, except Big Gus, totally ignored them. Over the years Big Gu had become a people watcher. His keepers nicknamed him "The other Mr Zabinski" because he seemed to be as interested in the behaviour of the human species as their boss was in animals.

Stefan was right; there was mayhem around the tyre. A succession of monkeys clambered up and taunted those below only to be promptly shoved off by a rival. It was hilarious and he was heartened to see Marcus joining in with the laughter.

"Let's have some of this cake," said Stefan.

"Okay!"

The two boys sat on a nearby bench in the shadows of an old abandoned farmhouse and windmill that stood just beyond the borders of the zoo. Both buildings had been unused for as long as anyone could remember and were now home to a huge flock of pigeons that the boys enjoyed observing from afar.

"Ah ha! Mr Zabinski junior – we meet again!" The boys looked up to see a smartly dressed man with a thick black moustache. He tipped his hat with one hand while holding a clip board in the other. He spoke in German but they had no problem understanding him. It was a language they'd learnt for years in school and, thanks to the influx of new boys, they'd had lots of recent opportunities to use. "I am Lutz Heck, remember? Director of the great Berlin Zoo; I have visited your father many times in recent years." He replaced his hat and attempted to stroke Apollo, drawing his hand away quickly as the rat, who often proved to be a keen judge of character, tried to nibble the offending finger. "I have come here to admire this wonderful zoo again!"

Stefan smiled politely but said nothing. Of course he remembered him. After his last visit his mother vowed never to let that "rude, arrogant, ignorant man" in her house again only for his father to reply "he may be a madman, but he is a very influential one!"

"I am returning to Berlin this evening and will report again to my colleagues what marvellous specimens you have here!" Standing behind Heck was a senior keeper, who often escorted important guests around the zoo. He gave Stefan a knowing wink over the V.I.P.'s shoulder, before fixing a pleasant smile on his face and ushering the man away.

"Who was that?" asked Marcus.

"One of my father's 'friends'" he replied with deep sarcasm.

"Well he gave me the creeps."

The crowds around them were starting to disperse now, and the boys decided to return to the villa. Stefan opened the cake box, picked up the *babka* and broke it in half, giving one part to Marcus and pinching a bit off his own piece for Apollo. All three of them munched as they ambled past the area where the giraffes and zebras mingled and stopped momentarily to admire the brown bears who were huddled together asleep in the corner of their cage. Eventually they reached the path that led up to the villa where Clyde, the peacock, greeted them with his feathery plumes on display.

"Stop," said Marcus suddenly.

"He's not going to hurt us," said Stefan. "You should know that by now, unless you're planning on counting those eggs—"

"No, not that..." he whispered, dragging his friend behind a nearby tree. "Look!"

Stefan looked to where his friend was pointing. Otto's truck was still parked in front of the villa. Next to it was one of the black rickshaw-cycles that were used to transport food and hay about the zoo. And there was his father directing the unloading of the cargo. "I don't remember packing any of those onto the truck," he said.

"They must have already been there, hidden under the canvas," Marcus replied.

The boys remained behind the tree until the final rifle had been unloaded.

SEVENTEEN

Marcus and Stefan crouched low in the bushes as the rickshaw full of weapons sped past them. Otto followed closely behind in the empty truck. Both boys were too shocked to speak – what could they possibly say? It was a full five minutes before they started to make their way sheepishly up the hill towards the villa.

Helda was coming in the opposite direction. She lived across the river, in a very poor district of Warsaw, an hour's walk away. Although she worked for the Zabinskis before Stefan was born, he didn't really know her. When he was younger she was a figure of fear, snarling at him whenever he made a mess and scolding him when he left food on his plate. In recent years she had become less scary, but he still couldn't warm to her. "Never judge anyone from their outward appearance," Stefan's father would say. But he found it hard to follow his father's advice – the best he could do was to try and ignore her. Marcus and Stefan stood to one side, to allow her to pass. She glanced down at them, briefly sneering at Apollo, and carried on down the hill without saying a word.

The boys entered the villa unnoticed and made their way towards the lounge. They had spent countless hours in that room together over the years, but today they barely recognised it. The familiar books and ornaments that normally lined the shelves had been replaced by the insect specimen jars and the carpet was covered in discarded newspaper. In the middle of the room, beside the empty trunks, stood the boys' fathers and to Marcus' distress, their mothers were nowhere to be seen. It was only when Apollo spotted his cage outside in the courtyard, charged down Stefan's arm and scampered across the floor that their presence was noticed. "Welcome to the chaos!" Jan Zabinski announced.

Suddenly the boys' mothers appeared from the courtyard. Lonia Tenenbaum charged into the room and hugged her son. "I am so, so sorry," she seemed to be saying. Marcus gasped for air in an ocean of relief, clinging on to his mother for fear of drowning.

"Those drains weren't as badly blocked as your grandmother first thought..." he heard his father mumble.

"Come!" announced Stefan's mother, grabbing her son's arm and slowly prising Marcus away from Lonia's embrace. "Let's leave the rest of this work to the men. I have some wonderful American soda water in the kitchen!" Then she whisked them both out of the room and across the hallway.

Marcus' head was still spinning as he sipped his drink while his mother sat next to him, silently stroking his hand.

"We saw that man from the Berlin Zoo, earlier," said Stefan, eager to ease the tension in the room. "Why was he here again?"

"He was making preparations," answered his mother.

"For what?"

"The conference we're hosting here next year. Don't you remember your father mentioning it? Most of Europe's zoo directors are coming and *that man* Heck is the main organiser – unfortunately."

Marcus felt the echo of his racing heart pounding inside his head. It had been so long since he'd overheard his mother storming out of the house and he could bear the uncertainty no longer. "I don't want to stay here." His voice was weak, but it demanded everyone's attention. "I am really sorry, Auntie. I hope this does not offend you. You know how much I like being here. But I really want to stay at home with my mother and father." Then he looked at his friend. "You can visit me and I will visit you. It will be just like normal. I don't care about Hitler and the war..."

"Of course you can stay at home with us," whispered his mother. "How did such a crazy idea get into your head?"

Marcus fought hard to hold back his tears and looked apologetically up at his friend. "Last night," he muttered. "I heard father say that Hitler hates Jews and that I should hide from him here. But that can't be right. We are all Jews. If it's safe for you to stay, then it will be okay for me."

"Hush," said his mother.

"And then I heard you leave in the middle of the night and…" but Marcus could no longer speak.

"There is no need to cry," said his mother. "Your father's little friends in those glass jars are going to move to the zoo, for safe keeping. That's all… I promise." Then she kissed him on his forehead and they felt each other's fear.

"You will never guess what Big Gus did today," Stefan's mother announced. "His keeper told me what happened – it's the funniest thing you'll ever hear!" She climbed up onto the table and stooped forward, tightly pursing her lips and pushing her face inquisitively towards Marcus, perfectly mimicking a monkey. Suddenly she started to whoop and holler. Then she knelt down, reached out for Marcus' hair and gently began to inspect it, just as a monkey would. Slowly he started to smile. "It happened this morning – we had only been open for an hour so there were very few people about. A family, mum, dad and two kids, started waving at the monkeys, like so many people do, and, well, Big Gus started to wave back. And the more they waved the more he copied them. This went on for a while until the man decided to get out his camera." Antonina Zabinski was stomping around the table now, as if it was a stage. "Well, he positioned his wife and children up against the cage and started waving like mad to get Big Gus to perform for his picture. So there they were, standing like lemons, waiting for the monkey to oblige… Apparently it went on for ages…"

By now Marcus' mother and the two boys were in fits of laughter as Antonina enacted each detail of the story.

"Oh dear..." she stopped abruptly. "I forgot to tell you something...." She suddenly leapt off the table and grabbed a tea towel and wrapped it around her head. "...this lady just happened to be wearing a straw hat that was decorated around the rim with beautiful flowers... And we all know how much Big Gus loves flowers!" Then she stuffed the tea towel in her mouth and leapt back onto the table to resume her monkey pose. Her audience were in stitches and she was relieved to see Marcus so happy again.

"Come!" she got down from the table. "It's time for a performance!" Then she held the boys' hands and led them back to the living room where Jan and Simon were crawling on the floor collecting up the discarded newspaper. They sat up abruptly to see what was happening. Stefan's mother lifted the piano lid, positioned her son on the stool and briskly flicked through the pile of music on the piano. She finally settled on the piece that she loved to hear him play the most – Beethoven's *Moonlight Sonata*".

Instantly, Stefan's father rushed out into the courtyard to get Apollo.

The scene could not have appeared to be more idyllic. The late evening sun shone through the open door and bathed the living room in a soft golden glow. Marcus attentively turned the pages of the music as his friend weaved his magic on the piano. Around them their parents danced like guests at a royal ball while an entranced white rat swayed gently on the piano.

But the boys both knew that none of this was real, they could sense the fear behind their parents' smiles. There were horrors on the horizon and it felt as if this could possibly be the very last perfect moment of their lives. Their childhood was slipping away. And as Marcus watched his friend's fingers glide over the keyboard, he couldn't help thinking that if something terrible was about to happen to Warsaw's Jews, then was it really so safe for them to remain at home when his father had gone to such lengths to protect his dead insects?

Part Two

September 1939

EIGHTEEN

September 1st

Despite the warnings of war from every radio station and newspaper, the beleaguered residents of Warsaw clung onto the dream of a last minute reprieve. Everyone, Jew and Catholic, prayed that, please God, at this eleventh hour, Hitler would decide not to attack. They dreamt of dismantling the sandbag-hills that had sprung up all over Warsaw. Maybe, just maybe, the soldiers that were stationed around the city could return to their barracks, alive, with their weapons unfired. If only the heavy artillery, positioned on so many street corners, could be wished away. But hope ended during breakfast.

"It has started," announced Simon Tenenbaum, slouching down at the kitchen table. Marcus had never seen his father look so exhausted and dishevelled. He'd been up all night pinned to the radio. "The Germans have bombed Wieluń," he continued, looking up at his wife and son in dread. "They are coming."

✡✡✡

Across the river, at the zoo, they didn't need a radio to confirm the outbreak of war. The keepers had been reporting unusual behaviour in the cages and enclosures for days now and, as

Antonina Zabinski often told her son, "We humans think we are so clever, but the rest of the animal kingdom knows far more than we do." Birds that were normally placid and quiet had been squawking for days with their plumage puffed up in alarm. The usually calm elephants that would happily feed from outstretched hands had become too aggressive to be with. Kasia even charged at Otto when he approached Tuzinka, her baby. There was an eerie stillness in the big cats' enclosure, where instead of proudly prowling their territory the lions and cheetahs sought refuge in shadows and furtively carried their meat into the secluded safety of their shelters. The monkeys were more manic than usual, shrieking and hollering all night – except Big Gus, who had retreated to a corner of his cage and sat with his head in his hands. Even Apollo was acting uncharacteristically – Helda noticed, with some delight, that he was not on Stefan's shoulder as he ate breakfast. "Where is your friend?" she asked – although Stefan wasn't sure if she was referring to Marcus or his rat.

✿✿✿

The Tenenbaums were hunkered in a neighbour's basement when the bombs began to fall on Warsaw; it sounded to Marcus like giant's footsteps getting ever closer. Each menacing thud triggered cries of anguish and fervent prayers amongst the others seeking shelter. Apart from Shlomo and his mother, he hardly knew any of the other people huddled together in the flickering candlelight. Instinctively he leant into his mother and she held him even tighter.

"Now we will see who are friends our," said a voice in the darkness.

"Never underestimate the strength of the Polish army," came another.

"They cannot hold out alone forever," responded the first voice.

"France and Britain have said they will defend us – let's wait and see what their words are worth."

"If they say they will come, they will come!" added a third.

"But when?" said another. "As the man said, we can't wait forever."

Marcus and Shlomo looked at each other across the dimly lit room, silently mocking the adults around them, while both clinging on to their mothers.

"We have waited for The Almighty to send the Messiah since the days of the prophets," came a quiet murmur from the corner of the room. "So we can wait a little longer for Great Britain's planes."

✡✡✡

Stefan was much closer to the first sounds of war. The Polish army had set up an anti-aircraft position in the grounds of the zoo and the air was punctuated by the relentless rat-a-tat of its fire. Jan Zabinski had insisted that every keeper should put their own safety above that of the animals, no matter how much they wanted to protect the creatures in their care. "You will be needed more when the shooting has stopped," he announced. "What help can you give to an injured or traumatised animal if you're dead?"

As Stefan scanned the frightened faces that had joined the family in their cellar, he knew that many had not heeded that advice, but he wasn't surprised. Most of the people who worked at the zoo openly valued the lives of their animals above their own. As he stroked the Apollo-sized bump on his jacket, he wondered what he would do in their position.

✡✡✡

The bombardment came in waves, but it had been quiet for over an hour now.

"When can we leave?" asked Marcus.

"There will be a siren," whispered his mother. "Then we will know that it is safe to go home."

"I'm afraid no siren will ever be able to guarantee that," said the man sitting opposite. "If the bombs don't kill us, the Nazis will finish the job when they get here."

"I really don't think there is any need for such talk," she retorted.

"Alas, I think you are being naïve, my good woman," he continued. "Have you not heard what they do to people like us? Do you expect Hitler's thugs to waltz into Warsaw with bagels and schnitzels for his good friends the Jews? Believe me, by the time they've finished with us, the survivors of the bombing will envy the dead..."

"My good man!" she was shouting now. "I will thank you to keep your vile ugly thoughts to yourself. Are you blind? Can you not see that there are children in here? If you have nothing worth saying, than I urge you to remain silent!"

Although the light from the candles was dim, the man could see in a glance that she had spoken for everyone. Mortified, he buried his face in his hands, ashamed.

It's too late for that, she thought. What had been said could not be unsaid – the damage had been done. Although what hurt far more was the fact that she had been powerless to prevent him from uttering those words and could do nothing now to lessen their pain. How was she ever going to be able to protect her son again?

✡✡✡

"No one would ever bomb a zoo, not even those crazy Germans!" said Otto pouring water into the glasses on the cellar floor. "Isn't Hitler meant to be an animal lover, anyway?"

"Not 'crazy'," said Helda.

"I beg your pardon…" Otto responded.

"Please do not call the Germans 'crazy'. You may disagree with their methods but you cannot argue with their motives."

The long lull in the bombing had lightened the atmosphere but Stefan sensed that the mood was about to change once more.

"Are you trying to be funny?" asked Otto with a seriousness that Stefan found hard to associate with him.

"On the contrary," came Helda's reply, with a definite air of defiance.

"More water," interjected Stefan's mother, carrying on the job that Otto had been distracted from.

"If you really believe what you are saying, then you are a traitor to your country!" said Otto. There was a gasp in the room. Given that Poland had just entered a war that threatened its very existence, such an accusation was about as strong as you could get.

"Don't you dare call me a traitor!" barked Helda. She was more animated than Stefan had ever seen her. "It is you who need to open your eyes. Can you not see what the Fuehrer is doing for Europe? Can you not see what he is doing for us all?"

This was probably the longest that most of the people in the room had spent in each other's company before. The zoo was such a huge place that it was possible for people who had worked there for ages to barely know each other. Such was the case with Helda the house keeper and Otto "the elephant king".

"You have no idea what it is like living amongst those Jews!" she exclaimed. "They speak their own language, they have their own shops, they eat their own food and, worst of all, they worship their own God! And there are so many of them – they breed like rabbits! Believe me, Hitler will be doing us all a favour…"

"I know exactly what it is like to live amongst Jews," said Stefan's father, slowly getting to his feet. He spoke in the soft, gentle way you would use with a toddler. "I grew up in The Old Town, most of my childhood friends were Jews, as are many of those I still consider to be my most trusted companions. So I can say, with some authority, that there is as much difference between you and me, Helda, as there is between you and any of your Jewish neighbours." His voice had now dropped to a whisper but he had everyone's attention. "And may I just add that if it wasn't for the generosity of Polish Jews that wanted their city to have the best zoo in Europe, no one here would have a job. I would thank you all to remember that the next time you look at the silver star in the side of this building." Then he calmly sat down, although inside he was fuming.

Stefan's mind was now reeling. If Hitler really hated Jews as much as Helda said, then where were all those bombs landing?

NINETEEN

September 9th

Marcus was struggling to make sense of his world – like so much of the city he once knew, it had been blown apart.

But he was no longer scared. Fear had now been replaced by something much darker – betrayal. Everything Marcus believed in had collapsed, like the many bombed out buildings that were now just rubble. He was suspicious of anything he heard. Now, when his parents assured him that everything would be fine, he knew it was a lie. When the radio spoke of how "victory was within our grasp", he knew that wasn't true either. And when his father solemnly promised that "not a single bomb" had fallen anywhere near the zoo, after watching exactly that happen from the attic window, he knew that trust was now dead.

✡✡✡

"And humans think they are the most advanced of species," said Stefan's mother with tears in her eyes. "Why? Because they can do marvellous things like this?" She stood in the doorway holding the limp body of a baby gazelle. There was no sign of injury. Like many of its fellow victims, the sheer terror of the bombing was enough to kill it.

Stefan knew exactly what to do next without being told – it had become a daily routine. He fetched a large canvas sack from the cellar and held it open while his mother gently slid the animal inside. It was important to remove the dead as quickly as possible to lessen the stress on the living, and light creatures such as this were taken to a nearby field and burnt at the end of each day.

He had bawled like a baby to begin with, but the horrors of the last few days had drained his tears. He had watched a dead Polar Bear being loaded on to the truck, its white coat streaked in red. He had heard the fearful cries of the llamas trapped inside their burning building and seen the anguish of their keepers as they tried, in vain, to douse the flames. And the sight of Tuzinka desperately nudging the motionless body of her mother still haunted him.

✡ ✡ ✡

Each morning there were fresh craters in Warsaw's streets from the previous night's raid, and yet more of The Old Town had disappeared. Those who were lucky enough to have escaped looked on helplessly as the dispossessed frantically pulled at the wreckage with their bare hands to retrieve as much of their life as they could. Once the search had been completed they gathered forlornly in the street, not sure what to do next. Occasionally horse-drawn wagons would pull up and the destitute souls would load their property on and leave. Marcus had grown numb to such scenes, just thankful that his house had not yet suffered a direct hit. As he joined the queue that snaked away from the only bakery in the district still open, he coldly cut himself off from the misery around him. Even the sight of a horse-drawn wagon heavily laden with the bodies of other dead horses was greeted with indifference.

The queue moved slowly and Marcus worried that he would have to go home empty handed, again.

"What's that?" came a yell. "Up there!"

Everyone looked into the cloudless sky. A lone plane was flying straight at them, low enough for Marcus to see each rivet. Panic shot through the crowd and everyone instinctively dropped to the ground. Marcus winced as the man behind stumbled and fell on top of him, wedging his body hard up against the shop window. The angry roar of the engine grew louder as the plane swooped even closer. The sound of metal crashing into concrete rang in Marcus' head as the machine gun spat out it bullets. Everything was over too quickly for fear to kick in. For a moment Marcus wasn't even sure if he was still alive, then all that he wanted was for that great fat oaf of a man to get off him. But he wouldn't budge. In the end Marcus managed to drag himself to his feet and looked down at the lifeless body that had unwittingly saved his life.

✩✩✩

Stefan woke from another restless night's sleep. He dragged himself out of bed and looked out of his window towards The Old Town. There had hardly been a single shell dropped on this side of the Vistula for a couple of days now, as the Germans concentrated their attack on the most densely populated parts of the city. He watched as planes buzzed overhead, like a swarm of giant mosquitoes waiting their turn to unleash their firepower. Occasionally a blast would flare up from the ground in response, but there was little that could be done to stop the relentless deadly relay. Pillars of smoke from countless fires along the skyline converged into a huge grey cloud that hung over the city, and Stefan couldn't stop thinking about his friend in the thick of it all. "Stay safe, Marcus," he whispered to himself.

TWENTY

September 16th

"Don't say it," said Marcus' mother. "I don't want to hear those words in this house! Not now—"

"Why not?!" replied his father. "We should shout it so loud that Hitler can hear us in Berlin!"

"Don't be ridiculous."

"I am being deadly serious," he replied. "A message needs to be sent out. You can bomb us and you can shoot us, but you can never win!"

"You're crazy. You have been listening to Polish radio for too long. We are surrounded – there is no hope now. The Germans will be here soon. Haven't you heard that all our soldiers have returned to Warsaw?"

"No – you're the crazy one round here, woman! It was a tactical retreat – and do you know what those troops have done?" Marcus' father was shouting now, something he rarely did before the war. "They have dug trenches around the city so deep, that no tank could ever cross. And where they couldn't dig, they have ripped up tram-rails and planted them in the ground as barriers. The Germans may think that we are beaten but we will always fight back!"

"You are a fool!" Marcus recoiled at his mother's

uncharacteristic harshness. "A deluded, blinkered, brainless fool!" Then she burst into tears, her body shaking uncontrollably. Even when her husband held her, and begged for forgiveness, the sobbing continued.

Marcus turned to leave the kitchen, unable to watch his parents struggle to console each other. But then he stopped and returned to the breakfast table. He grabbed the calendar that had caused the argument in the first place. Today's date was circled in red ink – Rosh Hashanah the Jewish New Year.

Marcus' bemused parents watched him drag a chair towards an open window. He climbed up and leant outside, holding the calendar up as high as he could. "Shan-nah-To-vah, Herr Hitler!" he screamed at the top of his voice. "Happy New Year, from Warsaw, to everyone in Berlin!"

✡✡✡

At the zoo, Jan Zabinski gathered his staff together on the driveway in front of the villa, with his son and wife by his side.

"Friends, as you know, our brave Polish forces have been unable to prevent the advance of the German army. The occupation of Warsaw is now inevitable. We face a time of great uncertainty. Our task is to do what we can for the surviving animals. Good luck to you all."

As the crowd dispersed, Stefan made his way to the courtyard, heading straight for Apollo's cage. The excited rat scampered onto his master's shoulder and remained there while Stefan cleaned Hercules' sty more thoroughly than he had ever done before. He refreshed all his bedding, replenished the water bowl and filled his trough with apples – his pet pig's favourite food. The entire operation was carried out to the accompaniment of Hercules's relentless snoring. "Ungrateful swine," joked Stefan as he replaced the broom and bolted the gate behind him.

✡✡✡

Although The Great Synagogue on Tłomackie Street was only a short walk from the Tenenbaum's house, they rarely went there. Even on the important religious festivals that punctuated the Jewish year, when the streets would turn into long streams of worshippers on their way to pray, they seldom visited. Their only surviving parent, Lonia's mother, Golda, had given up trying to persuade them to attend more frequently. "At least you're sending your son to Bar Mitzvah lessons," she said. "For that I must be thankful!"

But tonight it was different. After two weeks of intensive German bombardment, focussed largely on Warsaw's Jewish district, the "final free" Rosh Hashanah before the impending German occupation had taken on an even greater significance than normal.

When Lonia informed her mother that they had decided to attend the service, she was delighted. "For this, I have Hitler to thank," she'd said. "Why it should take such a disaster to get you all to synagogue, only The Almighty knows." She had insisted on accompanying Marcus and his parents to the synagogue and arrived at their house a full hour before everyone was ready.

When the family eventually set off to join the throng there was no sense of celebration – the atmosphere was more one of defiance.

"It's the largest synagogue in Warsaw," Marcus' father said to his son as they approached the huge green dome of the Great Synagogue. "It was built about sixty years ago by my grandfather's generation. It created quite a stir, I can tell you. Some people thought it was too big – too showy. They complained that the four columns at the front made it look too much like a Christian church. And can you see the Star of David up there?"

"Like the one at the zoo?" added Marcus.

"Yes, that's right. A few people said it was not a fitting symbol to put on a building – that the star was too closely linked to magic and mysticism. I tell you, the arguments around those two interlocking triangles destroyed some life-long friendships…"

"But that star is all over the place now," said Marcus.

"Things have moved on," said his grandma Golda, who had been listening intently to their conversation.

"We'll meet here after the service," said Marcus' mother as she made her way towards the entrance that led to the women's section of the synagogue. But Golda stood still, staring up at the building. "Come on," urged her daughter. "If we wait any longer we might not get a seat." But her mother did not reply.

Then to everyone's surprise she knelt down beside her grandson and hugged him, pointing up at the Star of David at the top of the domed roof. "They have stolen it from us," she said. "The Nazis, they force Jews to wear stars to set them apart. For Hitler it is a mark of shame. But he is a fool – it must be worn with pride." Then she said something that would stay with Marcus forever. "Please God you should live to see a time when the whole world sees it like that." Then she kissed him lightly on his forehead and turned to accompany her daughter.

✡ ✡ ✡

"I did not become a zoo director for this," said Stefan's father as he doused the pile of corpses with paraffin. His mother had placed each animal on the funeral pyre with immense care. Wings of birds that had succumbed to the stresses of the bombardment had been lovingly smoothed down, all traces of blood had been cleaned from the bodies of the larger creatures and their limbs and heads had been laid at an angle that made it look like they were sleeping.

"When so many people have forgotten how to be humane," she said to her son, "the rest of us need to remain civilised to help them remember." Jan let his wife's words hang in the air before dropping a flame on the pitiful mound.

As the fire took hold, Stefan looked across the nearby river to the other part of Warsaw, where bigger more ferocious bonfires had also become a nightly ritual.

✡︎✡︎✡︎

The planes struck at the end of the service, when the crowd outside the synagogue was at its most dense, creating a wave of panic and setting off a stampede of terror. The old and weak were pushed to the ground in the chaos, tumbling helplessly down the stone steps. And when the shooting began the screams were unbearable.

Marcus felt his arm being grabbed. "Run!" yelled his father. "Run!" There was no time to think and no time to breathe. "Crouch down here!" yelled his father, throwing Marcus against a wall, trying to shield him from the mayhem. But where was his mother?

The attack came in waves. During each lull Simon Tenenbaum tried to guide them both home. And when they barged through the front door, Marcus was instantly elated to see his mother there waiting.

"She's gone!" Marcus had never heard such a chilling cry before. "They've killed her – she's gone!"

TWENTY-ONE

September 25th

Warsaw was in flames. Entire areas of the city had been turned into wasteland, and the stench of death was everywhere. Thousands of homeless families listlessly roamed the streets from soup kitchen to bread queue, numb to the devastation around them. Those with homes that were still inhabitable opened their doors to the destitute, and it wasn't uncommon for three or four families to be living together in a one-bedroom apartment.

Marcus' house had been untouched, but his grandmother's death had broken his family. He desperately wanted to comfort his distraught mother, but soon realised it was futile. He'd tried everything to cheer her up, he even sang her favourite songs, but she was inconsolable. And she didn't want to be hugged – even when she finally relented and allowed him to hold her, Marcus realised it was no use. And when the sadness of failure became unbearable, he had to stop trying – which broke his heart.

Stefan had been sitting at his father's desk, holding the shiny black phone against his ear all morning. He wasn't normally allowed to use the telephone but his father had finally relented to let him at least try to contact Marcus. But it was useless. At first he dialled the Tenenbaums directly, but failed to get a connection. Then he tried contacting the central exchange to be put through by an operator, but that proved equally fruitless. The lines had obviously been destroyed, but Stefan kept trying nonetheless – anything was better than doing nothing at all.

Eventually he replaced the handset and started to play with a glass paperweight on the desk in front of him, rolling it slowly from hand to hand. Then he made goalposts from two wooden pen holders and tried to swerve the glass sphere round an inkwell goalie. Apollo noticed and scampered down Stefan's arm to take a closer look and quickly became involved in the game. Stefan realised that the harder he flicked, the wider it swerved and the more energetic his pet became. But then Apollo barged into the paperweight and deflected it onto the inkwell, splattering a shower of black ink over a pile of papers. In a panic Stefan frantically tried to soak up the stains with his shirt sleeve, but that only smudged the page even more. For a fleeting moment he even considered using the guilty rat to mop up the mess but then he spotted some blotting paper and started to dab. "It's a good thing my father didn't see that!" he whispered to Apollo, gently placing him on his shoulder. Then Stefan's attention was diverted by the list that was written on the paper:

- 20 machine guns and ammunition
- 12 anti-aircraft rifles and ammunition
- 150 pistols and ammunition
- 100 sticks of dynamite
- 10 reels of fuse wire

Below the list was a roughly drawn sketch of the zoo with arrows leading from each item to various locations in the grounds. If Stefan's guess was correct, the weapons he and Marcus had witnessed mysteriously being unloaded from Otto's truck a few weeks earlier were now in the hippo house, the giraffe enclosure and under the lions' cage.

October 5th

Marcus was surprised to see Shlomo in the crowd outside his front door and rushed out to greet him. He looked very pale and, for some reason, was holding a battered wicker shopping basket, bulging with clothes.

"They didn't get you then," Marcus said to his friend.

"No, but it was a close shave! Who are all these people?"

"Relatives, I think," replied Marcus. "I've never met half of them before."

"Why? What's happening at your house? Is it some sort of party?"

Marcus was stunned but tried not to show it. He'd assumed Shlomo had come for his grandmother's funeral like everyone else, but he was wrong. "Er... not really," he replied.

"Marcus, we're waiting – come!" called his father's voice from the house.

They had so much to share but there was no chance to talk. "I've got to go," Marcus said, after a tongue-tied silence. "I'll see you soon."

"Okay," replied Shlomo, as his friend turned back towards the house.

A small hunched figure with a grey scraggly beard stood in the open doorway. He was the rabbi who was preparing Marcus and Shlomo for their Bar Mitzvahs, but today he had a more sombre duty to perform. Behind him, in the hallway of the house, was a long rectangular coffin covered in a black shawl.

It was customary for Jewish funerals to be held as quickly as possible, but due to the huge number of deaths in Warsaw in recent weeks, the family had had to wait until now to bury Marcus' grandmother.

A handful of people paused in respect as the procession approached the battered streets of the Jewish District on their way to the cemetery. Shlomo was amongst them, clutching his basket of clothes. Marcus was holding his mother's hand as they followed behind the wagon that carried the coffin. She hadn't uttered a word since that terrible night, and he was relieved that she'd allowed him to keep his grip all the way to the graveside.

It was a beautiful summer's day. The city was eerily quiet and it was strange to see the pure blue sky untainted by clouds or aeroplanes. The hellish bombing had now stopped, but the invasion of the city by the victorious German troops had begun. Soldiers wearing the Nazi swastika had been on the streets for a few days and the first reports of random attacks on Jews had already started to spread through the community. Marcus' father had seen Poles in food queues being encouraged by Germans to abuse the Jews who were lining up with them, yelling "we will really teach you how to hate these vermin, now!"

But for the next few hours at least, it was safe to be a Jew in Warsaw. Several funerals were taking place simultaneously and a long queue of mourning families had built up outside the cemetery gates. And they had Adolf Hitler himself to thank for this sudden window of calm – because while Marcus' grandmother was being buried, the German leader responsible for her murder was attending a victory parade two miles away in Pilsudski Square, an event that every German soldier and Jew-hating Pole in Warsaw wouldn't miss for the world.

Part Three

October 1939

TWENTY-TWO

"I don't want to go," said Stefan.

"Nor do I," replied his father. "But I am still going."

"But why do I need to go with you?"

"It will help you to understand…"

"Understand what?"

"What has happened and what is about to happen…"

"But I already understand. I've seen what they've done to our zoo and I have seen what their planes have been doing to Warsaw every day. What more is there to know?"

"Trust me. Once you see, you'll understand. Now put that rat away and follow me."

Stefan returned Apollo to his courtyard home and reluctantly joined his father outside the front of the villa.

"Hold this," he said to his son, handing him a bag bulging with freshly baked bread. "This is for later on." Then they set off to walk towards the bridge that spanned the Vistula to enter the main part of Warsaw for the first time since the bombing began.

"Can we visit Marcus when we're there?" asked Stefan.

"Maybe," replied his father. "We'll see."

Stefan hardly recognised the world he was now entering. One of the parallel bridges that spanned the river had been blown away; its mangled metal remains crudely jutted out of the water. Bloated bodies of dead horses floated beneath them, and the burned out shells of abandoned vehicles dotted the banks. Some people held cloths over their noses to block out the stench from the water, and as they neared the end of the bridge Stefan too chocked as the harsh bitter smell of the battered city struck the back of his throat.

Pilsudski Square was huge. It was said that the entire population of Warsaw could fit in it. When he was much younger, Stefan remembered crossing it with his father, on their way to the nearby park. Then it had seemed to take forever.

"What are they doing?" he asked his father, pointing to a line of men standing in the centre of the square.

"Sweeping," replied Mr Zabinski.

There were about twenty men, dressed in rags, each holding a broom, being screamed at in German by a soldier holding a rifle. "*Schneller*! Faster!" he barked. "The Glorious Fuehrer, your new leader, will be here soon. Don't you want him to see what a beautiful city you have?"

Stefan's father took his hand and led the way to the park. It was unrecognisable; encamped on the once manicured lawns were hundreds of homeless victims of the war, and dishevelled children with gaunt hungry faces roamed around begging forlornly for food.

"Give me that bag," said Stefan's father. He reached inside and gave a loaf to the nearest child. Then another pair of hands appeared. Soon a small crowd of silent, sad-faced children had gathered round. Hunger had stolen their voices and they could hardly bring themselves to look up. Most rushed away guarding their food like starving animals in the wild, while a few older children tore their loaves in half to share with younger brothers and sisters. But all too soon the bag was empty, leaving a cluster of poor children with nothing. "I'm really sorry," whispered Mr Zabinski. "That's all I have."

As they made their way out of the park, all Stefan could think about was his friend.

"Stef!"

At first Stefan dismissed it as just a sound.

"Stefan Zabinski, it's me." Then he recognised it – Pawel; the bully he'd spent so much of his life avoiding. "They bombed my house, Stef… it's all gone."

"And your family?" asked Mr Zabinski, standing beside his son. "How are they?"

"We were all in a shelter when they struck, sir," replied Pawel.

"At least that is good news."

His father turned to walk away, but Stefan stayed rooted to the spot. This was probably the first time he'd really looked Pawel in the eye. Where had the ogre he used to cower from gone?

"Who do you blame?" he heard himself ask.

"Sorry?" replied Pawel.

"Whose fault is all this, the Germans or the Jews?" and he pointed at the hordes of other people in the park who had lost everything.

After a long pause, Pawel shook his head and looked down at the ground, "I really don't know what to think anymore," he said.

Stefan turned to join his father and they made their way back towards Pilsudski Square.

"You are a good man," came a booming German voice from behind Stefan's shoulder. A soldier in a smart black uniform approached Mr Zabinski with his hand held out expecting it to be shaken. "I saw what you were doing. Thanks to people like you, maybe these poor Polish children will not starve."

"And it is thanks to people like you that their parents are no longer here to feed them," he replied, leaving the soldier's hand unshaken.

TWENTY-THREE

Marcus was still holding his mother's hand at the graveside as the family solemnly filed past. In normal times their consoling words would be accompanied by a reassuring hug, but now that death was a daily occurrence, most people could offer no more than a gentle nod.

The last person to console Marcus' mother was the rabbi. "May The Almighty comfort you amongst the mourners of Zion", he said, a phrase that had been used at Jewish funerals for centuries. She remained still and silent. But unlike everyone else, the rabbi did not walk away. Marcus noticed that beneath the rim of his large black hat the old man's eyes were shut tight. "Your mother, she was a marvellous person," he whispered. "I knew her well – we grew up together. I remember your wedding like it was yesterday. Such a lovely day! Such a wonderful family." Then he reached out and gently cupped Marcus' chin in his hand. "She was so proud of her grandson," he continued. "She called him her 'Brightest Star'. He reminded her so much of your late father, may his soul rest in peace. Did she ever tell you that?"

"Frequently."

Marcus' heart began to race at the first word his mother had uttered for three weeks.

"He is your future, Lonia," said the rabbi. "He is all of our futures." Then he left.

At first she didn't move, but Marcus knew that things had changed when she gently squeezed his hand. Then she knelt down and held him, reaching out for her husband as well. "Let's go home," she said at last.

By the time Stefan and his father had returned to Pilsudski Square, endless rows of stern-faced German soldiers were standing to attention along its edge. But despite the crowds there was an unnerving silence. How could so many people be so quiet?

"Stay close," whispered Jan Zabinski as he steered his son towards the group of fellow Poles that had gathered in the corner of the square. Some had come out of pure curiosity, while others wanted to stare their tormentors in the eye. Most people looked on impassively, although there were a few towards the front who held homemade flags bearing the Nazi swastika. Stefan wondered if Helda was amongst them.

"There he is!" called a voice. A sudden ripple of anger and expectation surged through the crowd. Gradually the chant of "*Sieg Heil! Sieg Heil!*" started to ring around the square and the crudely made flags at the front began to wave.

Jan Zabinski leant forward so that his mouth was practically touching his son's ear and whispered, "Here comes the most odious man on the face of the earth." Then an open-topped vehicle appeared at the far end of the square, slowly gliding past the ranks of soldiers. Standing in the front passenger seat, dressed in a black leather coat was the unmistakeable figure of Adolf Hitler, looking even more severe than he did on Marcus' father's insect jars.

His cold, blank expression didn't waver as the car swept around the square, soaking up the admiration of his troops. Eventually it drew to a halt, and Stefan heard what he thought at first was distant clapping, but was actually the sound of a thousand boots marching in unison – the victory parade had begun.

"Do you think Marcus and his family are here?" asked Stefan.

His father gulped at the naivety of his son's question. The awful truth was that he wasn't even sure if Marcus or any of his family were still alive, but that was the last thing he wanted to tell his son. "No," he replied. "If I was a Jew I reckon I'd stay as far away from Hitler as I could."

The procession seemed to be never ending. Row after row of troops bearing banners emblazoned with the Nazi swastika paraded before them and Stefan stared open-mouthed at the huge array of weaponry on display. Then, a distant rumble overhead sent a shiver through the crowd. All eyes instinctively looked skywards as gasps greeted the arrival of the same planes that had brought so much destruction to the city. Even the Poles with the homemade flags fell silent.

"Let's go," said Stefan's father. "I think we've seen enough."

"Can we visit Marcus now? It's only a short walk away."

And because there was no way of explaining why they shouldn't go without alarming his son unduly, he agreed, secretly praying that his darkest fears weren't about to come true.

✡ ✡ ✡

Marcus' family were on their way back from the cemetery when the flypast roared overhead, but they hardly noticed it. There was a far more urgent matter to attend to.

"I know her," said Marcus' father, looking down at the throbbing bundle of rags on their door step. "Her husband is a technician at the school."

"Well we can't leave her here," said his mother gently kneeling down beside the woman. Then she gasped and quickly stood up. "She's holding a baby!"

Marcus' parents looked at each other in alarm. Then his mother knelt down once more, this time close to the woman's ear. "What has happened?" she whispered. There was no response. "Come let me hold you." Marcus watched as his mother gently coaxed the sobbing woman closer and hugged her like a child. The baby in her arms began to cry – at least it was still alive, although from the weakness of its whimper, only barely. "It's a new-born," announced Mrs Tenenbaum.

"Ten days," said a broken voice from the rags.

"Come, let's go inside," said Marcus' father pushing the front door open. "You'll be safe with us." Even as he said these words he knew they were mere hot air – he could no more guarantee safety than he could turn back time.

And so the Tenenbaums acquired two new house guests – Greta Gutman and "child". Within an hour Marcus' father's study had been turned into a bedroom.

"Look what I found in the loft!" announced Mr Tenenbaum carrying the cot that Marcus had slept in as a baby.

"I didn't think that was ever going to be used again!" said his wife.

Once the frail infant had finally settled, Greta started to tell her story.

"I had been in labour for some time when the air raid siren went off. The hospital suffered a direct hit. There was chaos. Some of the nurses carried me to the basement. It was terrible – so painful. In the end I gave birth to my son in a dark damp room, on a cold tiled floor." There was a distance to her words; her voice was drained of emotion. "Then there was a second hit and all the lights went out. I thought I was going to die. I think the building must have collapsed because the basement was suddenly full of rubble. We were sealed off."

"How long were you down there?" asked Lonia.

"God only knows," replied Greta, "maybe days. I don't remember much. But they found us… and my baby was still alive. I thought it had to be a miracle!"

"And your husband?" asked Mr Tenenbaum. "Do you know where he is? Does he know he is a father?"

Greta sat in silence for a while staring vacantly into the middle distance. Then she continued even more dispassionately. "When

I saw the devastation outside I started to panic. What hell was I bringing my child in to? So I went home. Where else could I go? But there was no home to go to. The whole block was destroyed. I had no idea where my husband was or if he was still alive. I was distraught. All the time this poor baby was whining…" she paused and her voice betrayed its first hint of emotion. "…and all I could think as I fed it was 'I am sorry I had you.'" This was clearly the first time the story had been told – it felt as if she was hearing it for the first time too. "But then another miracle! This morning, as I was standing in line for some soup, I saw my husband in another queue nearby. At first I thought I was dreaming, but no it was him. What could I do? What would you do? After all that had happened at last something good! So I called him. 'Moshe, Moshe, it's me!' Then he looked up. At first he was confused, but then he realised and his face lit up. One minute he was alone in the world and the next he had us back. He yelled in excitement – how happy he must have been." Then she paused again, but not for long. She was almost finished now; just a few more breaths and she could stop. "The Nazis guarding the queues were angry! What has a Jew got to be happy about? So he was smashed in the head with a rifle. But the fool tried to get to his feet. If only he'd stayed on the ground – maybe they would have just kicked him. But no. He stumbled towards us 'My child!' he called out. "At last!" But they were his final words. There were two shots and he was dead on the street."

In tears, now, Lonia Tenenbaum held her new houseguest, but she had no words of consolation to offer – there were none.

"So yes, Mr Tenenbaum," Greta said in conclusion. "Moshe did know that he was a father, but only for a few moments."

Then there was a harsh knock at the door. Nobody moved. Surely the Nazis hadn't come for this woman as well? Wasn't it enough that they'd shot her husband? Then the flap of the letter box flipped open and a familiar voice called through the hole.

"Stefan!" screamed Marcus. "It's Stefan!"

TWENTY-FOUR

"Marcus?" Stefan stood transfixed in the doorway. What had happened to his friend? He looked so thin and gaunt. Where was the hero that rescued Apollo from the tree?

"Jan, welcome!" Marcus' father rushed to greet them, overjoyed at this sudden opportunity to bring some normality into their lives. "Let me introduce you to Greta Gutman. She lives with us now, with her baby."

On their way from the victory parade Stefan and his father had seen stray dogs feeding on the carcasses of horses and entire rows of houses that had been reduced to rubble by the bombing. They'd gagged on the stench from the piles of discarded waste rotting on street corners, and seen desperation etched on people's faces. And now they were expected to greet this frail, ghostly figure as if everything was as it should be...

"We were just about to take coffee," said Marcus' mother, ushering Greta and Jan into the kitchen. "Please – you have to join us... come!" Then she turned to the boys. "You two run upstairs and play."

So Stefan followed his friend to his room, as he had done countless times in the past, and perched on the edge of his bed.

"Did they get the zoo?" Marcus asked anxiously. "I saw the bombing on your side of the river. How are the animals?"

"We've lost a lot – the zoo was hit quite hard," replied Stefan – but not as hard as here, he thought. He couldn't bring himself to talk about the nightly bonfires or the carnage he'd witnessed in the lion house and the bear enclosure. It all seemed so trivial now.

"And what about your mother and Otto and everyone else… are they okay?"

"Yes," replied Stefan. "Guess what?"

"What?"

"I know where those weapons are?"

"Weapons?"

"The ones we saw being unloaded from Otto's truck."

"Oh, yes, I'd forgotten about that…"

Stefan shot to his feet, delighted to have something genuinely exciting to tell his friend. "I found this sheet of paper… well Apollo found it really… I was trying to phone you… the lines were down… we were playing football on my father's desk… not real football, obviously… we weren't actually standing up there; that would be stupid! We were using a paperweight, and…" Stefan stopped mid-story and smiled; it was wonderful to see his friend laughing again. "We saw Pawel," he continued.

"When?"

"Earlier on, in the park." Stefan added. "He's been bombed."

"Was he okay?"

"I think so," replied Stefan. "He was in a shelter with his mum when they struck. I'm glad they didn't get you!" he added.

Marcus decided not to mention what had happened to his grandmother. He didn't want to talk about the near miss outside the bakery either. "Let's go and find Shlomo!" he announced, jumping to his feet to leave the room. He had been desperate to see their friend ever since the brief encounter, earlier on, at the funeral.

"Ok. Great!" said Stefan, following behind.

"Where are you two going?" said Marcus' father as the boys charged towards the front door.

"We're off to Shlomo's," said Stefan.

Marcus' mother suddenly appeared in the hallway. "What's going on?"

"The boys are going out for a while," said her husband.

"Do you think that's a good idea?" she replied nervously.

"Er... what do you think, Jan?" Marcus' father called into the kitchen.

"About what?" replied Stefan's father.

"Whether the boys should go out for a while..."

"Well it's all a bit late now," said Marcus' mother by the open front door. "They've gone."

TWENTY-FIVE

Shlomo's flat overlooked Traugutta Park, normally a ten-minute walk from Marcus' house, in the northern Żoliborz area of the city. But it didn't take long for the boys to abandon their usual short cut over the railway footbridge in the nearby fields; it was no longer there. Instead they had to use the main Gdansk Road that bordered the Vistula.

"Do you think we should turn back?" said Marcus.

"Why?" replied Stefan. "It's not much longer this way."

"But is it safe? Look at all those German uniforms."

"Don't you want to see Shlomo?"

"Of course I do!" replied Marcus. "But I'm not sure if it's safe…"

"They're not going to bother with kids," said Stefan.

"How do you know that?" asked Marcus.

"I saw thousands of them marching past Hitler in Pilsudski Square this morning. Now that they've won, why should they do anymore fighting?"

Marcus grabbed his friend's arm.

"You saw Hitler?"

"Yeah!" said Stefan, with the authority of an expert. "He was just standing there saluting his troops. I don't think we've got anything to be frightened of now – from where I was standing he didn't look very angry."

"But I'm Jewish – the Nazis hate people like me," said Marcus.

"Stop worrying! Anyway, how are they going to know that you're a Jew, you look just like me?" said Stefan, pulling his arm free. "Look, you can turn back if you want to. I want to see how Shlomo is."

"I saw him this morning," said Marcus, he's fine.

"Where did you see him?"

"He came round to my house," replied Marcus, but that was as much detail as he was going to divulge; if he told Stefan about the funeral then he would have to tell him about the air raids. And that would be far too painful – for both of them.

"That's fine then!" exclaimed Stefan. "If he could pop over to you, then it must be perfectly safe to visit him!" Finally convinced that he was right, he turned away and carried on along the road. And Marcus had no choice other than to follow him. Every part of him knew it was the wrong thing to do, but how could he just let his friend walk alone towards the enemy?

Although the barrier was up at the level crossing, where the railway met the road, there was still a long queue of people at the gate. As the boys approached they could see that a group of German soldiers were questioning everyone before allowing them to pass.

"What are they doing?" whispered Marcus.

"Checking papers, I guess," said Stefan.

"But I don't have any papers," said Marcus. "Only grown-ups carry stuff like that."

"Then we've got nothing to worry about – they won't expect you to have them!"

So they joined the end of the queue.

Then they heard the urgent whisper of a man's voice. "Boys!" At first they ignored it – why would anyone want to speak to them? "Boys – what are you doing here?" It was Mr Rokus, their maths teacher.

"We're visiting Shlomo, sir," replied Stefan.

"Are you crazy?!" said the man. "Especially you, Marcus... does your father know you're here?"

"Er, yes... we..."

"*Halt die Klappe*!" boomed a voice from the front of the line. "Shut up!"

"It's too late to leave now," whispered Mr Rokus. "They'd only get suspicious. Just stay close to me!"

So Marcus and Stefan did as they were told and stood beside Mr Rokus, but they had no idea why. At first they thought it was merely further proof of just how mad this man really was – that even outside school he couldn't stop bossing children about. Stefan tried to sneak a sniff of his breath, suspecting he'd been drinking again. But they soon saw the reason for his caution.

"What are they doing?" whispered Stefan.

"Looking for Jews," Mr Rokus replied. "Now keep your mouths shut. Not a single word until we get past!"

As they moved further along the queue, they could see a truck parked next to the soldiers. On the back were about a dozen Jewish men and a few boys the same age as Marcus, huddled together in fear, with two uniformed guards pointing rifles at them.

"Are these your sons?" asked the soldier as he scanned Mr Rokus' identity papers.

"This one yes," he replied resting his hand on Stefan's shoulder. "And this one is my nephew."

"Good," he replied, folding the documents and returning them to Mr Rokus. "Next!"

The three of them walked swiftly away from the checkpoint, only daring to breathe when they turned a corner and were out of sight. "That was close," said Marcus. "Thank you Uncle Kurt!"

"You don't realise how close it was," replied Mr Rokus.

"What do you mean?" said Stefan.

"If that soldier could actually read Polish he would have seen that my papers clearly state I am single and don't have any children. It shows that our guests are not as clever as they like to think."

They said their farewells to Mr Rokus, assuring him that they would use a safer route when they returned to Żoliborz, and made their way to where Shlomo lived.

"I'm really sorry, Marcus," said Stefan when they were finally alone. "I really shouldn't have made you come. They could have taken you away…"

"It's gone," said Marcus, looking over his friend's shoulder.

"What are you talking about?"

"Shlomo's block of flats," he replied. "It's not there."

Stefan turned to look at the mountain of bricks that confirmed what Marcus was saying. "But you said that you saw him this morning, so he must be okay."

"I did… and he was. But I had no idea that this had happened to his home."

"Didn't he tell you?" asked Stefan.

"Well, we really didn't have much chance to talk," explained Marcus. "You see, it was my grandmother's funeral and…"

And as Stefan listened to the tragedy that had struck his friend's family and of how close he had come to being killed in a bread queue, he realised how wrong he had been to say that there was nothing to be frightened of now.

TWENTY-SIX

"Where have you two been?" said Marcus' mother as the boys came into the house. "It was getting so late… we were worried!"

"Shlomo's been bombed out," said her son. "We couldn't find him."

"But I thought he was here this morning…"

"He was," replied Marcus. "But I don't know where he is now."

"How was it out there?" asked Mr Tenenbaum, appearing from behind his wife. "Did you have any problems with the Nazis?"

Marcus shot his friend a glance. "No problems at all, really – it was fine."

"They're probably all still in Pilsudski Square, waving at their Fuehrer!" added Stefan. "And we saw Mr Rokus as well!"

"Kurt?" said Marcus' father. "How is he?"

"Oh fine. He sends his regards and…"

"We have to go now, Stefan," interrupted his father emerging from the kitchen. "It is crucial we are home before it starts to get dark."

"When can we come again? When can Marcus visit us? He can sleep in my room, father. You know how much space there is!"

"We will see."

Marcus' father opened the front door just wide enough to see through the crack. "It's clear," he announced. "With any luck you'll be back at the zoo within the hour."

Stefan and his father slipped out so quickly there was barely any time to say goodbye.

"We have to be very careful," Jan Zabinski said to his son as they made their way towards the bridge that crossed the Vistula. "Walk briskly, but don't run. Stay with me at all times and don't, whatever you do, say a word."

Stefan felt a sudden urge to tell his father about what had really happened earlier that afternoon, but decided against it. "But why...?" he asked as innocently as he could.

"Just do what I say," snapped his father, guiding him into an alleyway. "No one must know that we've been visiting the Tenenbaums. The last thing we want is to cast suspicion on them." Jan could see that his son was confused. "Look – from now on Warsaw is a divided city," he explained. "The Nazis are on top, we Poles are in the middle and the Jews are at the bottom. Open friendship between Jews and Poles can be dangerous for both parties." Then he glanced furtively around to ensure the coast was clear. "There is one more thing," he said, opening the bread bag to reveal a tightly wrapped bundle at the bottom. "At no cost must the Germans know about this."

"What is it?" whispered Stefan.

"A baby," he replied. "That woman in Marcus' house made me take it. I really had no choice."

There was a bundle of towels at the bottom of the bag. Stefan nervously took a corner and carefully peeled it away to reveal the precious cargo asleep inside. Before he could say a word, his father gently resealed the white cocoon and gripped the handles of the bag. Then he took his son's arm and casually stepped out of the alleyway.

German soldiers seemed to be everywhere. Some were rolling spirals of barbed wire across the road while others attached posters and leaflets to any surface that would take a nail.

Any hope that the pair could slip past unnoticed were dashed as they approached the bridge. Since this morning a heavily guarded barrier had been established, just like the checkpoint Stefan had encountered earlier on with Marcus. He began to feel sick.

"*Herzlich willkommen!*" Stefan held his breath as his father bellowed loudly in his best German accent at the nearest guard. "Welcome to Warsaw! What part of The Fatherland do you come from?" And where did he get those cigarettes from? "I was in Berlin last year, visiting the wonderful zoo in the Tiergarten. Are you familiar with it?"

At first the startled soldier was lost for words. He looked like an anxious school boy floundering to answer his teacher's question. And he was staring very suspiciously at the cigarettes on offer.

"Oh, I understand," said Mr Zabinski. "You're not allowed to smoke on duty. Well, why don't you take a couple and smoke them with a friend later," sliding two of the cigarettes into the breast pocket of the soldier's jacket.

"*Halt!*" snapped the soldier, pushing Stefan's father's hand away with the muzzle of his rifle and pointing it straight at his chest. "*Öffnen Sie die Tasche!*" he shouted, insisting that Mr Zabinski open the bag he was holding.

"Okay, okay. I am so sorry to have upset you!"

"*Schnell!*" the soldier was starting to panic now – as was Stefan, although he was desperate not to show it.

"What is going on here?" A more senior officer approached to see what was happening. Stefan noticed his father's face instantly brighten. "Ah, good day. I was just telling your colleague here of my visit to the Berlin Zoo. What a spectacular place, I especially loved the elephants. Have you been?"

"Of course!" replied the officer. "I went there many times as a child and now it is a favourite with my own children."

"I seem to have unsettled your comrade, here. I am most dreadfully sorry."

There was a brief exchange between the two soldiers and the younger man withdrew his rifle, snapped his heels together and briskly moved to guard another part of the roadblock.

"Some of these youngsters have trouble controlling their tempers," joked the officer. "He probably thought you were hiding a family of Jews in that bag of yours!" and the two men burst into laughter.

"Look, why don't you take the whole packet?" Stefan's father said to the officer. "Share them with your colleagues at your convenience. I won't tell the Fuehrer if you don't!"

Then the senior officer winked, tapped his nose knowingly and promptly slipped the cigarettes into his pocket. "I wish you a pleasant evening," he said as he lifted the barrier for them to pass through.

"And the same to you, my friend," replied Mr Zabinski.

Neither father nor son spoke until they reached the other end of the bridge.

"What would have happened if they found the baby?" Stefan asked.

"You don't want to think about it," replied his father.

✡ ✡ ✡

The thing that struck Stefan, when his father opened the bag back at the villa, was his mother's lack of surprise. While others panicked, she looked for solutions. He knew that they would never have coped with the horrors of the last six weeks without her talent for staying level headed in a crisis.

"'God has sent you to save him,' that's what she said to me," explained Stefan's father. "'You are his only hope for a life' she pleaded."

He handed his wife the basket and sat on a chair in the hallway with his head in his hands.

"'But he is your child,' I said, 'How can you give him up?'"

Stefan's mother gently lifted the baby out of the bag and held it close to her chest.

His father carried on. "'But that is the wrong question,' she

107

replied 'Rather ask how can I give him a life when I no longer wish to live myself?' Then she grabbed me, with tears streaming down her face. She begged me to take him… 'He is so weak – I can do nothing here for him – this is his one chance. You must do this – you must!'"

"That poor, courageous woman," said Stefan's mother, gently loosening the towelling. "I wonder if this little man will ever know what a brave person his mother is." Then she turned to make her way to the kitchen. "Contact Otto's wife, ," she said to her husband. "Franciszka is bound to be able to help."

Jan went to his study and Stefan was suddenly alone in the hall. He looked around at the paintings and ornaments that adorned their home, each still in their normal place. He scanned the undamaged walls and glanced up at the ceiling, where not a single flake of plaster had been dislodged, and he looked through the unbroken windows to a world where no soldiers were waiting to ruin his life. Then he wandered out into the courtyard, gathered up Apollo and leant into Hercules' sty. "Do you know how lucky we all are?" he whispered, stroking the nose of his pig.

TWENTY-SEVEN

Stefan stared out of his bedroom window, still haunted by the harrowing scenes he had witnessed earlier on. Suddenly muted footsteps from the gravel driveway below grabbed his attention. He leant out of the window and peered down to see a small group of people approaching the house. A shaft of light flashed across their faces as the front door of the villa opened and they quickly filed in. Stefan immediately recognised Otto and his wife, but he didn't know the others.

Eager to see what was going on, Stefan dashed out of his room and crouched on the landing to peek through the banisters at the hallway below. He watched his father greet his guests, hang up their coats and guide them into his study, although Otto and Franciszka stayed in the hallway. Immediately Stefan's mother joined them from the kitchen, holding a bundle wrapped in a white blanket – it was the baby. Instantly Otto and Franciszka embraced in an explosion of emotion.

Then Otto joined the others in Jan's study and the two women went into the kitchen with the baby, leaving Stefan staring at the empty hall. He quickly closed his bedroom door and sneaked downstairs to find out what was going. He darted into the longue and sat silently at the piano, straining to decipher the murmurs from the study next door, but he couldn't follow what was being said, so he decided to risk standing in the hallway. He casually chose a book from the shelves and leant against the wall, positioning himself beside the coat stand. Feigning to read, he focused all his attention on the animated discussion spilling out into the hall.

"The old farmhouse?" asked his father.

"Yes – the one with the windmill beside it," replied Otto.

"When?"

"This morning."

"How many?"

"Three car loads. Ten, maybe a dozen men, I'd say."

"Soldiers?"

"Not all of them – some were wearing plain clothes."

"Gestapo officers, I should think – the secret police. What were they doing?"

"Hard to tell – but it looked as if they were inspecting the building. They were there for at least an hour. Some of them were measuring the windows and doors, while others wrote notes on their clipboards."

"I reckon they're planning on moving in… probably using it as a barracks. It's in the ideal position – over here on the quiet side of the river, but still close enough to the main part of the city."

"It looks like we're about to get new neighbours, then!"

Stefan turned another unread page…

"We'll have to move the weapons from the zoo," this was a male voice that Stefan had never heard before. "We can't risk them being discovered."

"I wouldn't worry too much about that," said Stefan's father. "They are well hidden. I doubt that the Gestapo will want to ruin their boots in the sewers and drains."

"Is that where you've stored them?"

"More or less, Feliks," replied Mr Zabinski. "Most of the guns are under the hippo house, the ammunition is in the old giraffe enclosure and most of the grenades are stored in the sewers under the lions' cage. I reckon they are pretty secure."

"If you say so, Jan," replied the man. "But the last thing we need is for some nosey Nazi to stumble upon them. That'll be the end for all of us!"

Stefan froze – well aware of what "the end" actually meant.

"The Nazis have only just arrived," this was a female voice that was also unfamiliar to Stefan. "It'll take them a while to get settled in and organised. They'll be too busy to worry about any resistance from us Poles."

"Don't underestimate the Germans' talent for organisation, Marda," said Stefan's father. "It didn't take them long to set up roadblocks all over the city today. Stefan and I had a pretty close shave on our way back from The Old Town... didn't we Stefan?"

Stefan slammed his book in panic and spun round to see his father leaning, arms folded, in the doorway of his study. "Good book, I hope!" he said. Stefan's jaw had suddenly turned to stone. "Tell me, when did you ever learn to read upside down?"

"Ah ha!" Otto suddenly appeared next to Jan in the door way. "We have a spy!"

"More like a hero!" corrected Stefan's father, lurching towards his son. "Do you know what this boy did today?" Then Stefan felt himself being dragged across the hall towards the study. "If a twelve year old boy can retain his composure when a twitchy German soldier is pointing a gun at his father's chest than there is hope for us all!"

The room was filled with spontaneous applause. Stefan's mother and Franciszka arrived, with the baby, to join in the celebration.

"How is the poor thing?" asked the woman standing beside Stefan's father.

"Very weak, Marda" replied Franciszka. "But I think it's just a lack of food. He seems to be medically sound. But it's wonderful," she added. "You don't know how happy you have made Otto and I. We had given up the dream of ever becoming parents and now this gift from God has arrived."

Stefan's mother put a comforting arm on her shoulder. "Let's hope that he is the first of many Jews that can be saved," she said.

Part Four

November 1939

TWENTY-EIGHT

At last Marcus' father returned home with some news.

"Who is Janusz Korczak?" he asked.

"He's a doctor," replied his father.

"So why is Shlomo living with a doctor? Is he ill?"

"No, he's fine. Dr Korczak looks after lots of children like Shlomo."

"But there are no other children like Shlomo-the-Bull in Warsaw!"

Marcus' father was pleased to see his son so animated, but he knew that it was not going to last long.

"Where is this place? Can we go and see him?"

"It's on Krochmalna Street."

"Brilliant – that's not far from The Café Sztuka!"

"It's an orphanage." Marcus suddenly looked confused. "It's where children go who don't have any parents…"

"I know what an orphanage is!" he said.

"Shlomo lost more than just his home during the bombing. I'm afraid his mother was…"

"No – there must be some mistake. How could he survive unhurt when they were together?"

"Shlomo was in the park when the bomb hit their building," corrected his father.

Simon watched in agony as the joy drained from his son's face and reached out to comfort him. "He's all alone now," Marcus said.

Shlomo's mother would call him her "little man". Her husband had died when she was pregnant – Shlomo once said that the best way to lose your father is never to have known him in the first place. But now he'd lost both parents.

"She was buried on the same day as your grandmother," said Marcus' father. "He was on his way back from the cemetery when he came to our house."

"He was carrying a basket full of clothes," said Marcus.

"He was looking for a home," said his father. "And we turned him away."

TWENTY-NINE

The next morning Marcus found his father unplugging the family radio from the wall. "What are you doing that for?" he asked.

"Read this," replied his father, handing him a piece of paper from his back pocket. "It's the latest decree from our German masters."

"All Jewish-owned radios must be brought to The Gestapo headquarters by 15th November," Marcus read. "Any Jew found in possession of one after that date will be imprisoned."

"Soon we will only be allowed to breathe in when they say so," said his father, carrying the radio towards the front door. "And if they don't permit us to breathe out again we will all suffocate."

"Let me come with you," Marcus pleaded. "We can go and see Shlomo afterwards."

"Why not," replied his father. "Hurry up and grab your coat."

"Why do they want our radios?" he asked his father, as they left the house.

"To silence the outside world; if the Germans become the sole source of information then their word becomes the truth."

As they walked along the street Marcus saw shopkeepers replacing broken windows with planks of wood salvaged from nearby bombsites. There were hordes of women and children fervently brushing dust and dirt from the pavements, desperately trying to sweep some normality back into the lives. He saw bagel sellers hawking their goods on street corners and the usual army of trolley men weaving in and out of the crowd, pushing their barrows as vigorously as ever, touting for work. "Let me push that radio for you!" one called out to Marcus' father. "Come on, old man, it's far too heavy to carry!"

"Who are you calling 'old man'?" his father joked. "I'm half your age. It is me who should be pushing you!"

Marcus was pleased to hear the lightness return to his father's voice, but it stopped abruptly as they approached the old court house, where the Gestapo had set up their headquarters. A huge swastika flag adorned the front of the building and a sinister row of baton-wielding guards lined the steps that led to the entrance. As they joined the long silent queue that snaked along the pavement, Marcus realised that most of the radios they were holding looked like theirs – apart from one much bigger set that had been brought in a pram and was wrapped up in a blanket like a baby.

"I wonder how long this is going to take!" whispered a voice.

"Why? Maybe you have an important appointment to keep?" quipped another.

"As it happens I do!" replied the first. "Chamberlain, the British Prime Minister, is coming for lunch!"

A ripple of chuckles began...

"Well I promised my wife I'd fetch home some smoked salmon," said another. "We're hosting Stalin and he refuses to eat anything else!"

The chuckles became giggles...

"That's nothing," added a third joker. "We're having Hitler for supper... but we haven't decided whether to fry him, boil him or eat him raw!"

This triggered an explosion of laughter.

"*Haltet eure Klappen, dreckige Juden!*" came a yell from the court house steps. "Shut your mouths, dirty Jews!"

Instantly order was restored – but not for long.

"Here come Laurel and Hardy," whispered a man beside

Marcus, as two men appeared on the steps of the building. They couldn't have been more different – one was tall and thin, with a jet black uniform while the other was barely half his height and several times wider. He was obviously not a soldier, but as the unlikely couple reached the queue his particular role became clear.

"*Dreck... Dreck...*" snapped the short, round man casting a clearly expert eye over the radios. "*Dreck... rubbish...*" Once a radio had been declared "*Dreck*", its owner was shunted out of the line by the soldier and directed towards a waiting truck to deposit the set.

Occasionally the radio inspector would pause, lift his round metal-framed glasses and pass a verdict of "*gut*". The owner was then taken to a second waiting truck.

Eventually he got to the pram and pulled back the blanket. Instantly his face lit up and he leant forward, practically pressing his nose against the radio. "*Electrola!*" he exclaimed. "*Amerikaner! Perfekt!*" Then he yelled in joy at the top of his voice – "My Fuehrer will be delighted! It will be in Berlin by tomorrow!" Then he grabbed the handle of the pram and charged off towards the old court house himself. This clearly alarmed and confused the soldier, who spun round so quickly to follow the old man that he tripped over his own feet and stumbled to the ground. The reaction in the queue was instantaneous, it was literally impossible not to laugh – which immediately turned the soldier's embarrassment into rage.

"*Haltet eure Klappen!* Shut your mouths!" he yelled from the ground, and his face turned as red as his armband. But the laughter continued. Furious, he quickly shot to his feet and swung his baton wildly onto the head of the nearest person in the queue. Instinctively a group of fellow Jews broke from the line to try to pull him off.

"Careful, he's reaching for his pistol!" shrieked a voice.

Suddenly a radio flew past Marcus, crashing into the officer's head, sending him back to the ground. It was quickly followed by a second, third and fourth – then the bombardment commenced. "You wanted our radios – so here they are!" called the crowd in delight.

What followed next was so predictable that when the event was relived in the following days, it was hard to believe that so many people could be so foolish. Marcus' father, who was one of the first to throw his radio, later tried to explain to his wife that he was lost in an intoxicating mix of frustration and revenge. But he knew how absurd it was to think that a handful of radios thrown in anger could ever avenge what the Nazis had done to their city.

It took a while before the other officers realised what was happening. But once the first pistol shot was fired, the conclusion was inevitable. Had there been a machine gun in the area the death toll would have been far worse.

"You stupid, stupid man!" said his wife as she tied the torn sheet around Marcus' leg. "How could you do this? Is it not enough that I have lost a mother to those animals? You think that maybe I should lose a son as well?"

Simon had no response. He sat at the foot of Marcus' bed with his head in his hands, not knowing whether to feel regret that he'd allowed him to come in the first place or relief that the bullet had merely grazed his son's thigh.

"It's fine, Mum, I promise. It barely hurts – I didn't even realise I'd been hit until we were almost home."

"You're crazy," she said charging out of the room. "Both of you!"

Marcus' father gently stroked his son's forehead. "Quite an adventure, eh?" he said and they smiled at each other.

"We didn't get to see Shlomo," he said to his father.

"We'll go another time, maybe tomorrow."

"That's if Mum ever lets me out the house again."

"Oh she will, I promise you," he replied. Then he edged a little closer and unbuttoned his jacket. "I picked up a souvenir. It fell at my feet when the radios started to fly." Marcus pulled himself up and gasped as he recognised the handle of the officer's pistol poking out from his father's inside pocket. "I think maybe its best that you don't tell your mother."

THIRTY

Winter began to bite and the future of the zoo looked bleak. Each day Otto spent hours driving through the streets appealing for donations and leftovers to feed the few remaining animals, but in a city that was struggling to feed itself he usually returned with an empty van. And when starvation claimed the lives of those creatures that had survived the war, instead of searching in vain for food, he began to distribute the carcasses to Warsaw's hungry residents. The zoo had no income and many of the keepers agreed to work unpaid, but such devotion and generosity was tested to the limit on one dark December day.

Stefan woke to see the zoo covered in a blanket of snow. He used to love days like this; the lions looked like old men with their white speckled manes and the giraffes used their enormous tongues to lick snowflakes from the roof of their enclosure. He once saw the monkeys having a snow fight and even joined in; Marcus was so jealous. But on this particular morning, the abandoned cages looked even sadder than usual. As he paused by the penguin pool, remembering how much they used to love the ice, he heard the low distant growl of engines getting closer. Instantly he turned to see a convoy of canvas-covered vehicles making its way through the main entrance of the zoo towards to the villa. By the time he had run home a grim welcoming committee had assembled. The visitors were clearly expected and the solemn expressions on the faces of his parents suggested that they were not particularly welcome.

The car at the front of the convoy drew to a halt and a figure in a fur-collared overcoat emerged. "Herr Direktor! It is good to meet again, although, alas, in such regrettable circumstances." It was Lutz Heck, the person Stefan and Marcus had met in the zoo all those months ago. No wonder his mother's face was colder than the weather.

"It is always a pleasure to meet with those who share a passion for the wellbeing of animals," responded Stefan's father. "But as you suggest, it is not easy to maintain that passion in the midst of so much death and destruction."

"Indeed, Herr Direktor, I deeply sympathise with you and I can only imagine how difficult it has been …"

"Then you should have visited us while your country was attacking our zoo," interrupted Stefan's mother. "I can assure you the awful reality would have exceeded anything your imagination could have conjured!"

There was no mistaking the anger in her words, but Heck had no intention of reacting to it. Instead he directed his attention to Stefan, who was now standing between his parents. "Ah, Master Zabinski! It is good to see that you are well!" Stefan did not reply – which was what he thought his parents would have wanted.

"Can we cut the small talk and get down to business," boomed a gruff German voice from the back of the car. "I have got twenty men waiting in these trucks and I don't want them to waste their entire day at the zoo. Quickly, get a move on!"

Heck suddenly looked flustered. "Er, yes. Well… as you know I, I mean, we have come here today to assist in saving the animals you have left…"

"You are interested in *saving* animals?" Stefan's mother asked sarcastically.

"Yes, look, there is nothing we can do now about the creatures you have lost. But you still have many animals that can be helped…"

"How do you know?" asked Jan Zabinski.

"Pardon?"

"How can you tell what animals are still alive from just standing here?"

Heck began to look extremely uncomfortable. "Well I am presuming that in a zoo as big as this…"

"Either you have already seen for yourself, which means that you have made recent clandestine visits to the zoo without my prior knowledge, or you somehow know that certain animals were deliberately left unharmed by the Luftwaffe."

Both accusations hung unanswered in the cold morning air and would have remained so, had the patience of the officer in the back of the car not snapped. The door flew open and a tall man in a black shiny leather coat charged out, pulled open Heck's collar and produced a piece of paper that he clearly knew was there. Then, without even looking at the Zabinskis, he proceeded to read – "Truck one, some elephant called Tuzinka is going to Königsberg – truck two, camels and llamas are going to Hanover – truck three, hippopotamuses are off to Nuremberg – truck four, lynxes and zebras to Schorfheide and trucks five and six, as many Przewalski horses as we can fit in, and they are going to Vienna. Any questions?" Even now he didn't look up from the paper. "Good. Your staff will assist this transportation in every way possible. I expect all my troops to be off these premises by 17:00."

"But that is impossible," said Stefan's father. "There is no way that these animals could be properly prepared for such arduous journeys at such short notice…"

"I will tell you what is 'impossible', Herr Direktor!" bellowed the officer. "That twenty highly trained soldiers waste any more of their precious time with dumb animals when there are thousands of even dumber Jews to be dealt with!" Then he returned to the car, slammed the door and leant through the open window. "Sort this out, Heck! Any animals that are not ready to leave by the time I return will be destroyed on the spot. Drive on!"

As the car sped away Stefan's father turned to the keepers

who had gathered in front of the villa. "We have no choice, my friends. For the sake of our animals, we must do all that we can to make them comfortable. Consider it to be the last good deed you will be able to do for them." Otto quickly stepped forward and organised the keepers into small work-parties and then set off towards the elephant enclosure to supervise the departure of his beloved Tuzinka.

Soon the only people left on the driveway were Heck and the Zabinskis. "I hope you are aware of what you are doing," said Stefan's father in a low calm voice. "You may or may not be responsible for what has already happened to my zoo. But if any harm comes to the animals you are stealing today, as we both know it surely will, then all the blame will be yours. I hope you can live with that." He didn't wait for a response and swiftly led his wife and son back into the villa.

THIRTY-ONE

Across the river, in The Old Town, the freezing temperatures were having a devastating effect. Coal was now strictly rationed and people struggled to heat their homes. Most people slept fully clothed to stay warm and some even broke up furniture for fuel.

But being cold wasn't the worst of Marcus' night-time worries. He would have gladly swapped whatever warmth he had to silence Greta Gutman's constant wailing. During the day she would stare blankly out of the window, but at night she howled pitifully. Although she slept in his father's old study downstairs, her screams echoed throughout the house. And, try as he might, Marcus could not block them out and he was left to wrestle with his demons in the darkness. Distressed and alone he couldn't help resenting being haunted by her grief…

"Why does she have to do that?"

"Don't be so heartless – think of what she's been through."

"Yes, but everyone has suffered. Look what happened to Grandma…"

"But she has lost her husband and given up her baby…"

"I know all that – but she's driving me mad and it's giving me nightmares…"

But the fact that she wasn't Shlomo angered him even more.

"It's just not practical," his mother had insisted. "We are struggling to feed four mouths as it is – a fifth would be impossible. At least Shlomo has a roof over his head and food on the table."

"But he is my friend!" Marcus had pleaded. "And anyway, he was here before her. We should have taken him in when he first came."

"You can't turn back time…"

"But it's true! And you wouldn't have turned him away. I know it – you would have taken them both in. Then there would have been five mouths to feed and we would have managed!"

"Marcus, please, you're not being reasonable…"

She was right – and deep down Marcus knew it. But he was cold and scared and very hungry; he was no more capable of being reasonable than he was of being happy. Which is precisely why he did what he did on that bitter December morning.

After breakfast Marcus went to his room and crammed some clothes into a suitcase. Then he attached some string to the handle and discreetly lowered it out of the bathroom window onto the path beside the house.

"Where are you off to?" asked his father as he came down the stairs.

"The bakery," he replied. "Yesterday mother queued up for an hour and when she got to the counter there was none left. It's so early now that I am bound to get a loaf."

"Well make sure you wear this on your arm," he said, handing his son a strip of white material with a blue star on it.

"Why?" asked Marcus.

"To show you're a Jew," replied his father.

"But I know that already!"

"You're not wearing it for yourself. You're wearing it because our German masters want you to."

"And what if I don't?"

"What a senseless question! Haven't you learnt anything over the last three months? Now put it on and stop complaining."

Marcus had every intention of taking off the silly armband as soon as he was out of the house. But when he realised that everyone was wearing one he knew that without it he would stand out from the crowd and attract attention. So he straightened the cloth to ensure that the star was facing outwards and smoothed it flat against his arm to make it as visible as possible. Then, pulling his hat tightly onto his head and flicking up the collar on his heavy winter coat, he took his suitcase and set off along the snow covered pavement.

Normally it would take no longer than fifteen minutes to get to Krochmalna Street, where Shlomo was staying, but the icy ground slowed him down. Suddenly his progress was brought to a halt by a shrill German voice in the road ahead.

"*Juden, holt euch Schaufeln*! Jews, take a shovel!"

Marcus instinctively darted behind a parked truck.

"*Schaufelt den Schnee weg, los*! Dig the snow, quickly!"

On the far side of the street he could see a line of elderly Jewish men, each wearing their brand new armbands, holding shovels in their hands. Angry German soldiers were walking along the line shouting at the top of their voices – "*Schnell! Schnell!*" Many of the diggers were clearly far too frail for such work and struggled to grip the handle. One particularly old man was unable to maintain his footing and kept slipping over and getting up again. This appeared to be a source of hilarity for the onlooking soldiers.

Marcus grabbed his suitcase and quickly scurried into a side street to take another route to the orphanage, more intent than ever on his mission to get to Shlomo.

THIRTY-TWO

Meanwhile, at the zoo, Stefan was helping to prepare Tuzinka for her journey.

"Königsberg isn't such a bad place to live," he heard Otto say to the elephant. "Maybe this is all for the best. There are too many unhappy memories for you here. See it as a fresh start." During the siege of the city the sight of the orphaned calf gently nudging her mother's lifeless body, as if she was trying to wake her up, broke the hearts of everyone who saw it. Otto had spent hours coaxing her away so that the huge bulk of the adult elephant could be removed from the enclosure, and even longer consoling her when the operation had been completed. He spoke then, just like he was now, as if she understood every word. "I hear there are many other elephants where you are going. You'll find a new mother in no time. I wish I could come with, but Franciszka and I have a new baby ourselves – we have responsibilities. So many parents have been lost in this terrible war."

Stefan felt he was intruding and decided to leave Otto alone to say his farewells. The snow was falling again, adding a fresh layer to last night's covering and the paths were completely white. As he approached the villa the front door was open, and he could see his father and Lutz Heck in the hallway, in deep conversation.

"Herr Zabinski, we are doing for the animal kingdom what Hitler is doing for humanity – creating racial purity. Just as the Jews have diluted the Aryan race by spreading their genes all over Europe – likewise, purebred creatures have been wiped out by unfettered crossbreeding with inferior species. Look at these magnificent specimens!" Heck was holding pictures of buffalo and horses for Stefan's father to see. "Have you ever seen such noble beasts before? They are the aristocracy of the animal kingdom and we have the unique chance to return them to their rightful place!"

"Doctor Heck, I am sure this is all very interesting, but I am a very busy man…"

"Herr Direktor!" Heck was shouting now. "I don't think that you have grasped the enormity of what can be achieved here. Your Przewalskis, along with the other superior samples we have found in your zoo and elsewhere, will be selectively bred to recreate creatures that have not been seen for generations. I cannot tell you how excited I am! It is a unique opportunity to correct the genetic errors that have infested our continent and create a superior, purer world – surely you must understand!"

"Oh yes, Herr Doctor, I understand completely," said Stefan's father. "I have no doubt that your work is crucial to you. Not many people have the chance to 'play God' and meddle with evolution in such a way."

"I think you are missing the point, Mr Zabinski," Heck exclaimed. "I'm proud to say that the Fuehrer himself is aware of my work! He considers it to be of the utmost importance – he says that the rebirth of such noble breeds will become an inspirational symbol of racial purity!"

"I am sure he does," Jan replied, manoeuvring his unwelcome guest towards the open doorway.

Stefan watched his father turn briskly towards his study, leaving Heck alone on the front step. Suddenly, Helda came into view. She was holding Heck's coat and graciously guided it onto his shoulders before handing him his hat. Even though the falling snow shrouded Stefan's view, her admiration for Heck was clear to see.

Stefan decided to avoid the house and walked around the frozen lake, where the snow-coated peacocks were tending their young. He went past Otto's deserted workshop and the eerily quiet buildings where sick animals were once cared for. No one had been to this part of the zoo for weeks and the snow here was as smooth as cream. Eventually he reached the rear of the lion house, wrenched open the door and carefully climbed the cold metal steps, which were as slippery as ice, that led up to the lookout post,.

Using the binoculars, Stefan had a spectacular view of the city. Through the veil of snow the Vistula was like a huge grey snake asleep on a cotton wool carpet and the speckled trees along its banks looked like rows of giant ice lollies. The jagged edges of the battered buildings in The Old Town had been magically softened and the Royal Palace in Saxony Park looked like it had been plucked from a fairy tale. Meanwhile in the zoo below, ugly black trucks with their stolen animal cargo slowly passed through the main gate, crunching their dirty trails into the snow.

Then Stefan was distracted by some movement near the old windmill and pointed the binoculars towards the once abandoned farmhouse. A cluster of men were carrying vast quantities of building materials through the main entrance and by the number of footprints in the snow it appeared to have been going on all morning. So these were the "new neighbours" that Otto and his father were talking about.

THIRTY-THREE

92 Krochmalna Street. That's all the information Marcus had to go on. He'd never been to an orphanage before so he had no idea what to expect – but he certainly didn't imagine it would be as big as his school. He rested his suitcase against one of the pillars at the entrance. Then, making sure that no one was watching, he wrenched two buttons from his coat, ripped the collar of his jumper and knelt down, scraping his knee against the stone floor until a hole appeared in his trousers. Next he grabbed a handful of snow-frozen earth and rubbed it into his hair, face and hands. Finally, he kicked his suitcase until one of its sides cracked and bit hard into his bottom lip. Yes, there was blood – now he was ready.

Slowing his walk to a stagger, he approached the building and knocked hard on the large wooden door. At first there was no response, so he knocked again.

"Can I help you?" called a woman from inside. Marcus didn't reply. "Who is this?" she repeated. Again, Marcus said nothing. He wasn't surprised that they were reluctant to open the door. This was a Jewish orphanage – he could have been a Nazi. "State your business!"

"Please," said Marcus as feebly as he could. "I need help."

Marcus heard the heavy scraping sound of bolts being unlocked and immediately cowered as the door opened only enough to peer through. He sobbed as convincingly as he could and the door widen further. Soon he was in.

"I am looking for Dr Korczak," whimpered Marcus. "They tell me he can help. My parents… I have lost them… They are gone…" To his surprise there was actually a real tear on his cheek.

"What is your name, boy?" said the woman, putting her hand on his shoulder.

"Marcus," he replied. "Marcus Gutman…"

"And who do we have here?" Marcus looked up to see a short bearded man with small round wire glasses approach.

"Marcus Gutman, Doctor. He has just arrived."

"Is he alone?"

"Totally."

The man sat on the floor beside Marcus, removed a handkerchief from his pocket and gently wiped his eyes. "I see you have been hurt. Tell me what happened?"

But Marcus had run out of lies and decided to rely, instead, on tears.

"Come with me," said the doctor, helping him to his feet and picking up the suitcase. "Let's get a hot drink inside you; you're as frozen as a snowman."

Marcus followed behind and entered a room full of children. Some were sowing, others were drawing and a few were playing cards. He quickly lowered his face in case one of them was Shlomo – the last thing he wanted was to have his cover blown. Immediately, two very young children rushed up to greet the doctor. As he patted them on the head, others came to join them and he was soon surrounded by a mob of children all eager to add to the huddle. "Stop! You'll crush me!" he called out.

"Marcus!" called a voice from the other side of the room. "What are you doing here?"

Marcus had to act fast and charged towards Shlomo with his arms wide opened. Then he hugged him, ensuring that his mouth was right next to his friend's ear. "I'm Marcus Gutman," he whispered. "Remember that – it's Gutman, not Tenenbaum."

"Ah, so you two know each other. That is good!" exclaimed the doctor. "Then, Marcus, you play cards with these boys here while I take your case up to Shlomo's room; I'm sure there's an empty bed in there."

"What's going on?" asked Shlomo when they sat down. "Don't tell me that the Germans got your parents as well! And what's all this Gutman-not-Tenenbaum stuff?"

Marcus couldn't bring himself to tell Shlomo that he'd run away from home; it would have dragged his friend into the lie, which was already taking on a life of its own.

"It's terrible, Shlomo," he stuttered. "I just don't want to talk about it..."

"I know what you mean," replied his friend. "I can't talk about it either."

"Pick up your cards then," came a voice from the other side of the table. "Are you two playing or not?"

So they all played cards and nobody spoke, which suited Marcus perfectly. Maybe that would be the best strategy from now on, he thought. Rather than killing off his parents in some dreadful invented scenario, perhaps he should pretend to be too traumatised to speak about it.

"Yes – no one is going to force me to talk."

"You'll never get away with it..."

"I might. I could even pretend to be mute..."

"That's crazy..."

"No it isn't. I don't really need to say another word from now on..."

"Marcus," called a voice from the door. "Can you come here for a moment? The doctor would like to have a word with you." Marcus obediently put down his cards and left the room, ready to embark on his vow of silence.

"Ah, Mr Gutman," said Dr Korczak. "How are you feeling? Better I hope."

Marcus smiled and half-nodded.

"I would like you to meet someone. He is in my office. Is that alright with you?"

Marcus nodded again; being voiceless was proving to be easier than he thought.

"I will leave you both alone," he said opening the door. "I'll be waiting outside if you need me."

Marcus entered the room and in an instant his plan had been blown apart. "Poppa!" he yelled. But that was all he could say. As he sobbed into his father's chest he was overcome with relief and guilt.

"It's a good thing your mother puts your full name into everything you wear," he heard his father say. "It didn't take the doctor long to realise what had happened when he opened your suitcase."

"I'm so sorry... I'm so..."

"Hush now," said his father. "We all have a lot to apologise for."

"But..."

"Enough talking," he said. "Let's go home."

The doctor accompanied Marcus and his father to the entrance of the orphanage. "Thank you for visiting us," he said with a smile. "Please come again, whenever you want. But next time, less of the amateur dramatics, eh?"

"Should I say goodbye to Shlomo?"

"I think it's best that I explain everything to him," he said.

As they made their way through the icy back-streets of The Old Town, Marcus couldn't bring himself to say a word. Eventually his father broke the silence. "So tell me, what was it like to be an orphan?"

"Dreadful," he replied.

It was almost dark by the time they reached their street. Marcus was extremely tired and he couldn't wait to get into his room. But then his father snatched his arm and pulled him to a halt. "Oh no – what now?" he gasped. "Right... stay calm. It looks like we have a visitor." At first Marcus had no idea what was going on, but then he too saw the soldier in the Nazi uniform leaning against their front door.

THIRTY-FOUR

"Simon Tenenbaum?"

"Yes that's me."

"My name is Ziegler. I would like to talk with you."

"What do you need to talk with me about?"

"Insects." Then, for the very first time, Marcus and his father saw a Nazi smile – it was a chilling experience. "I beg your pardon," he said, stepping away from the door. "I appear to be blocking your way."

Marcus' father fumbled in his coat pocket for his key and struggled to slot it into the lock. His mother and Greta Gutman were standing like statues in the hall.

"There's a German outside," murmured Marcus' mother. "He wants to see you."

"I know," her husband replied, closing the front door behind him. "How long has he been there?"

"About an hour. I told him you were out, but he said that he'd wait. It's to do with that radio incident isn't it!?"

"He said he wanted to talk about insects!"

Marcus clung to his mother like a raft in a stormy sea and yearned for his pre-war life. There was a grinning Nazi outside the front door; how was anyone expected to make sense of that? And clearly his father was equally bemused – encounters between Germans and Jews were strictly command-and-obey affairs but this man was waiting calmly outside. He even appeared to be quite pleasant. It had to be a trap – maybe he knows about the gun...

Then the front door slowly swung open again. "I am aware of your work, Doctor Tenenbaum, and share the same interests," called the Nazi into the hallway.

Doctor? No one ever called Simon Tenenbaum that, although it was true. Not even Jan.

"Herr Doctor," he continued, seeming to sense Marcus' father's fear. "I can assure you that I am not here in any official capacity. Please believe me when I say that, under different circumstances, if I were to find myself in Warsaw I would have sought you out. If it was possible, I would have come to your home today in civilian clothing..."

Marcus hugged his mother and started to panic. Clearly his father had been singled out for a specific reason – and three months of Nazi rule had taught him that being singled out by Germans is never a good thing.

"My principal interest is Coleoptera," said the Nazi at the door. "Ever since I was a child I have been fascinated with beetles. At university I studied zoology and read your paper on the beetles of the Balearic Islands. It was fascinating."

Simon Tenenbaum had never been so scared in his life. Why would a German officer do so much background research in an attempt to appear so plausible? What terrible fate have they planned for him?

"Your classification of the Carabidae family was so interesting – I have read it many times."

"Ah, you mean my work on ladybirds..."

"No, Herr Doctor, ladybirds are the Coccinellidae family, as you well know. Carabidae are ground beetles that spend most of the day under rocks and stones and come out during the cooler night-time to feed on tiny bugs. They are usually metallic, black and shiny and their elytra, the casing that protects its wings, is often grooved, but not, as you point out in your paper, always. Have I passed my test?"

Marcus' father was stunned. It was totally incongruous to hear accurate scientific descriptions coming from wearers of that uniform. He couldn't help but stare open-mouthed at the unclassifiable creature in front of him.

"Interestingly, in beetles such as this, the first leg segment extends backwards over the first abdominal segment and…"

"Alright, alright. I am convinced!" He held his hand up and shook his head in disbelief. "You can stop now, Mr Ziegler."

The soldier was clearly relieved. "It is an honour to meet you, sir," he said holding his hand out for Marcus' father to shake.

"Mr Ziegler, you are clearly a learned man and, no doubt, a true student of entomology. But that does not stop you from being a German soldier standing in the doorway a Jew's house. And if you expect me to shake the hand of such a person while a crowd of my neighbours are looking on, then I would say that you must be the only human specimen that has less common sense than a ground beetle!" Ziegler pulled his hand away swiftly, clearly embarrassed. "If you want to continue this conversation further I suggest that you come inside. But I cannot invite you in as if we are friends." He leant forward. "I suggest that you start to behave in a way that is more fitting to your uniform…"

A sudden look of realisation spread across Ziegler's face. Then he narrowed his eyes and took a deep breath – "You dirty, stupid Jew!" he yelled then he lunged at Marcus' father pushing him back into the hallway, cracking the door hard on its hinges. Instinctively Greta Gutman dashed out of the hallway and Marcus' mother screamed. The German officer slammed the front door and quickly knelt down to help Simon Tenenbaum back to his feet. "Are you ok?" he asked with genuine concern.

Marcus' father couldn't stop himself from smiling at the expression of total confusion on his wife's face. "This is not what it seems," he said, knowing that Ziegler couldn't understand Polish. "I think this is a genuine Nazi insect lover!"

Marcus' mother took her son's hand and turned towards the kitchen. "I do not care why he is here; just get rid of him as quickly as you can!"

"I am sorry to have caused you such inconvenience," said the officer. "What I would really like to do is view your collection. I have read so much about it and…"

"I am afraid that is not possible," interrupted Mr Tenenbaum.

Watching on from the kitchen Marcus could see the German's face suddenly harden. "Look, I have apologised to you for causing such distress, and as you are a Jew I appreciate how you must feel towards me, but, well, I don't think you have very much choice!"

Marcus' father smiled to himself; how quickly even the politest Nazi can revert to type.

"Let me repeat, it is not possible for you to view my collection. I am afraid that is final!"

"Why are you being like this?" shouted Ziegler. "I have already answered your clever-Jew questions to demonstrate my sincerity and now you are trying to play more games with me! Please do not forget who I am and what you are! It is well within my power to confiscate every last one of your insects and have them taken to Berlin. I am sure that my old professor would be delighted to make room in his department for such a famous collection!"

"Be my guest!" Marcus' father was relishing this sudden sense of power. "But you will have to visit Warsaw Zoo to collect them." It was Ziegler's turn to look shocked now. "Because that is where they have been stored for safe keeping – which is the reason why it is not possible for you to see them. Do you understand me now?"

Ziegler took a few seconds to compose himself, aware that he had made a fool of himself and reached out for the door, eager to leave as quickly as possible. "But I am sure I can organise a private viewing," Marcus' father continued. "The director, Mr Zabinski, is a personal friend of mine. I'm certain that he will be only too pleased to oblige."

Ziegler was still rigid with embarrassment and couldn't bring himself to look Simon Tenenbaum in the eye. "I will get word to him and put the arrangements in place. Alas, as I am sure you will appreciate, I will not be able to accompany you there to be on hand to answer any questions you may have, for obvious reasons." He paused for a while to emphasise the absurdity of the strict restrictions that Jews now lived under. "But I can assure you that Mr Zabinski will be a more than adequate replacement."

"Thank you, Herr Doctor," Ziegler mumbled sheepishly. "I am most grateful. And please accept my apology…"

"Please do not bother, Mr Ziegler. No apology at all is far better than an insincere one." He reached into his pocket and took out a piece of paper. It happened to be the latest list of German restrictions on Warsaw's Jews. "Please write on the back of this how I can make contact with you after I have spoken with Mr Zabinski."

Ziegler took the paper, wrote the required information on the back, and left the Tenenbaum household as quickly as he could.

THIRTY-FIVE

After the theft of the zoo's remaining residents Stefan's father was inconsolable and spent most mornings walking alone amongst the empty cages. "It is one thing to have tried and failed to save a dying animal," he lamented. "But to standby powerlessly while such a terrible crime is being perpetrated is unbearable."

So, in the dead of night, Antonina Zabinski set about saving her husband from his despair.

"Wake up, Stefan, there's work to do. Now get dressed and come downstairs as quietly as possible."

"What's wrong?"

"There's no time to explain. Just put on some clothes and come down to the hall. We've got to act fast before your father wakes up."

As he rushed down the stairs he saw his mother and Otto with several other keepers, wrapped up like Arctic explorers. "Put on your coat and grab this," she said thrusting a shovel into his hand. "We've got to work fast."

Stefan only realised how early it was when he saw the moon hanging in the cloudless sky. A steady flurry of snow had fallen over night and each stride left an ankle-deep footprint. "We only have an hour," said his mother and instantly the assembled troop dispersed throughout the zoo.

"What's going on?" asked Stefan.

"Oh, you'll see," she replied, taking his hand.

Things only started to make sense to him when they passed the frozen pond. "Let's start digging," announced his mother. "We're about to make a lion!" Which is precisely what they did. The thick snow moulded as easily as clay, and soon two life-sized white lion statues stood at the foot of the concrete mountain where their real cousins once roamed. Stefan adorned their manes with hay and used stones for their eyes. But the morning sun was starting to peep over the horizon and there was no time to admire their handiwork. They hurried back to the villa, passing a brand new colony of white penguins, a gigantic white stallion and the world's first genuinely white white rhinoceros on the way.

"Oh no – he's coming!" Stefan's mother gasped, grabbing his arm. "Quick, get behind this tree."

"What if he thinks they are all ghosts?"

"Then he's crazier than I thought!"

It was the huge white seal that caught Jan Zabinski's attention first – the keepers had attached a giant beach ball to its nose. Stefan and his mother watched from a distance as the baffled zoo director clambered over the wall to get close to it. They couldn't see his face, but the spring in his step suggested he was amused. Then he saw the zebras, with their black-ribbon stripes and the giraffes (which were actually ribbon-less zebras with broom-handle necks). "I can hear him laughing," Stefan said.

As he approached the lion house Stefan couldn't bear to stay hidden any longer and rushed up to his father. "We made those, poppa, do you like them?"

"They are magnificent!" he replied.

Soon all of the keeper-sculptors gathered round their director and each new discovered work of art became the focus of ever more raucous laughter.

"I wonder whose idea this all was!" exclaimed Jan Zabinski, embracing his wife.

"It's good to have you back," she replied.

When the crowd approached the elephant house there was a collective gasp as they admired how realistic Otto's statue looked. "He has recreated his Tuzinka," said Stefan's mother. "A true labour of love!"

"But where is he?" asked a keeper.

"I've no idea," added another. "I haven't seen him since we first set off."

So everyone started calling "Otto! Otto!"

"Hush," said Stefan's father. "I can hear something – it sounds like the monkeys have returned to their enclosure." He led the group up the hill to the huge cages where Big Gus and his fellow primates used to entertain the visitors. And as they approached the hollering got louder.

Suddenly an explosion of hysterical laughter filled the morning air and Stefan pushed through to the front of the crowd to see what had caused it. There, positioned right next to the "Please Don't Feed the Monkeys" sign was a large snow figure whose paper-bag hair, grooming-brush moustache and broken-branch salute made him unmistakably a snowman Adolf Hitler.

At once Otto appeared from his hiding place at the back of the enclosure pushing a wheel barrow piled high with snowballs. "Roll up, roll up!" he cried. "Come and try your luck on the Nazi Coconut Shy!"

Soon a barrage of missiles bombarded the snow-Fuehrer until it had been utterly destroyed. And the snowball fight continued for most of the morning, reviving a sense fun in everyone that had been long locked away.

"You did all this, you wonderful woman," Stefan's father said to his wife.

"Well, thank you, my good man," she replied before splatting a handful of snow in his face.

THIRTY-SIX

Stefan's father didn't join the fun. Instead he stood on a wooden crate in the middle of the monkey house – he had an announcement to make.

"We had so many exciting plans for our wonderful zoo," he said as everyone gathered closer. "But now the future is uncertain. Each night we dream that our country is free, only to wake up to see that our unwelcome guests are making themselves more and more at home!" he pointed to the old farmhouse, which was quickly becoming one of the most impressive buildings this side of the Vistula. "The sad truth is that no one is going to pay to see animals carved from snow. We must find another way to survive, my friends, and the answer lies in the stomachs of our new neighbours!"

"Pigs!" exclaimed Otto, standing beside his employer.

"You're damned right they are," added a fellow keeper. "Every last rotten one of them…"

"Not the Germans," said Stefan's father. "Otto is talking about the animal. Three truckloads are on their way here from Denmark right now."

"Why?" asked a keeper.

"So we can breed them and sell them to the Germans."

"But why would we want to breed pigs for Nazis?"

"So we will charge them double and our fellow Poles will be able to buy cheap meat and the zoo will remain open."

"But what do we know about breeding pigs?" asked another keeper.

"I'm sure you'll learn," replied Stefan's father. "Anyway, we have a resident expert here; have you seen how huge Hercules has become?!"

As the Zabinskis made their way back to the villa something was troubling Stefan "So we're going to breed pigs for food," he said, trying to clarify what he had just heard.

"That's right," replied his father.

"They will have to be slaughtered..."

"Of course! Not even Nazis eat live animals!"

"So what's going to happen to Hercules?"

"What do you mean?"

"Will he be killed as well?"

Stefan's father placed a hand on his son's shoulder. "I promise you, no one is going to lay a finger on your pig!"

"Mr Zabinski," Helda was waiting in front of the villa. "There is a telephone call for you. It is from your Jewish friend, Mr Tenenbaum. He says it is urgent."

"Can I talk with Marcus?" asked Stefan. "Poppa, please... At least ask how he is..." But his father had already rushed ahead into the house.

"I'm sure he is fine," said his mother. "Don't worry."

Rather than walk past Helda, who was standing in the doorway, Stefan decided to go and see Hercules in the courtyard behind instead.

"I would not count on it." He stopped dead in his tracks; the dour housekeeper so seldom spoke to him that it was a shock whenever she did. "Don't be so sure that your friend is still fine. Remember I live near The Old Town. I see what happens. Maybe your friend is the lucky one... maybe he is the one Jew in Warsaw that the Germans are leaving alone... maybe he can become invisible and walk along the street unseen... if so, then he is fine." Then she looked up at the metal Star of David that was embedded in the wall at the corner of the villa. "But your mother is right about not worrying – don't bother wasting your energy. After all, he is only a Jew!"

✡✡✡

"Please let me come."

"It's far too risky."

"But I'll stay in the truck, I promise."

"Stefan, please… Just accept what I say."

"But you're going to see Marcus…"

"I don't know that for sure. I'm meeting his father at The Sztuka. I have no idea what'll happen after that."

"But I miss him, poppa."

"I know you do," said his father. "We all do. Now go and practise the piano… you know how much that cheers you up."

THIRTY-SEVEN

Jan Zabinski parked his truck in a side street opposite the
entrance to The Sztuka Café. He barely recognised the city; war-
torn buildings had become make-shift shelters and the most
derelict sites were now dumping grounds for uncollected rubbish.
Even with the windows shut, the stench of decay was unbearable.
And winter was adding to the misery; shivering, hungry children
huddled together on street corners for warmth, each taking turns
to break away from the group to beg from passers-by.

His friend had tried so hard to sound cheerful on the phone
earlier. "We need to talk, I'll meet you at The Sztuka at five o'clock.
Wait till I arrive before you go in – make it look like a chance
meeting. It will be so good to catch up with you again."

And there he was; at first Jan did not recognise him in his
heavy winter coat. The armband with its light blue star made him
indistinguishable from every other figure on the street. Jan took
a deep breath and climbed down from the truck, suppressing the
overwhelming urge to greet his friend effusively, mindful not
to attract any undue attention. His concern and affection was
expressed through the length and strength of their handshake.

"Simon, it is so good to see you."

"You too, Jan." he replied, opening the door of the café.

The Sztuka was as full as ever, but there was very little food on
display. "I will get the drinks," he said to his friend. "You find us
some seats."

Simon Tenenbaum chose a table in the corner of the room; sitting with your back to the wall ensured you would not be overheard. Many fellow Poles would happily report any loose talk to the Germans in order to gain favour; merely being suspected of plotting against the Nazis could be fatal.

"I have met a friendly Gestapo officer," whispered Simon to his friend. "I have a feeling he could prove to be useful to you, Feliks, Marda and the Polish Resistance."

"That's interesting," Jan replied. "Tell me more."

Keeping his mouth hidden behind his coffee cup, Simon described his meeting with Ziegler. "Young, naïve and gullible... a Nazi who agrees with Hitler but is probably uncomfortable with his methods... wants to appear to be a decent human being... I reckon he'd be easy to manipulate. He even let me call you from his office!"

"He must really trust you! And you say he wants to view the collection?"

"Yes – he appears to be quite knowledgeable. I said you'd pick him up from my house when he gets off duty this afternoon, in about an hour's time."

"So he's not just a foot soldier then."

"Far from it; he organises work parties of Jews as forced labour in various factories about the city. He has quite a bit of influence."

"Very interesting," said Jan, slowly replacing his cup on the table.

Many years earlier, when Jan and Simon were at university together, they used to come to this café for snacks between lectures. It was where Simon first met his future wife. "How are Lonia and Marcus?"

"Coping," replied Simon. "Although it's hard for us all to fill each day since they closed Zamenhof."

"I know," said Jan. "We're struggling to find another school for Stefan."

"At least the Nazis think your son is worthy of an education," said Simon. "Jewish children have been banned from attending schools altogether. A few of us teachers are planning on starting secret classes."

"That'll be risky."

"Everything is risky for Jews nowadays! But when this mess comes to an end, we're going to need as many good brains as we can find. We can't afford to lose a whole generation of children."

"Good luck," said Jan. His friend had always been an optimist and it was typical of him to be involved in activities that looked to a better future.

"How are things at the zoo?" asked Simon.

"Oh, we're also coping," Jan replied. "But it is hardly a zoo now. Thanks to Lutz Heck most of our animals have been taken to German zoos. He says they are merely on loan – we even have the documentation to prove it!" He lifted his cup to his mouth once more. "So if you are ever short of toilet paper let me know and you can happily use it!"

"So what are you going to do?" asked Simon.

"Breed pigs," answered Jan, clearly baffling his friend. "There are thousands of German stomachs that need filling in this city. Some are now our neighbours in the old farmhouse next to the zoo. Hopefully we can earn enough from supplying them to be able to re-open after the war."

The two friends sat in silence, revelling in the sheer pleasure of being able to share some time together, no matter how fleeting.

"I'd better be going then," said Simon eventually. "We don't want to keep our good friend Mr Ziegler waiting."

"Can I give you a lift?"

"No, that would look far too suspicious. Jews only walk in this city. With all the exercise we're getting, you'd think we'd all be fit as fiddles!" he joked.

Jan remained in the café long enough to allow Simon time to get home. When he finally walked out of the door he brushed past the gaunt figure of the pianist Wladyslaw Szpilman, on his way in about to perform. As Jan walked across the street to his truck he wondered how long it would be until he and his friend would be able to share in such pleasures again.

An hour later, as Jan parked outside the Tenenbaums' house,

the strange sight of his friend standing casually beside a uniformed Gestapo officer immediately startled him.

"Let me make the introductions," said Simon Tenenbaum as Jan climbed down from the truck. "This is the esteemed director of the Warsaw Zoo, Mr Jan Zabinski." There was a strange tension in his voice. And as he spoke he was gently nudging the Nazi forward, ensuring that the encounter took place in front of the vehicle. "His great reputation, along with that of his zoo, has spread across Europe and, had it not been for the war, he was due to host this year's international conference of zoo directors." Ziegler bowed his head briskly as a mark of respect and shook Jan's hand. "Mr Ziegler is a student of entomology with a particular interest in beetles," Simon carried on. "I hope that you will find my collection both informative and surprising – there are some very rare specimens there. I look forward to discussing them with you on your return..."

"Thank you, Herr Do..."

"...and I am sure that Mr Zabinski will be only too pleased to be your guide. Although, I can assure you that his good lady wife, Antonina, is almost as knowledgeable."

Jan wondered why his friend was talking so much. Was it down to nerves? He seemed to be prolonging these formalities for as long as possible – as if he was playing for time.

"So farewell!" he said at last, shaking both Jan and Ziegler's hands again. "I wish you both a pleasant journey and an entertaining afternoon."

Jan held the door open for his passenger. Then he suddenly saw Lonia moving away from the rear of the truck and furtively go to stand beside her husband. The anxiety on their faces made him suspect that something very dangerous had just taken place.

Then the penny dropped and Jan knew that he was carrying a far more precious cargo in his truck than the man sitting next to him. He watched the reflection of his friends in the side view mirror, and knew that it wasn't him that they were waving goodbye to.

THIRTY-EIGHT

In winter night-time falls on Warsaw as quickly as a dropped cloak, and by the time Jan had turned onto the road that led to the Vistula the city was in darkness. Only the occasional flash of a passing headlight illuminated the face of his passenger.

"I hear that you and Mr Tenenbaum studied together at university?"

"That is correct."

"So you have known him for many years now."

"Correct again."

"You must be very close, then. Almost like brothers, you might say. Yes?"

So the interrogation begins, thought Jan, gripping the steering wheel tightly and fixing his gaze firmly on the road ahead.

"After all, only a trusted friend would be permitted to look after such a valuable collection. He must hold you in the highest esteem."

Jan had expected to be grilled on his friendship with Simon but he didn't think the questions would start so soon. He thought there would have been some light-hearted banter designed to gain his confidence, but this young officer was clearly as inexperienced as Simon had suspected.

"We have enjoyed a long professional relationship, Mr Ziegler. His expertise has been invaluable to me over the years and I like to think that my knowledge has assisted his work as well."

"But he is a Jew, Mr Zabinski. Is it common for Jews and Poles to collaborate in such a way?"

Jan slowed down to join the queue that snaked back from the checkpoint at the entrance to the bridge. Soldiers were searching each waiting vehicle with their torches, but Jan was sure that the presence of his VIP passenger would exempt him from such an indignity – something that Marcus' parents no doubt considered when stowing him away in the back of the truck.

"Surely the knowledge contained in a brain is more important than its race or religion," Jan said. "Otherwise why would an officer of The Reich, like yourself, read the work of a Jew like Tenenbaum?"

"It is one thing to benefit from a Jew's knowledge; it is another to befriend the person."

Jan struggled to hide his contempt. "Maybe so," he replied. "But as I said, Mr Tenenbaum and I have enjoyed a good professional relationship over the years. Besides, I had been trying to convince him for some time that a collection like his should be on public display and not ferreted away in a private study. Between you and me, I consider it to be something of a triumph to have secured it for the zoo." His words tasted sour, but if this Nazi suspected that he and Simon were friends, it would be disastrous.

"Papers!" barked a voice through the window.

"I don't think that will be necessary soldier," said Ziegler pulling rank by thrusting his face into the beam of the torch. "And please inform your comrades that we will be coming straight through, I am far too busy to wait in line like a common Pole!"

Jan swallowed hard and smiled to himself. It was going to be a pleasure to deceive such an arrogant man. He manoeuvred the truck out of the line and drove towards the front of the queue, passing a cluster of soldiers standing to attention in respect to the officer beside him. If only they knew that they were also saluting a Jewish child, being smuggled away right under their noses.

Then, as they approached a second group of guards, Jan suddenly spotted an opportunity. "Good evening, my friend!" he exclaimed, seeing the soldier he and Stefan had encountered when the checkpoint was first established. "Have you heard from Berlin lately? Has your son visited the elephants in the zoo, or is he waiting for you to return to take him there?" The soldier beamed a smile of recognition and approached the truck.

"Good day to you again, sir!" said the soldier, but froze when he caught sight of the Gestapo officer in the passenger seat. "*Heil Hitler!*" he barked, clearly worried that he was about to be rebuked for being too familiar with a Pole.

"You know this man?" Ziegler asked Jan.

"We met some time ago," he replied. "I saw him apprehend two Jews who were trying to leave the city disguised as Poles. I was amazed at how quickly he realised their identity papers had been forged. And when we spoke later and I discovered he was an animal lover like you, we hit it off immediately!"

"Excellent," said Ziegler, clearly impressed. "What is your name, soldier?"

"Standar," he replied. "Lieutenant Standar."

"Congratulations, Lieutenant," Ziegler took out a notebook from his inside pocket and wrote a few brief notes. "I will be recommending you for some leave when I return to my office. Hopefully your son won't have to wait too long for his father to take him to the zoo again!"

The soldier saluted again, clearly elated, and Jan drove onto the bridge inwardly triumphant. Not only had he succeeded in cementing Ziegler's confidence, he had also won the gratitude of his new friend Lieutenant Standar.

Obviously convinced that the zoo director wasn't one of those strange "Jew-loving Poles" Ziegler sat in silence for the rest of the journey, which suited Jan as it gave him time to consider the best way to deal with his secret cargo. He knew that Marcus would

153

have been told to stay still for as long as possible, but he couldn't remain in the truck forever.

As he drove through the snow-dappled gates of the zoo Jan decided to turn left, away from the villa.

"Come over here, Otto!" he called as they came to a halt beside a field where a group of keepers were constructing the shelters that the pigs were going to live in. Otto lumbered through the mud and approached the truck, managing to conceal his alarm when he saw the uniform in the passenger seat. "I think there's something wrong with this 'dopey' old truck again. Could you check the back? It's making that 'grumpy' sound again!"

Otto immediately decoded what he was hearing. "No problem, boss," he said as casually as possible. "Just leave it with me!"

Jan got out of the truck and quickly ran round the front to open the passenger door for his guest. "I've no idea how long this old wreck will last – it's impossible to get spares nowadays."

Ziegler climbed out of the cabin with caution, careful not to tread in anything that might tarnish the shine on his pristine boots. Jan quickly steered him along the snow-covered path and led him away from the truck as quickly as possible. "It would be a pleasure to take you on a tour of the zoo," he said. "But I think you would soon grow bored with looking at empty cages. Most of the animals that managed to survive the war have been kindly rehoused by Lutz Heck. We still have a few specimens but—"

Ziegler stopped in his tracks "Doctor Heck? The director of Berlin Zoo?"

"That's right. Have you heard of him?" replied Jan, well aware of the German zoologist's reputation in his country.

"Of course I have!" said Ziegler.

"Oh, he is an old friend. We go back a long way – a wonderful man…" Jan had never enjoyed lying so much.

"I had no idea how well connected you are!" said Ziegler.

"Oh, you know what animals lovers like us are like," he said placing a friendly hand on the officer's shoulder. "Once we find a kindred spirit we tend to stick together."

"Father!" called Stefan's voice as the two men approached the villa.

"Stefan!" exclaimed his father. "Quick, get your coat on. Otto is about to work on the truck... the engine's playing up again. You know how much you like helping him. Hurry, he's by the pig field."

"But how's..."

"Stefan," snapped Jan, desperate to stop his son from mentioning Marcus. "Don't waste your time talking; I'm sure Otto would appreciate your assistance! Now go, and I don't want to hear another word!"

"Do you have many children?" asked Ziegler as they entered the villa.

"Just the one," he replied. By now Stefan had put on his coat and was gawping in the hallway at their unexpected guest. "This is Mr Ziegler, Stefan," he said and was relieved when his son was too shocked to ask any more questions. "Now, off you go!"

Helda was standing at the entrance to the kitchen, totally flabbergasted. "They'll be one extra for supper tonight," he announced.

Part Five

December 1939

THIRTY-NINE

Stefan's mind was in a spin as he trudged past the field of semi-circular shacks that were waiting for the zoo's latest arrivals.

"There's a Nazi in the house!" he said to Otto who was securing the latch on a large wooden trunk at the back of the truck.

"I know, I saw him. Now come and help me with this."

"But why?"

"Because it's too heavy to carry myself, of course."

"No, I mean, why has my father brought a Nazi home?"

"I have no idea," replied Otto. "But whatever happens, he mustn't see what's hidden in here." He dragged the trunk to the edge of the truck and turned it so that Stefan could grab the handles on its side.

"It's guns, isn't it?" Stefan whispered. "Poppa said there was something wrong with the engine, but he was only pretending wasn't he?"

"Look," Otto said mimicking Stefan's hushed voice. "If you help me carry this to the lion house, I promise to let you see what's inside. But we've got to act fast!"

Otto led them across the field between the pig stys, and by the time they reached the lion house their shoes were caked in mud.

"This is really heavy," said Stefan. "How many weapons are there?"

"Only one," said Otto, gently lowering the trunk onto the ground.

"It's a bomb, isn't it?" asked Stefan excitedly.

"Don't be so impatient," said Otto, opening the heavy wooden lid. "Take a look for yourself."

As Stefan pulled back the blanket that covered the secret cargo, his heart began to race. At first, in the faint moonlight, he couldn't see very much. There didn't seem to be a nozzle so it definitely wasn't a machine gun. Maybe it was a bomb... but it was huge and it somehow seemed to be moving.

"Marcus!"

"How's that for a secret weapon?" said Otto, lifting the petrified boy out of the truck.

"What are you doing here?" asked Stefan. "How, I mean why, I mean..."

"I really don't know," Marcus said, clutching a suitcase close to his chest. "Everything happened so quickly... No one told me anything..."

"They probably didn't want to frighten you," said Otto. "The less you knew the better."

"I think they were worried that I'd run away again," said Marcus, tears rolling down his cheeks.

"You ran away!?" said Stefan. "When? Where to?"

"I went to find Shlomo," he sobbed. "He's in an orphanage..."

Stefan didn't know whether to be pleased at his friend's surprise arrival at the zoo or if he should console him in his sadness? "At last we can live like brothers," he heard himself say.

Marcus nodded, but he wasn't able to smile.

Suddenly they heard the sound of scraping metal – the drain cover beside their feet was opening. "Quick, over here!" Stefan's mother's face looked up at them. "This way," she said and then she vanished like a rabbit down a burrow.

"What are you waiting for?" urged Otto.

Stefan scampered down the metal ladder to join his mother in the sewers below. Marcus quickly joined them and looked up just in time to see Otto's smiling face disappear behind the

160

closing drain-cover. There was a split second of total darkness and then Stefan's mother turned on her torch.

"What's happening Auntie?" said Marcus.

"I've spoken to your mother," she replied. "They just want you to be safe. It's all for the best, I promise."

"There was no time to say goodbye," he said. "And now it's too late."

"Hush," she whispered, trying desperately to sound as reassuring as possible. "This won't last forever, you'll be home soon." She directed the torch along the tunnel in front of her. "Now follow me and mind you don't slip. And try not to breathe in too deeply – the smells down here are disgusting!"

It felt as if they were trapped inside the belly of a giant snake. Stefan always knew there was a network of sewers beneath the zoo that flushed all the animal waste into the Vistula, but he didn't think he'd ever be in it. And as he coughed and gagged on the putrid air, he wished it would have stayed that way.

The boys stuck close to Stefan's mother as they edged their way through the darkness, pinching their noses as tightly as possible.

"I think I'm going to be sick," said Marcus.

"Just hold your breath for a few more seconds," she replied. "We're almost there."

There was a shaft of light shooting down from the roof of the sewer in front of them. As they approached, they could see an identical set of steps to the ones at the lion house. "Guess where we are now," said Stefan's mother. Neither boy had the faintest idea. "Well, let me give you a clue," she was suddenly whispering. "If Stefan called out the name of a certain pet we would probably hear a rat squeak!"

"We're underneath the courtyard outside our house!" said Stefan.

"Correct," replied his mother. "Now wait here while I make sure the coast is clear."

As she climbed the ladder the boys leant against the wall of the sewer. "What's in the suitcase?" asked Stefan.

"I've no idea – I didn't pack it." Marcus unclipped the locks and held it under the shaft of light that was stronger now that the cover overhead had been opened. There was a note on top of his clothes. "*Stay safe…*" – it was his father's handwriting. "*We love you very much. Give Uncle Jan the parcel.*" Marcus rummaged around at the bottom of the case and found a solid bundle of paper. He instantly knew what it was – the handle, the nozzle, the trigger-cover… he was holding the pistol his father had picked up.

"Come up now, boys," whispered Stefan's mother from the top of the ladder. "Take it slowly and be as quiet as possible." Marcus clutched his suitcase and let his friend go first. They were eager to breathe the fresh night air and flush away the sewer grime that lined their lungs. "Keep your heads down," she warned.

The drain cover in the courtyard was situated between Hercules's pen and Apollo's cage. The huge pig was a heavy sleeper and his steady snore was undisturbed by the arrival of three unexpected guests crouching by the entrance to his sty.

"We'll be safe here," whispered Stefan's mother.

Through the window they could see Jan Zabinski holding one of Marcus' father's insect jars close to the soldier's face; they were clearly deep in conversation.

"Will I be staying here with Hercules?" asked Marcus.

"Do you really want to live with a pig?" replied Stefan's mother. "I'll ask Otto to build you a sty in the field, if you wish. Then you'll have lots of them to play with!"

"The zoo is being turned into a pig farm," Stefan explained, noticing the look of confusion on his friend's face. "Otto's getting everything ready for their arrival."

"I've prepared the basement room for you," she added with a smile. "You're going to be our little secret under the stairs!"

FORTY

"We'll never see him again," said Lonia Tenenbaum. The sun had started to rise, but Marcus' parents hadn't noticed. They had hardly moved from the kitchen table since watching their son disappear in the back of Jan's truck yesterday. Greta Gutman had joined them in their painful vigil. On the table was the sheet of paper that had convinced them that their son would be safer at the zoo. It was a leaflet that had been distributed throughout Warsaw by their German rulers entitled *The New Jewish District*, displaying a detailed street map of the city with a thick black line around a tight cluster of streets in the middle.

"Soon these will be the only streets where Jews will be allowed to live," Simon said.

"They can't do that…" she replied, but both of them knew that they could.

The leaflet went on to explain the reasoning behind this directive. It was a "health measure", designed to prevent the spread of typhus – the "Jewish Plague."

"More and more Jews arrive every day in Warsaw," Lonia added. "There's not enough food to eat and even less water to drink and wash in. What do they expect? The Germans have created a living hell – it's a recipe for disease and disaster. Tell me how cramming everyone into a few square miles is going to help?"

"They are not doing this for our good," said her husband. "A Nazi doesn't care if a Jew dies. All over Poland Jews are being herded like cattle into ghettos, and now they want to make one here."

Lonia grabbed the paper from her husband's hand, screwed it up and threw it on the floor. She dashed out of the kitchen in tears and Simon followed to console her. But Greta Gutman stayed at the table, barely registering her hosts' distress – she had already lost everything.

FORTY-ONE

Marcus woke up but remained perfectly still. He'd been given strict instructions to be as quiet as possible, "I really don't want to scare you," Stefan's mother had said before she locked the door the previous night. "But it would be disastrous if the Germans found out you were hiding down here – for us all."

It was so dark in the basement that Marcus wasn't sure if his eyes were open. He felt under the sheet for the bread and water he'd been left. "You must make it last all day," he'd been instructed. "This evening, once Helda has gone home, we will bring you some more."

The movements above his head suggested it was now morning. He followed the footsteps as they passed from one side of the ceiling to the other, trying to work out who they belonged to. He decided that the lighter quicker steps were Stefan's. He kept his mouth shut tight in case the sound of his breathing seeped up through the floorboards; but there was nothing he could do to quieten the thumping in his chest.

Slowly he became accustomed to the dark and was able to make out the boxes that had been piled up against the far basement wall to create the space for his mattress. There was a chair in front of them and beside that he could see the outline of his suitcase. Should he have mentioned the gun last night?

Life went on above Marcus' head but he had no concept of time passing. Sometimes the muffled voices that occasionally invaded his black basement world were distinct enough to understand, but mostly there was silence. He thought about his grandmother and Greta Gutman's husband. He thought about poor Shlomo's mother and the man in the bread queue who had saved his life. He thought about all the other people who were no longer alive, and was alarmed when he realised that all this was passing through his head without leaving a trace of sadness. Maybe this is what dying is like – just lying still in the darkness and feeling nothing? At least this way he wouldn't feel the pain that all those other people felt. He would miss his parents, yes, but then who was to say that he was ever going to see them again anyway?

Then he heard Stefan playing the piano. Each note was as clear as a word, as if his friend was talking to him. And as the music played, he focused on the light that framed the basement door and smiled; not because he was happy, but because he wasn't dead.

He reached for the bread by his side and was surprised to find that it had gone and there was barely any water left either. Yes, there were crumbs on the pillow beside his mouth, but he couldn't remember eating or drinking a thing.

FORTY-TWO

To pass the time, Marcus decided to measure the boundaries of his basement world with tiptoe steps and discovered that the room was a perfect twenty-four foot-length square. Apart from his mattress, the boxes piled against one of the walls and the chair with his suitcase on (and the toilet bucket in the corner…) the room was surprisingly sparse. Stefan's mother had probably removed everything he could have bumped into before he'd arrived.

"Shlomo could have been here."

"What do you mean?"

"If he started living with us on the day of the funeral, my parents would have had to put both of us on the truck."

"You can't be sure – it would have been harder to hide two people in the back."

"But they wouldn't have split us up… that would have been cruel."

"In that case, they wouldn't have smuggled either of you out – if he'd have moved in then you'd still be there."

"Still, I wish he was here now…"

"You're a fool; it's much better to be on your own."

"But it's so boring…"

"So you'd rather be dead than bored? Have you forgotten what it's like over there?"

"Well at least I'd have someone to talk to…"

"You must be mad!"

"I must be – why else would I be whispering to myself like this?"

Marcus lay back down on his mattress and fixed his stare on the light-flex hanging down from the ceiling. Stefan's mother had removed its bulb last night in case he'd been tempted to turn it on, although his eyes had become so accustomed to the gloom that he barely noticed the dark anymore. He found himself drifting in and out of sleep until being awake felt exactly like dreaming. Occasionally blind panic wrenched him out of his slumber and for a few terrible moments he was gripped with fear and confusion, briefly forgetting where he was and what had happened to him.

To relieve the boredom he started to sing the section of the Torah he had learnt for his Bar Mitzvah over and over again in his head, and was surprised at how easily it came to mind. Its gentle tones seemed to sooth him and when Stefan started to play the piano in the longue overhead, it felt like his friend had decided to accompany him.

Every now and then he remembered the gun and vowed to hand it over to Stefan's father as soon as he could.

The lock on the door clicked open, but Marcus had no idea whether it was a dream.

"It's me!" came a voice. "Helda's gone home." Stefan's silhouette filled the open door. He was holding a tray with a flickering candle in the middle that cast a spooky shadow onto his face. "I've brought your supper and some cards to play with."

"What's that disgusting smell?" asked Marcus, placing his hand over his nose.

"Pigs," replied Stefan, handing his friend the plate of food. "They arrived this morning and I've been helping Otto and the others unload them."

The light from the flame brightened his room, and Marcus realised how much had been hidden from his view in the dark all day. Behind his mattress Stefan's mother had hung a familiar photograph of him with his parents and on top of the boxes that lined the far wall was a row of all the toy cars that he and Stefan used to play with when they were much younger.

"Eat up," urged his friend. "It's vegetable stew – your favourite. Mother made it especially!"

Its deliciousness jolted Marcus back to his pre-war life and he thought about the countless times their two families had dined together – but he couldn't feel happy. All he could think about was his parents, imprisoned in their own home on the other side of the river. What were they eating for supper that night?

"Cut the cards," said Stefan. "Let see who goes first."

FORTY-THREE

Simon Tenenbaum entered the kitchen and sat at the table, deliberately scraping his chair on the floor to announce his arrival, in the hope that Lonia would turn away from the window. With every passing day she'd found it more and more difficult to speak to her husband, and blamed him for the constant pain of regret she now lived with. With Greta Gutman by her side, she refused to face him.

"We will be leaving this afternoon," he said sheepishly. There was no reaction. "Janusz Korczak will be here to collect us." Still his wife didn't move. "The orphanage has moved to Chłodna Street, where the ghetto will be. They have some attic rooms we can use. I'm going to be teaching there from now on."

"What are you talking about?"

"We only have a few hours to get ready."

"You're crazy," Lonia started to leave with Greta Gutman close behind, but Simon stood up and blocked the door.

"Get out of my way," she insisted.

"I don't think you heard me."

"Oh I heard you alright. But I have no intention of listening to another word."

"Be reasonable — "

"Reasonable? 'Reasonable' would be Marcus still living with us, 'reasonable' would be refusing to speak with Ziegler every time he comes, 'reasonable' would be staying in this house ..." She was in tears now and Greta Gutman's hand was on her shoulder.

"I have arranged for Kurt Rokos to live here while we are gone. We can trust him, Lonia. If we wait to be evicted by the Nazis, they will hand our keys to whoever they like. This way we know we will have a home to come back to."

Later that afternoon Janusz Korczak arrived with a borrowed ambulance and Kurt Rokos came to help with the loading. But there was no time for long goodbyes. Lonia and Greta stayed in the back with the suitcases while Simon sat beside Janusz in the passenger seat. "Stay safe, my friend," was all Kurt could think of saying as he watched them drive away from their home.

FORTY-FOUR

While Marcus relived the same uneventful day over and over again in his basement world, the dangers overhead were increasing. Now that the Danish pigs had settled in, the Nazis from the neighbouring farmhouse began to treat the zoo like their own private park. To make matters worse, Ziegler was now turning up unannounced to browse the insect collection.

"We must have a way of letting Marcus know when there's a German on the premises. He has to take cover in his room in case one of them decides to wander down to the basement," Stefan's father said to his son.

"How can we do that?"

"Choose a piano piece to play whenever a Nazi comes near," he replied. "Make it really loud, so that Marcus will hear it through the floorboards."

"The last part of the *Moonlight Sonata*," said Stefan immediately. "I love playing that really loudly!"

"Good choice!" said his father. "Tell him to stay hidden until you stop playing and the coast is clear."

So from then on, Stefan became his friend's early warning system.

"What a marvellous pianist your son is!" Ziegler said one day as Jan greeted him. "Every time I come he seems to be practising. And he plays with such power!"

"Yes," replied Stefan's father, stepping aside for his unwelcome guest to enter the villa. "We are all very proud of him." But Ziegler remained in the doorway with a troubled look on his face.

"Follow me," he said after an anxious pause. "I wish to show you something." Ziegler led Stefan's father to the front of the villa. "Then he pointed up at the wall. "What is that Jewish star doing there?"

"Alas it cannot be removed."

"But why is it there in the first place?"

"It is a very long story, my friend…"

"And I would like to hear it," said Ziegler, folding his arms across his chest.

"My predecessor was a well-known gambler," started Jan. "He frequently hosted card games here at the villa. He had many Jewish friends; some of them were extremely wealthy…"

"Of course," Ziegler butted in. "What else would you expect?"

"Precisely," Jan continued. "Well, many years ago the zoo had fallen upon hard times and was in danger of having to close. So he invited some of his Jewish friends to a night of poker and managed to cheat them out of a fortune. The Jews found out what had happened and tried every means to get their money back. Of course the police refused to take their complaints seriously – who would believe the word of a Jew?"

"Absolutely!" said Ziegler.

"So the zoo was saved by stolen Jewish money! And to taunt them even further the director had this star made as a reminder of his triumph. The Jews tried to have it removed – rumour has it that, one night, they even broke into the zoo and tried to take it down themselves – but they were defeated again! It had been so deeply embedded into the wall that it simply could never be removed. The only way to take it away would be to knock the wall down. So, you see, this Jewish star is a constant reminder of the famous night the richest Jews in Warsaw were swindled out of a fortune. Quite a tale, don't you think?"

"Indeed!" exclaimed Ziegler.

That evening Jan took great pleasure in telling his wife how easy it was to trick the German officer.

"I didn't know you were such a good liar," she said.

"Ziegler is a Nazi," said Jan. "He believes that all Jews are greedy, money-obsessed parasites. As long as he thinks that I might believe such nonsense as well, he will accept whatever rubbish I tell him."

FORTY-FIVE

In the attic apartment at the top of 33 Chłodna Street, Marcus' parents and Greta Gutman unpacked the suitcases in silence.

"It's bigger than I expected," Simon said at last.

"Stop fooling yourself," said his wife. "I'm just happy that my mother is no longer here to see this!"

"Believe me, we are the lucky ones," he replied. "Most families have had to share. Many are living five, six, maybe more, to a room."

"Don't treat me like one of your pupils," she snapped. "I am not blind. I know what is happening around me. But please, I beg you, never use the word 'lucky' to describe our situation. I would swap all this for a hole in the ground if I could have my Marcus back."

Simon gently stroked his wife's arm. "And I would gladly dig that hole with my own bare hands if I thought that would help."

"Moshe and I lived on this street when we first got married," Greta Gutman was standing by the window. She rarely spoke, but when she did her mouse-like voice had the impact of a lion's roar. "I can see the apartment from here. I think maybe you are lucky."

Suddenly there was a loud knock on the door and it immediately flew open. "Is he here?" It was Shlomo, breathless from racing up the stairs to the attic. "Marcus, where is he?"

"He is at the zoo," said Lonia, holding her husband's hand. "Safe."

FORTY-SIX

The only thing that the zoo's new arrivals shared with Hercules was their appearance. He was as placid and tame as a puppy, while they treated all humans as mortal enemies. One keeper complained that he felt far safer working with lions. It was Stefan's mother who discovered the way to calm them down. "Try singing to them as you approach," she suggested one day. "It will distract their attention." As usual her instincts were right and soon the pigs' grunts were accompanied by the sound of Polish folk tunes – which provided an endless source of amusement for passing Germans.

Jan's scheme to sell the pigs to their neighbours was working well, but it was a constant struggle to find sufficient food for the animals in a city that could scarcely feed its humans.

"Then you must be made a priority-industry!" exclaimed a particularly tall officer when he heard about this problem. "These animals are crucial to our work here. We have named them 'Hitler's Pigs'!" An image of Hitler, ankle deep in mud, inspecting a regiment of pigs in Nazi uniforms with their trotters held out in salute, flashed through Jan's mind. "It is of the utmost importance that they are fed well – I will see what I can do!"

The following week the same officer approached Stefan's father. "You are aware that we are establishing an area in the city where only Jews will be permitted to live?"

"Yes," replied Jan, who had heard about the Nazi plan to establish the ghetto.

"Every day more Jewish vermin are being moved into that area. The district will be sealed off by November at the latest."

"Sealed off?" enquired Jan.

"Yes. Once they are relocated, a wall will encircle the area. Like rats all Jews carry infectious diseases and this will ensure that they only contaminate each other."

"I see."

"And are you aware," continued the officer, "that in the eyes of a Jew there is nothing filthier than a pig?"

"Yes, I have heard of this," said Jan.

"Then you will, no doubt, appreciate the humour in what I am about to tell you!"

I'll try, thought Jan, but I can't promise anything...

Then the officer produced an envelope from his jacket pocket. "This document authorises you to go anywhere in Warsaw to obtain food for your animals. It specifically mentions areas where Jews live. *Obergruppenführer* Heydrich himself has signed this authorisation – he is particularly amused by the idea of taking food from Jews and feeding them to pigs!" The stern-faced officer suddenly broke into a broad grin, which stretched and reddened a deep scar on his chin, making it look as if he had three lips. "That is funny, no?"

"No... I mean, yes, of course. Very funny," said Jan taking the letter. As he looked at the signature of Reinhard Heydrich, one of the most senior members of the Nazi party, he immediately realised the potential significance of the document.

"I hope this will make things easier for you now," said the officer.

"Oh yes," said Jan. "It will be extremely helpful. Thank you!"

FORTY-SEVEN

"This is just like being some sort of prisoner."

"Don't be so ungrateful, these people have saved your life."

"I know, I know. But how much longer am I going to have to live like this? "

"I think you're being very selfish, Marcus. Just be glad that you're safe…"

"But am I? I spend all my life down here, because there are people up there who would kill me if they knew where I was. I don't call that safe."

"Well there's nothing you can do about it."

"Yes there is."

"What do you mean?"

"Think about it – lately they have stopped locking that door at night. I could leave this room whenever I want…"

"You can drop that idea right now…"

"But it would be so easy to escape!"

"Don't be mad, Marcus. You wouldn't survive five minutes out there…"

"Oh wouldn't I? You know that I have the run of the house when everyone's asleep…"

"What are you talking about?"

"Don't tell me you don't know what I mean! I do it every night…"

"I'm not listening…"

"I creep up the stairs, dance in the hall, take food from the kitchen…"

"La, la, la… not listening…"

"And I still have that gun… I even took it out once and pretended to be a cowboy!"

"Stop it now! You're mad if you think you should leave here and risk getting caught by the Nazis…"

"But I've worked it out… I have a plan!"

"Well, whatever it is, you can forget it right now!"

"Those sewer tunnels; I bet they lead outside the zoo. They must go past the lion enclosure and the monkey house, under the Gestapo headquarters in the old farmhouse and right to the Vistula…"

"You are mad, aren't you? All that time by yourself down here has damaged your brain…"

"I could easily grab some food, enter the sewers from the drain in the courtyard and get to the river in no time…"

"Then what? Smear some mud under your nose and march past the checkpoint on the bridge pretending to be Hitler?"

"I could easily swim across the river…"

"That's enough now…"

"You know I could make it – I've swum twice that distance before…"

"Marcus – are you awake?" whispered Stefan from the door.

"Yes, of course, come in…"

"Only, I heard something – I thought you might be talking in your sleep or something."

"No. I was awake. I was probably talking to myself. I do that sometimes…

"Yeah," said Stefan. "It must get really boring down here sometimes."

Stefan put the plate of food he was holding on Marcus' mattress and took out the pack of cards he always brought with him. "What's the score now?" he said shuffling the pack and dealing the cards into two piles of ten.

"I'm winning thirty-three to twenty-seven…" said Marcus.

"Then prepare yourself for the come back!" said Stefan.

FORTY-EIGHT

Simon had been a teacher for twenty years but had never taught anyone younger than eleven before. "We are like bees!" he said nervously to the circle of five year olds looking up at him from the floor. "And 33 Chłodna Street is our hive! Everyone has a job to do – no one ever stops!" To his relief they seemed to be listening. "Cooking, cleaning, sowing, teaching, learning, looking after the sick…" What was he so worried about? This was going to be so much easier than he'd expected. He started to relax – but not for long.

"Who makes all the honey!" called a girl from the back.

"There is no honey," replied Simon.

"I like honey," said another. "Can I have some?"

"Bees sting don't they? I don't want to be stung!"

"Don't worry," said Simon anxiously. "No one is going to get stung."

"I can sting you!" exclaimed a boy. "Look!" and he pinched a nearby girl her on the cheek.

"Now stop that right now!" said Simon.

"He stung me – it hurts!"

"Let's chase him out of the hive!" called a second boy.

"No…"

"Yes! Let's get him!" said another, springing to his feet.

"Sit down, all of you!" snapped Simon as three more children stood up.

"This looks like fun!" called Janusz, popping his head round the door. "Can I join in?" He let out an enormous buzz and joined the swarm of children circling ever faster around the room. "Welcome to our world!" he said, scooping up the nearest child and placing her on his shoulders.

While Simon was trying to tame bees, Lonia was taking needlework lessons. "I haven't done this since I was a girl!" she said sucking hard, yet again, on her stabbed thumb. The seaming workshop was the busiest room in the orphanage. With over a hundred children to clothe, everything they wore was patched up until its material was too threadbare to take a stitch and then cut up into patches for mending.

Madam Stefania, the deputy director of the orphanage, patrolled the room with a stern face and stopped behind Lonia, making her feel like an incompetent school girl. "Did your mother never teach you how to backstitch?"

"I'm showing her what to do," said Greta, sitting beside Lonia. "She'll get the hang of it soon."

"I certainly hope so," Stefania snapped, grabbing the hem of the skirt. "This repair would barely last a day!"

"She is like that with everyone," said a fellow seamstress from across the room after Madam Stefania had left. "But I promise you, she has a heart of gold."

✡✡✡

As he followed Janusz throughout the day, Simon realised just how accurate his earlier description of the orphanage had been; it was a hive of activity. There were children painting, dancing, singing and cooking.

"Who is that?" asked Simon as he pointed to a religious Jewish man sitting on the floor with a group of children.

"That's Rabbi Ziemba," replied Janusz. "He often comes in to tell Yiddish stories. Some of our children barely know a handful of Polish words. It's important that we make their life here as comfortable as possible..."

"I'm sure I know him," said Simon, surprised. "I think he's the rabbi that was preparing Marcus for his Bar Mitzvah."

181

✡✡✡

"This is a madhouse!" exclaimed Lonia, later that evening in their attic apartment.

"You're right," replied Simon, putting on his overcoat. "But compared to the rest of Warsaw it's an island of sanity!"

"Where are you going? You know how dangerous it is on the streets for a Jew at this hour."

"I'm meeting Ziegler," he replied.

"That only proves you are mad!"

"Trust me, Lonia. I know what I'm doing."

"That's what you said this morning when you agreed to teach the kindergarten!"

"Believe me," he said. "After surviving that experience there's nothing a Nazi could do to frighten me!"

A few moments later, Simon was hunkered in the shadows of a doorway opposite the building where Ziegler worked, thinking about how much his beloved, battered city had changed. In recent months the huge brick wall that would define the borders of the Jewish ghetto had zigzagged its way relentlessly across streets and between buildings. In time the entire area would be sealed off from the rest of Warsaw. Some people actually thought this was a good thing – as if the wall was going to protect them from the evil world outside. "Nowadays a Jew can only trust a Jew," they would say. "In here, at least we will know who our friends are." But Simon thought that such talk was naïve. From the very beginning he had thought that Hitler had to be stopped before it was too late, but that moment had past long before the first bomb fell on Warsaw.

Simon watched the steady stream of officers emerge from the building opposite, careful to stay out of the light. Eventually he recognised the figure of his insect-loving "friend" coming down the steps.

"Come," said Ziegler, dispensing with all pleasantries. "I have a surprise for you."

FORTY-NINE

"Let me put your clothes on," said Marcus.

"What are you talking about?" Stefan replied.

"We're about the same size."

"We're not – you're much bigger than me. But anyway, why do you want to wear my clothes."

"So we can swap places – just for a while," replied Marcus.

"What do you want to be me for?"

"Because I'm fed up with being me!" said Marcus. "Anyway, it's so late; no one will notice."

"I think my mother has guests, this evening. They're in the lounge…"

"Then I won't go anywhere near there…"

"But what about your hair – mine is blonde and yours is black."

"I'll wear a hat…"

"That's really silly."

"Let's cut the cards for it," said Marcus picking up the pack. "If you win I'll drop the idea – promise."

Stefan suddenly felt sorry for Marcus – his poor friend's life had been turned upside down. "Alright," he conceded. "But only for a few minutes…"

"Twenty…"

"Ten…"

"Fifteen…"

Marcus nodded and picked up the cards. "You shuffle and cut first."

Stefan took the deck, mixed it up a few times and placed it on the bed. Then he swiftly grabbed the pack. "Jack!" exclaimed his friend.

"Not bad," said Marcus as he slowly lifted the pack up to his mouth and kissed the top card for luck. "Ace – I win!" and he punched the air as if he'd just scored a winning goal. "I have my freedom back for a quarter of an hour!"

"I'll go and get the clothes," Stefan said, defeated, as he made his way to the door.

"And don't forget that hat!" Marcus added.

As soon as his friend was gone Marcus retrieved the three other aces he had hidden under his bed and returned them to the pack, silently thanking his father for showing him that trick.

"You cheated."

"So what."

"But he's your friend."

"What harm have I done?"

"What if he finds out?"

"You know he won't!"

Marcus looked at himself in the mirror that hung on the back of his door. "I must stop doing that," he said to himself aloud.

FIFTY

"Where are we going?" said Simon. Both previous night-time insect discussions with Ziegler had taken place on a secluded bench, and there was no reason for him to suspect that tonight would be any different. He certainly didn't expect to be bundled onto the back seat of a car and covered in a blanket.

"Keep your head down and don't move," replied Ziegler from the driver's seat. "I'll let you know when we have arrived."

There wasn't the slightest hint of menace his voice, which frightened Simon intensely. Perhaps he had misjudged this young German and that boyish innocence was just the mask of a cold, hard man of violence. Many fellow Jews had suffered at the brutal hands of the Gestapo. Their reputation for cruelty was well known – from casual street beatings to capture and systematic torture.

"How long will we be gone?" Simon asked. "My wife will be worried…"

"Hush!" snapped Ziegler. "I will tell you when it is safe to speak. Until then, shut up!"

Simon's heart sunk. How could he have allowed himself to get into such a situation? Suddenly the car drew to a halt and the idling engine made the whole vehicle shudder. Ziegler shared a short exchange in German with someone outside and an intense sense of powerlessness made Simon's blood run cold. Then they set off again, jolting violently as if the car was travelling over metal ramps.

"Try and guess where we are!" called Ziegler, but Simon couldn't bring himself to speak. "I will give you a clue," he continued. "If I stopped right now and pushed you out of the car, you would probably drown." Simon still couldn't respond and the air of jollity in his captor's voice merely magnified his anxiety. As a boxer, in his younger days, he would turn his fear into anger, which made him a formidable opponent. But here his fists might as well have been bound with rope – he had never felt so weak.

"Get up!" commanded Ziegler. "Then you will see for yourself." Still Simon couldn't move. "Dr Tenenbaum!" he shouted. "Have you fallen asleep back there?" Then Simon felt the blanket being whipped away. "Now sit up and look out of the window, then tell me what you can see!"

Gingerly, Simon prised his cheek away from the cold leather seat and looked up to see the iron girders of the bridge flashing past the car window. He instantly knew what this meant. "We're going to the zoo," he exclaimed.

"Got it in one!" laughed Ziegler. "Oh I do like surprises!"

Simon's fears took on a whole new dimension. He had braced himself for an interrogation; maybe they wanted more information on Janusz? He'd even resigned himself to the inevitable brutality he was going to encounter, convinced that his years in the ring would prepare him for the worst. But now he would gladly have accepted the most horrible of tortures for what he was about to endure. It was obvious what had happened; Marcus had somehow been discovered and everyone, Jan, Antonina and Stefan included, was about to suffer the consequences.

FIFTY-ONE

"We're like twins!" said Marcus standing beside his friend and staring into the mirror on the back of the basement door. "Even our parents wouldn't be able to tell us apart!"

"You're crazy," said Stefan.

"You're right!" Marcus opened the door onto the stairs that led up to the hall – a part of him wanted to say a proper farewell to his friend, but he knew that if he did he probably wouldn't have been able to leave.

"Wait," said Stefan.

"Why?" replied Marcus with one foot already on the bottom step.

"It's almost six forty five and the grandfather clock in the hall is about to strike. So when it strikes seven o'clock, in fifteen minutes, you'll know your time is up."

"Ok," said Marcus impatiently, still unable to look his friend in the eye. "If you say so…" Then, after a tense few seconds, the chimes began and Marcus set off.

At the top he could see Stefan's mother through the half open lounge door laughing with some friends. Otto's wife was there, holding her new baby. He dashed into the kitchen, grabbed some bread and forced it inside his shirt. Then he reached down and pulled the sock on his right leg as high as it would go, checking the Gestapo gun hidden inside.

He knew that his disguise would never fool Stefan's mother, so taking the short cut to the courtyard through the lounge was out of the question. He decided to use the front door instead. Once outside Marcus darted around the side of the villa and stopped abruptly before he got to Hercules' sty; if he startled the pig its snorts would surely alert Mrs Zabinski. He tip-toed to the drain and opened the cover as silently as possible. As he lowered himself onto the ladder he felt the pistol in his sock press hard into his leg.

In the sewers he could hardly see his hand in front of his face. He was going to have to rely on instinct to trace the route past the lion enclosure, under the old monkey house and then out towards the river. His heart began to race and his heavy breathing echoed off the walls around him.

Then he stopped. What was he doing? Stefan was right – he was crazy.

"Don't give up – there's no turning back now!"

"But this is madness. How can I be sure this is going to work?"

"You can't. But how can you be sure someone won't find you in the basement? At least this way you're in control…"

"But I don't feel in control…"

"Stop worrying and get moving!"

As Marcus trudged along the tunnel, the weight of his doubts increased with each step. If he turned back now, he might just get to the villa before the clock struck seven and no one would ever know what he'd tried to do.

"Whose there?" came a terse whisper from the darkness. "I know there's someone, now reveal who you are!"

Marcus was so frightened he wanted to cry. At least it was a Polish voice; almost certainly Otto, but it still meant he'd been caught. Quick-fire thoughts shot through his head; he'd be taken back to the villa, told off for trying to escape and putting everyone's lives in danger by risking the Nazis discovering that a Jew had been given shelter here.

"If you don't make yourself known I will shoot," snapped Otto. Marcus could just about see his old friend's unmistakeable silhouette, illuminated by a shaft of light from a drain cover overhead. "I am aiming a gun at your head. This is your last chance to reveal yourself before I fire…"

"It's Grumpy!" Marcus heard himself say. "I have come to help!"

"Stefan, is that you?"

"Yes," croaked Marcus.

"Go home now!" snapped Otto. "This is no job for a child. And be careful from now on – there's a difference between being brave and being stupid. Tonight you have been both. It nearly cost you your life. Promise me you won't do anything like this again and I won't mention it to your father!"

"Ok."

"Right – now go!"

Marcus didn't wait a second longer and charged back towards the courtyard drain, tripping and slipping at every stride. He desperately grasped the ladder and pulled himself up. Forgetting to slide the cover back gently, the screech of scraping metal startled the pig, triggering a succession of loud growling snorts that filled the night air. He kicked the cover shut in panic and stumbled out of the courtyard just as Stefan's mother was emerging from the back door to investigate the noise.

Marcus frantically scampered round to the front of the villa and his heart sunk like a stone when he realised the door was locked. There was no way in. Just as he was about to drop to his knees in defeat, he suddenly heard the sound of wheels on gravel and looked up to see the glare of highlights coming towards him. Like a startled deer he turned and darted behind the nearest bush.

Convinced that he hadn't been seen, he pushed his hands into the branches in front of him and forced open a gap to spy through. It was a Nazi staff car. Then he gasped as he recognised the officer getting out of the driver's door. What was Ziegler doing here so late? He widened the opening and leant further into the bush to get a view of the V.I.P. he was helping out of the rear passenger door. It had to be someone really important to be chauffeured by such a high ranking officer. But there was nothing that could have prepared Marcus for the moment he realised just how important he was…

FIFTY-TWO

Jan was too engrossed in his work to hear Ziegler's car pull up outside the villa. No "uninvited guest" had ever called after dark, so when the bell rang he assumed that it had to be Otto, back from moving those rifles under the lion enclosure. He remained at his desk in the certain knowledge that his wife would answer the door. The first hint of anything out of the ordinary was when the bell rang for a second, much longer time. It was unlike Otto to be so impatient, Jan thought looking up from his papers.

"Alright, alright!" he heard Antonina call from the hallway. "I'm on my way."

Then there was a firm knock on Jan's office door and, much to his irritation, it flew open before he had a chance to respond. "We have guests," said his wife.

"Herr Direktor!" exclaimed Ziegler, striding past Antonina into the office. "I trust I am not disturbing you at this late hour."

Jan shot up from his chair. "Of course not, Herr Ziegler, it is always a pleasure..." But then he spotted Simon over his shoulder in the open doorway and his mind exploded in confusion. "Mr Tenenbaum," he gulped, steadying himself against his desk. "Both of you... How unexpected..."

"I thought you would be surprised," exclaimed Ziegler, clapping his hands in childish delight. "I do so like surprising people!"

"Am I to assume that my insect expertise is too rudimentary for you!" joked Jan.

190

"Oh no, no," replied Ziegler looking genuinely hurt. "Nothing could be further from the truth."

"Then why have you brought Mr Tenenbaum here tonight?" Jan could not bear to look Simon in the eye. They hadn't seen each other for so long and it was agonising to appear so detached when he just wanted to embrace his friend.

"He is not here tonight as an entomologist," said Ziegler. "He is here as a Jew!"

These harsh words sent shockwaves through the room; this had to be about Marcus...

"Something needs to be settled tonight, once and for all, and I suspect that we all know what I am referring to. I have tried to overlook the matter, but each time I come here it is harder to turn a blind eye. And after recently being contacted by *Oberscharführer* Schultz, it cannot be ignored any longer. I gather you are familiar with this man, Herr Direktor."

"I'm afraid that name is new to me..." Jan replied.

"Very tall, dark hair, quite a wide scar on his chin..."

"Ah yes, I know who you mean now. He is stationed in the old farmhouse next to the zoo."

"Precisely," replied Ziegler.

"And he is the officer who obtained this for me," said Jan reaching onto his desk for the letter granting permission to enter the ghetto to obtain food for his pigs.

"He got you this?!" Ziegler was clearly astonished at what he was holding.

"Yes!" replied Jan. "We are now a 'priority-industry'!"

"But this is signed by *Obergruppenführer* Heydrich!" Ziegler said uneasily. "I had no idea Schultz was so highly connected." He took a moment to collect himself and then carried on. "Well, he has expressed a concern to me that can no longer be ignored." He folded the letter and handed it back to Jan. "Gentlemen, I would be grateful if you would both accompany me outside." Then he turned briskly and strode into the hallway, only to stop again abruptly at the sight of Otto's wife nervously putting on her coat while Antonina stood beside her holding the baby. "What a beautiful child," said the German. "May it grow up in a world without war."

"We can all agree on that," said Antonina, returning the baby and opening the front door.

Everyone filed out into the night and there was a rustle in the bushes on the far side of the driveway that none of them noticed.

"It is this!" said Ziegler pointing up at the Star of David embedded in the outside wall. "Its presence can no longer be tolerated."

"But as I told you, Herr Ziegler, it is impossible to remove it without taking down the wall."

"So you say," replied the German. "But *Oberscharführer* Schultz has informed me that it has become the source of considerable unrest amongst his men and I have assured him that I would deal with it. That is why I am here tonight."

"With respect, Herr Ziegler," said Simon, straining to contain his relief that none of this appeared to have anything to do with Marcus. "Where do I fit in here?"

"This is a Jewish star," exclaimed Ziegler. "I gather its presence here symbolises the greed that so typifies your race. Does that not humiliate you?"

Jan quickly noticed the baffled look on his friend's face. "I have told Herr Ziegler the story behind the star," he interjected. "About the night that many of Warsaw's wealthiest Jews were swindled out of their fortunes."

"Of course," Simon responded, seamlessly picking up the theme. "And my father was one of them," he added.

"Excellent!" exclaimed Ziegler. "Now let's get down to business!" and he re-entered the villa leaving everyone else in confusion.

Franciszka took the opportunity to leave with her baby and made her way towards the pig field, where Otto would be waiting to take them both home. Jan followed Ziegler into the villa, but Antonina deliberately held back to steal a precious moment with Simon before they went inside as well. And from behind a bush in the shadows, Marcus sighed in frustration and placed the gun on the ground. He only had that Nazi's head in his sights for a split-second – if he'd have stood still for just a little while longer he'd have blown his brains out for sure.

FIFTY-THREE

Marcus was determined to kill the Nazi and get to his father – nothing in the world mattered more. Quickly checking that the coast was clear he left his hiding place behind the bush and darted across the driveway towards the rear of the villa. Hercules was sleeping deeply again, and he positioned himself behind the sty, resting the barrel of the pistol on its roof, ready to fire when the time was right. He had a perfect view of the scene inside.

Ziegler had gone straight into the lounge where the insects were displayed. "So you insist that this star cannot be easily removed."

"Correct," replied Jan. "I suspect that the whole wall would need to be demolished and the entire front of the villa rebuilt!"

"What a pity!" replied the German. "Then we are left with no option than to do precisely that!"

"That's ridiculous," Jan protested. "Surely it could just be covered over…"

"Alas no," Ziegler continued. "This option has been considered and rejected. If it were merely hidden it would still be there, and it is the star's very existence that is the problem."

"Be reasonable," said Jan, straining to contain his temper. "You are proposing the destruction of half of my house!"

"Furthermore I have been instructed to inform you that unless the offending object is removed within the week, *Oberscharführer* Schultz will not be purchasing another pig from you!"

"I can't believe that!" snapped Jan. "A few days ago he was saying how vital our animals are to the war effort. And besides, there isn't another pig farm within miles of here."

"You misunderstand me," said Ziegler. "I did not say that he would be taking his custom elsewhere. I said that he will not be purchasing any more pigs from you. It will not be difficult to find a German pig farmer to relieve you of your duties."

Simon looked on in despair. He still had no idea why he had been brought to witness all this. But that was about to change.

"Herr Direktor, I like to think that I am an honourable, reasonable man," said Ziegler, walking towards the insect specimens. "Maybe we could come to some sort of deal." He slowly reached inside his jacket, produced a sheet of densely typed paper and handed it to Simon. "If your friend agrees to sign this contract, I will take legal ownership of the entire collection and we will not have to demolish your house."

"So all of a sudden the star can be tolerated!" said Jan. "A few moments ago, its very existence was the problem."

"I am sure *Oberscharführer* Schultz can be persuaded to agree to merely covering the damn thing," he said dismissively. "But only if the Jew signs. Otherwise the bulldozers will arrive and you can wave goodbye to your home and your pigs!"

"And you think that these are the actions of an honourable, reasonable man?" said Jan very deliberately.

Ziegler laughed anxiously and walked slowly to the far side of the room, clearly beginning to lose his composure. All evening he had been playing up to the intimidating image of his uniform, but he was starting to struggle to keep up the performance. He'd expected to be driving back across the river by now, the proud new owner of the most comprehensive private collection of insects in the world. But his scheme wasn't running as smoothly as he'd hoped and he was starting to lose his nerve.

"Let's play cards for it," stuttered the German, noticing one of Stefan's many packs on the piano in the far corner of the room.

"What are you talking about?" said Jan.

"Look," said Ziegler flicking through the pack. "I'll place two cards in my hat... a king and a queen... and we can get the Jew to pick one out. If he chooses the king, then I get the collection and you lose your house and the pigs but if he takes a queen you keep everything. Collection, house, pigs, star... the lot!"

"That's preposterous!" said Jan. "Out of the question!"

"Ok," said Simon, at last breaking his silence. "But only for the insects. After all, to be frank, that's all you really want."

"No," said Jan. "I can't let you do this."

"What good are they to me now?" he said to his friend.

"Agreed!" announced Ziegler taking off his hat and flicking through the cards before Jan could change Simon's mind. "Let's do this now!"

"This is only for the insects," said Simon. "Whatever happens, Mr Zabinski will keep his pigs and his house, agreed!"

"Yes, yes..." said Ziegler, gasping like a toddler in a sweet shop.

Jan took a pen from his pocket and quickly made some amendments to the contract and handed it to Ziegler. "Sign here then."

The officer took the revised contract, read it carefully, took Jan's pen and signed. Then he handed the paper to Simon, who added his signature without reading a word.

"Ok," said the German, holding out his hat. "King I win, Queen you win."

Simon knew, of course, that there were two kings in the hat. It was an old trick that both he and Jan had seen many times before. As he picked out a card he could see that the young German was practically bursting with excitement.

"Ooops!" said Simon suddenly flicking the card across the room. "Oh dear, I am so nervous I can hardly stop my hand from trembling!"

Ziegler put his hat down and set off to retrieve the card, but Jan took a firm grip of his wrist. "Oh there's no need to go over there," he said. "Let's just see what card is left behind in the hat. If it's a queen then you must have won!" Then he reached in to pull out the remaining card. "Well, I never – it's a king! So the card Mr Tenenbaum must have picked out was a queen. It seems that you have lost Herr Ziegler!"

As the young German stood in the middle of the room with his mouth gaping open, Jan grabbed the rest of the pack, picked up the card that Simon had flicked across the room and casually started to reshuffle the pack before replacing them on the piano.

"Isn't it ironic that I should be so lucky with cards when my father lost his fortune with them in this very house?" said Simon removing a beetle specimen form the shelf and placing it in Ziegler's hands. "This is for you. You see, we Jews can be generous as well as greedy." Then he turned to Jan and shook his hand. "It was good to see you again, Mr Zabinski. Maybe when you are in the ghetto collecting food for your pigs you can pay a visit to Janusz Korczak's orphanage on 33 Chłodna Street. We always have plenty of food left!"

"I can imagine!" Jan replied with a wink.

"Come, Herr Ziegler," I think it is time you took me home."

The room emptied and no one heard the frantic clicking from the courtyard outside as Marcus repeatedly pulled the trigger of the gun in the hope that it would finally kill his father's captor. There were bullets in the gun, he could clearly see them, but it still wouldn't fire. It was the first real gun he had ever held, so how was he to know there was a safety catch?

Angry that he had failed to kill the Nazi for a second time, he knew he had to get out of sight as quickly as possible. He could hear the voices of the three men in the driveway at the front of the house and instantly realised that the only hope of getting back to the basement without being seen was to dash through the lounge and charge across the hallway as quickly as possible...

"Where the hell have you been?" said Stefan as his friend finally flew through the door and landed on his mattress.

"You're not going to believe this, Stef, I promise you..."

FIFTY-FOUR

The attack came two days later. It could have been Ziegler's idea, the vengeful act of a humiliated man, or equally Schultz may have been behind it. Either way, officers who emerged from the Gestapo's farmhouse headquarters carried it out. Otto spotted them marching purposefully past the pig field towards the villa, holding machine guns. Although Nazis were a common sight on the zoo grounds, they were normally sharing a joke or an off-duty cigarette; this was obviously different. Dawn had only just broken and the soldiers that were stomping through the early morning mist were clearly on a mission.

Inside the villa none of the Zabinski family had yet emerged from their rooms and downstairs, in his basement hideout, Marcus was still asleep. Helda was alone in the kitchen – she was the only person inside the villa who heard the order to take-aim barked out in a harsh German voice – "*Zielen!*"

The raid lasted less than a minute, but it reverberated in the hearts of those who lived through it forever. No bullet was fired at any person and no one was injured; the chosen target was the Star of David embedded in the villa wall. Although no blood was spilt, for the attackers the assault was as much a matter of life and death as any battleground conflict.

For everyone inside the villa, it was a sickening reminder of the bombardment of their city the year before. Paralysed by panic and fear, the Zabinskis clung to each other on the upstairs landing as the relentless sound of bullets crashing into brick and ricocheting off metal echoed throughout the house. In the basement Marcus had no choice but to face his fears alone. He was forced to relive the night his grandmother had been murdered by the Luftwaffe and the day a stranger in a bread queue had shielded him from death. In the kitchen Helda was flat on the floor, sheltering under the table. The wall that housed the Star was directly outside, and a cloud of plaster dust filled the room. For her this was just like the nightly air raids, spent in cramped, damp cellars; pressed up against neighbours that she'd long lived beside but hardly knew. Like everyone else in the villa, she was yet to discover the reason for this attack.

When the guns fell silent, the brass casings of hundreds of bullets were scattered over the driveway, which was coated with the red residue of shattered bricks. As the firing squad retreated, the traumatised residents of the villa emerged to join the zoo workers who had been drawn to the scene. Outrage and bewilderment spread through the crowd gathered in front of the damaged wall at the realisation that all this mayhem had been targeted at the Star of David.

"This is madness," said Otto.

"Totally crazy," agreed Jan.

"Come, let's clear things up," said Antonina, briskly taking her son's hand. Stefan's thoughts were with Marcus, all alone in the basement. He toyed with the idea of dashing down to see how he was, but with Helda around it was far too risky, so he joined his mother on the ground, to help gather up the small metal tubes that littered the driveway.

"What a dreadful mess," said Otto, placing a reassuring hand on Jan's shoulder.

"It is," agreed Jan. "But it was also an awful waste of time and effort."

"What do you mean?"

"Well, look at the star – it may well be dented, but it's still there. They wanted to destroy it, but look, so much brickwork has been blown away that it's far bigger than before!"

"You're right," agreed Otto and the two men crouched on the floor to join the clear up operation.

"I regret having to say it, but I knew this would happen." Helda's voice was so seldom heard in public that at first no one realised who was speaking. "I have always thought that a Polish zoo was not the place for a Jewish sign and prayed for this day to come. From the moment the German's moved in next door, I knew it was only a matter of time. Now finally these courageous soldiers have done something to remove it…"

"Courage?" barked Otto getting to his feet. "If you are describing the actions of those Nazis as 'courageous' then, I am afraid to say, you have completely taken leave of your senses…"

"I would thank you not to address me in such tones," she replied. "You may have felt comfortable working under the glare of such an ugly thing, but I for one have never approved of it."

Everyone's eyes focused on Helda and she began to tremble with embarrassment. "Let me assure you that I am not the only person who feels this way. The world needs to recognise that the Jews are no more than vermin!" She was shouting, now. "When this war is over, and Herr Hitler has finally established order in Europe, then you will wish that you had stood up to be counted like I have!" Then she stepped slowly towards her employer. "Mr Zabinski – I have always considered you to be fair and honourable. I have given many years of loyal service to you and—"

"Stop," said Jan. "Please do not say anymore, Helda. I want you to think long and hard before you decide to leave. You know how difficult work is to find in Warsaw. Before you walk away from here, consider what it will mean for you and your family." Helda stood like a statue. "Go home and consider your decision. If you choose to come back then there will always be a position waiting for you here."

Eventually she replied. "Thank you," she held out her hand for Jan to shake. "Whatever happens, Mr Director, I will always think of you as a decent man."

FIFTY-FIVE

By the time the Ghetto wall was finished conditions were so cramped that, in places, up to seven people were sharing the same room. The Tenenbaums were fortunate to have their attic, although it was only exclusively theirs at night-time; during the day it doubled as a classroom. Occasionally the rabbi came to prepare boys for their Bar Mitzvahs.

"With respect, rabbi," Simon once said. "What is the point of these lessons? None of these boys have families to organise Bar Mitzvahs for them. Are they not just wasting their time?"

"A Bar Mitzvah is more than just an excuse for a party!" replied the rabbi. "It marks the moment when a boy becomes a man, both in the eyes of God and in the eyes of the boys themselves. And when these troubled times are over, my friend, we Jews are going to need as many men as we can get!"

Jan had become a frequent visitor to the orphanage. He was one of the few Poles officially permitted to enter the ghetto, to collect food for the pigs, and made a point of visiting his friend as frequently as possible. He and Otto quickly became familiar faces at the heavily guarded gates and they were often waved through without even having their papers checked.

Of course Jan never actually took anything from the orphanage. He had persuaded Ziegler to arrange for him to collect food that had been left by German soldiers, using Simon's insects as inducement. Every time he made a collection he loaned Ziegler a different specimen to display in his office, swapping it over on each visit. "That way my pigs will get a steady supply of food and you will see a wide variety of insects – what could be better?!" Ziegler had approved the arrangement without hesitation.

It was during a visit to the orphanage, when talking with Simon at one end of the attic while the rabbi was teaching a group of boys at the other, that Jan came up with an idea that he instantly knew was probably the craziest thought he had ever had. Everyone he told about it gasped at its audacity; it was madness to try such a stunt under the noses of the Nazis. But, inevitably they too found themselves drawn to the plan and soon realised that, whatever the risks, they would do everything they could to make it work.

✡✡✡

It was on his next visit to the orphanage that Jan approached the rabbi, after the Bar Mitzvah class had been dismissed.

"It's going to happen in ten days' time," Jan said. "Everything is in place!"

"So you're going through with your madcap scheme?" replied the rabbi.

"Of course!" replied Jan. "Did you ever think I wouldn't?"

The rabbi just smiled. "If I called you a *'meschugene'* would you know what I meant?"

"Oh yes!" laughed Jan. "And you wouldn't be the first person to call me that!"

FIFTY-SIX

The sight of German soldiers strolling through the zoo grounds had become so common that Stefan spent most of the day on look-out duty and his piano-alarm was regularly heard. Although Helda's departure had made Marcus' discovery less likely, he still spent practically all day in the basement. After his crazy dash for freedom he hadn't put a foot outside the villa, so when Antonina brought him a coat and gave him five minutes to get ready, he was totally bewildered.

"Where am I going?"

"Out," she replied.

"Where to?"

"Oh you'll see," came the answer.

"Am I going home? Is the war over? Will I see my parents again? Tell me, tell me, tell me…"

"You're going to have to trust me," she said ruffling his hair.

"Is Stef coming too?" Marcus asked.

"He is!" replied Antonina. "We all are! But I wouldn't bother asking him what's happening, because he knows as little as you do! Now hurry up." Then she left the room.

"Do I need to pack my suitcase?" he called.

Antonina paused halfway up the basement stairs to consider her response. "No," she finally replied. "You won't need to bring anything with you."

"So I'll be coming back here then?" he probed further, but Antonina was no longer there to reply.

When he emerged into the hall the look of confusion on his friend's face confirmed that Antonina had been telling the truth when she'd said that Stefan didn't know what was going on. Jan was standing by the open front door holding a specimen jar from the insect collection. Outside was the truck, heavily loaded with at least ten large wooden barrels. Otto was standing amongst them. "Okay – all clear!" he called.

"Stefan first," said Jan. "Quickly now… just do what Otto says."

Marcus watched his friend climb onto the back of the truck and clamber towards Otto and then disappear into a barrel.

"Next!" Otto commanded. Marcus dashed towards the truck. "Quick, in this one. Just crouch down and don't make a sound!" He turned his head towards the barrel next to Marcus'. "And that goes for you too, Stefan! Not even a whisper from either of you!"

The barrels were damp with a faint smell of rotten food, and thin shafts of light cut through the gaps between the wooden planks. As the truck began to drive away from the villa they began to wobble.

"Good morning, Herr Direktor!" came a German voice. "I see you are taking your wife with you today to collect food for our pigs!"

"Correct," said Jan. "There may come a time when I can't go and she needs to learn the ropes!"

"Of course!" came the response and the truck moved off again.

The boys in the barrels tried to trace the truck's progress from what they could hear and the vibrations of the vehicle. Soon it began to jerk slowly as if they had joined a line of slow-moving traffic.

"Papers… ah, Herr Zabinski – the pig-man!"

"Good morning!" Jan replied.

"Off you go!"

Then the truck picked up speed again – but not for long.

"Herr Direktor!" it was Ziegler's voice. "That must be a particularly heavy insect – it appears to require three people to carry it."

"I wanted to see how this food-for-insect system works," called Stefan's mother. "So I'll know what to do myself, if my husband can't make it here himself, for some reason."

"Very wise, I'm sure," said Ziegler.

Then the engine cut off and there was a clunking sound as the bolts at the back of the truck were slid open.

"My word, that's a lot of barrels!" called Ziegler. "I doubt that we'll be able to fill them all today!"

"Never mind," said Jan. "Our pigs will be grateful for whatever you have!"

The boys heard the thud of feet stomping around on the back of the truck and the sound of barrels being dragged on the metal floor. After a few minutes of silence the barrel-dragging resumed, but this time it was accompanied by the strong smell of food – clearly they were no longer empty.

"Here's the giant stag beetle you brought me last time," said Ziegler.

"I hope you enjoyed it," said Jan. "And here's your latest companion!"

"A giant rhinoceros beetle – how marvellous!"

"Take care of it, won't you!" said Jan.

"Of course I will," answered the German. "Have you got any more food collections to make?"

"I think I'll try the orphanage on Chłodna Street," replied Jan as the engine spluttered back into life. "They're bound to have something for me to take away! Goodbye!"

"Farewell!" replied the German.

FIFTY-SEVEN

A few minutes later the truck pulled into the courtyard at the back of the orphanage. Otto lifted the lid from Stefan's barrel and immediately leant inside, his finger pressed hard against his lips. Stefan instantly understood and climbed out as quietly as he could. His eyes took a short while to adjust to the daylight, but by the time his feet touched the ground he could see clearly, and what he saw made him want to scream out with joy. Instead he rushed silently into the waiting arms of Lonia Tenenbaum, who was sobbing uncontrollably. It suddenly dawned on him why everything had been cloaked in such secrecy. He could see the small, bespectacled figure of Janusz Korczak, and next to him was Shlomo, beaming with happiness.

"I am so glad you are well," Stefan murmured into his friend's ear as they embraced. "I have missed you so much."

"Me too, Stef," said Shlomo.

Then Stefan noticed the hordes of faces peering out from the rows of windows behind them. There were children of all ages and adults as well – and none of them made a sound.

"It's time to go inside," whispered Janusz, ushering Shlomo and Stefan towards the building. "Hurry now," and soon they were part of the throng of spectators.

And then Marcus appeared at the edge of the truck, like an animal emerging from hibernation. Stefan couldn't remember the last time he had seen him out in the open. He looked like a prisoner finally being released from his cell.

Then Lonia charged at the truck in an explosion of emotion and the air was filled with anguish and joy. Mother and son embraced so tightly, as if they were saving each other from drowning. And then Simon joined them and the family was complete. But there were no cheers of delight from the onlookers – hugging their parents was something that none of them would ever do again.

While every eye was focused on the Tenenbaums, Otto and Jan dragged the barrels from the back of the truck towards the house. Stefan's mother had been baking for days and by the time everything had been unloaded, the tables in the dining room appeared to be heaving with enough cakes and biscuits to feed half of Warsaw. Homemade streamers and colourful decorations adorned the walls and as the excitement began to grow, some music struggled to be heard from a gramophone player in the corner.

Gradually all the residents of the orphanage filed into the room. And in the centre, waving his hands above his head and swaying to the music was the rabbi, dressed in a long black robe, adorned with silver stars. On his head, instead of the black *kippah* he usually wore was a large, black, furry hat that made him tower over the many children who were gathering round him in delight. Soon everyone in the room was circling him in a growing frenzy of singing and dancing.

"I never thought you'd pull it off," shouted Janusz to Jan, straining to make himself heard above the noise. "Look at the happiness you've brought to this place!" Before Jan could reply he was grabbed by the arm and yanked away to join in the mayhem. He turned to identify his assailant and was heartened to see the beaming face of his life-long friend staring back at him. "You're a miracle-worker!" was all he could hear of Simon's words.

As the last of Antonina's cakes were eaten the rabbi returned to the centre of the room, but this time he wasn't singing or dancing. On his shoulder were the sacred Torah scrolls – the focal part of most Jewish religious observance. Quickly, a table was dragged from the edges of the room for him to rest it on. Then, in a powerful booming voice, he began to chant the prayers that always preceded the reading of the Torah in synagogue, and a hush descended on the room. You didn't need to be particularly religious to be moved by the scene that was unfolding. Beyond these walls the Nazis were imposing the most terrible restrictions on every aspect of Jewish life. Gatherings such as this would have been viciously broken up if discovered. For everyone present the rabbi's voice was a defiant song of freedom. Then he began to recite a list of names, and gradually the entire Bar Mitzvah class gathered around him. Then he turned his head towards Marcus, took a deep breath, and sung out his name and a chorus of approval rang around the room.

So while Europe was under the spell of a man whose hatred of Jews knew no bounds, here in the heart of Poland, a small group of Jewish boys were celebrating their Bar Mitzvahs. While the mortar in the ghetto walls was yet to dry, a ceremony rooted in thousands of years of tradition was taking place under the noses of men who strived to devise ever more brutal ways of making Hitler's plans a reality. A surge of pride swept through the room.

One by one, the class stepped forward to recite what they'd been taught. Before each boy began, the rabbi placed a white *tallith* on their shoulders, the prayer shawl that symbolises the wearer to be a man. Some of their voices were frail and faltering while others were strong and bold – but each was greeted with cheers of appreciation.

"Do your best," whispered the rabbi to Marcus as he approached, mindful that he hadn't been coached for many months. He turned to see his apprehensive parents and smiled to himself. How were they to know that he had sung what he was about to recite in his mind countless times in his secluded basement world? His voice was as loud and clear as a bell; when he finished the room exploded in delight.

Marcus went to embrace his proud parents and suddenly realised they were both wearing coats. Then he noticed the suitcases by the door that led out to the courtyard where the truck was waiting. "Are you coming with me?" he asked his mother. She couldn't reply, but the look on her face was all the answer he needed.

"It's getting dark," said Otto. "If we leave it too late they're likely to search our truck. We've got to go now!"

Janusz was standing by the door. "Good luck," he said shaking Simon's hand. "You'll be missed my friend."

"Shlomo, come with," said Marcus to his friend.

"I'll be safe here," he replied. "I'll see you after the war. I promise."

"Hurry," said Jan. "Follow me!"

Otto was waiting at the truck and helped Marcus' mother onto the back and then lifted her into a waiting barrel. Stefan was next.

"Help me with these bags," said Marcus' father to his son. "They're quite heavy."

One by one, they handed the suitcases to Otto who slotted them into another barrel.

"You're next young man!" said his father.

Marcus clambered up, darting quickly to the barrel he'd hidden in on the way there. As Otto replaced the lid, he couldn't remember the last time he'd felt so happy.

And as the truck slowly bumped its way over the cobbled streets of The Old Town, towards the ghetto gates, Marcus felt the weight of the world lifting from his shoulders. He was never going to be alone again.

Each time the truck stopped, Marcus held his breath. But somehow he knew that they were not going to be searched. Even the occasional muffled German voice didn't alarm him. And when the metal grid on the bridge across the Vistula shook the wheels of the truck so violently that his barrel almost toppled over, he knew they were safe.

Then they stopped and Marcus heard the opening and slamming of doors – they had arrived! He manoeuvred himself into a crouching position, ready to jump up like a jack-in-the-box to amuse his waiting parents. Outside he heard barrels being scraped and voices being raised. There were even a few screams. Hurry up, he thought, my knees are aching.

Eventually, he saw his lid move and sprung to his feet. "Surprise!" he called. But the scene that awaited him was not the one he'd expected. There was Stefan, standing beside Otto. And there was his mother, holding onto Antonina and crying like a baby.

"Your father left this in his barrel," said Jan handing Marcus a note.

My dearest Lonia and Marcus,
I can't tell you how happy I am to know you are safe.
I look forward to the day we can be together once more.
I hope you understand why I had to stay.
I am needed here.
With all my love S xxx

Part Six

January 1941

FIFTY EIGHT

And so it began.

The day after the "The Great Bar Mitzvah Escape" (as it was now called) Jan invited some fellow members of the Polish Resistance to the villa for a meeting. "We are a zoo with no animals," said Antonina, handing out slices of homemade apple pie. "Maybe it's time to put those empty cages and shelters to good use?"

"It is one thing hiding a mother and child from the Nazis," said Feliks Cywinski. "What you are proposing is on a much bigger scale."

"We are not planning on opening a hotel!" replied Jan. "Think of it more as a holding operation. Simon will identify people who are willing to risk escaping from the ghetto and I'll bring them here to stay until we can find a safe house for them outside Warsaw."

"We will need false papers," said Marda Walter from the other end of the table. "Everyone that gets out will need a totally new identity."

"The Resistance have people who can organise such things." Jan said.

"But what about the Nazis in the old farmhouse?" asked Feliks. "They treat this place like their own."

"We'll use the sewers!" said Antonina, pouring some tea. "The tunnels under this zoo are ideal for moving people about in secret. Nothing ever needs to happen in view of the Germans.

And besides," she continued, passing a slice of cake to Stefan who was sitting at the corner of the table, "we have a special alarm that alerts us to danger!"

"What's that?" asked Marda.

Antonina winked at her son and he left the kitchen to make his way to the lounge.

"My word!" said Marda in amazement as the famously fierce final movement of Beethoven's *Moonlight Sonata* filled the air. "Is that really Stefan?"

"It certainly is," said his father with pride. "Whenever he plays like that, everyone knows there's a Nazi nearby."

"The boy's a genius!" said Feliks, helping himself to the final slice of pie. "He's as gifted a pianist as his mother is a cook!"

✡✡✡

The plan worked like a dream. Jan's regular visits to the ghetto made him and Otto so familiar that the guards never searched their truck on the way out. Although, as Jews caught leaving the ghetto without permission were instantly shot, it wasn't easy for Simon to find people who were willing to take that risk. When he did, it took about a week for false papers to be created. As very few Jews were blonde, Antonina and Marda would occasionally dye the escapees' hair in an attempt to help them look 'less Jewish'. They did everything they could to help them pass as regular Poles; they even taught children the Lord's Prayer in Polish; something a Jewish child would never normally know.

Soon, in addition to Marcus and his mother in the villa basement, the Zabinskis were playing host to a variety of Jewish "guests" who were hidden in the concealed shelters behind the bear enclosure, the pheasants' cages and the lion house. And Stefan became as familiar with the zoo's sewer system as he was with its paths. Using the drain cover near Hercules' sty as the "main entrance", he borrowed a flashlight from Otto's workshop and regularly delivered food, blankets and clothes to the new arrivals.

"Let me come with you," whispered Marcus as they were playing cards one night. "No one will know."

"My father will never agree," replied his friend. "It's far too risky."

"But if the Germans don't see you, then why would they see me?"

"That's not the point," said Stefan. "If they *did* find you… well, you can imagine what they'd do."

What are you two whispering about?" called Lonia from the other side of the room. Marcus loved having his mother with him. He no longer had to speak to himself for company, and he was glad to be able to comfort her when dark night-time fears for his father's safety overwhelmed her. But it also made it practically impossible to keep secrets…

"Oh nothing, Mum, honestly."

FIFTY-NINE

But things were about to change.

One unseasonably warm February morning, as Stefan's piano alarm swept through the villa, Jan watched from his office window as a huge black car came to a halt on the driveway outside. To his surprise he saw Ziegler opening a passenger door for a much older (and obviously superior) officer. As they strode briskly towards the front door, it was clear that this visit had nothing to do with insects.

"Please, sit down," Jan said to his guests as he ushered them into his office.

"No, we will stand," snapped the senior man.

Jan started to worry; if it turned out that the rescue operation had been discovered, he would be killed for sure. They'd torture him first to find out who else was involved, but in the end he'd be shot – it's what happened to Poles who protected Jews.

"This is official business, Herr…"

"His name is Zabinski," prompted Ziegler.

"Zabinski," echoed the officer.

How could this have happened? Maybe Helda had known about Marcus all along and couldn't keep quiet about it anymore? The Germans paid generously for information that led to the capture of Jews, and any qualms she may have had about revealing her suspicions would have been easily outweighed by the need to feed her family. Or perhaps Simon had been caught and forced to confess to everything under torture? Jan recoiled at the thought. This plan had been his idea and if anything had happened to his friend, he would never forgive himself.

"May I offer you some refreshment?" Antonina had spotted the Germans' arrival and was carrying a tray of drinks.

"Thank you, Mrs Zabinski," said Ziegler.

"No time!" snapped his stern superior officer. "Leave us!"

Jan avoided eye contact with his wife as she left the room – he didn't want to see the fear he knew she would be feeling.

"We need to talk about a rather delicate matter," mumbled Ziegler.

"Who is playing the piano?" asked the older man.

"It is my son," replied Jan.

"He is a fine player."

"Indeed he is, Herr Kommandant," confirmed Ziegler. "Every time I have visited this house he is practising."

"I admire such focus in a child," said the officer. "You must be very proud of him."

"Indeed," replied Jan.

"As I said, this is rather a delicate matter," said Ziegler. "But then, we have come to know each other well in recent months and I feel there is a level of trust between us."

"Listen to me, Zabinski," interrupted his superior officer with an air of menace. "If you breathe a word of what you're about to hear to anybody else, you will be putting yourself in considerable danger."

"Herr Zabinski is an honourable man," said Ziegler. "I am sure we can rely upon him to be discreet and cooperate."

Jan tried to remain as calm as possible, while struggling to read their intentions.

"Next week we are privileged to be hosting *Reichsführer* Himmler in the headquarters next to this zoo. He will be staying there over night," said the Kommandant. "I am sure I do not need to explain the significance of such an event."

"Of course not," replied Jan. His head was reeling now; Himmler was about as close to Hitler as you could get – many saw him as the evil brain behind the Nazi's anti-Jewish policies. But why would he need to know about his visit?

"It is vital that we pay our respects by entertaining him in a way that is fitting to someone of such importance," said Ziegler "And I gather from *Oberscharführer* Schultz, that in recent weeks the quality of the meat that he has purchased from you has declined considerably. No doubt you would say that you are doing your best under very trying circumstances. But nonetheless…"

"…let me get to the point," barked the senior officer. "Herr Ziegler informs me that there is a particularly large pig that lives in your courtyard – one that dwarfs the scrawny specimens in the field."

"Yes," replied Jan. "That is my son's pet…"

"We want it," said the Kommandant. "It would make the perfect centre piece for the banquet being organised for *Reichsführer* Himmler."

"But it is my son's pet…"

"That is of no relevance to us, Herr Zabinski."

Jan's thoughts started to unravel. This had nothing to do with hiding Jews. Simon was safe and the smuggling scheme was still intact. But this was no time to relax.

"I am sure we can find you another suitable animal, Herr Kommandant," said Jan.

"The only creature on the farm that is anywhere near the size that is required is your boar."

"I really must protest!" said Jan.

"Mr Zabinski!" shouted the officer. "I was led to believe that you are a man of intelligence. I should tell you that ever since I heard about that despicable star on your property I have had my doubts, and you can thank Herr Ziegler here for vouching for your good character, otherwise I doubt that this villa would still be standing!"

"But it is quite an old beast," Jan continued. "I doubt that the meat on it would be very good..."

"Silence!" yelled the officer, his face growing red with anger. "What have I got to do to make your slow Polish brain understand? I don't really care if its meat is as tough as leather. We need a huge roasted pig on a platter to carry into the banquet, in true traditional style in honour of *Reichsführer* Himmler, and that is precisely what we are going to have!" Then he turned to Ziegler. "Go and kill it now! And aim for the neck – we need to keep its head unblemished."

"Yes, Herr Kommandant!" replied Ziegler extending his hand in salute. Then he left the room unbuttoning his holster.

Antonina was in the hallway and she had to step back to avoid the officer storming passed her into the lounge where Stefan was still playing. "What's going on?" she asked Jan.

"They're taking Hercules," he replied.

"No!" she cried. "Stop them."

"I tried..." started Jan, but Antonina had gone. She was charging towards the courtyard, barging in front of the startled German.

"You cannot do this!" she said, standing between Ziegler and the pig.

"Get out of the way, woman," barked the Kommandant.

But Antonina had other plans. She dashed towards Hercules' sty and pushed open the gate. "You will have to shoot me first!" she shouted, standing beside the startled animal's head.

"Mama!" called Stefan, who had left the piano in panic and was standing by the doorway.

"Antonina!" yelled her husband. "Come away!"

"If you wish to sacrifice yourself for this pig, it is your decision," said the senior officer. "Either way we will take the creature. You have ten seconds to stand aside and then you will both be shot!"

"With respect, Herr Kommandant," said Ziegler nervously "There is no need to..."

"Silence!"

"Mama!" called Stefan, who had started to cry. "Come away!"

"No!" said Antonina defiantly.

"I cannot do this!" said Ziegler visibly shaking. Then he replaced the pistol into his holster.

The tension in the courtyard was unbearable.

"Are you mad, Ziegler?" snapped the Kommandant.

"No – but I think that you are over reacting here!" Ziegler responded. Then he turned to Jan. "Herr Zabinski, I trust that you will agree to this request and make the suitable arrangements!"

"Er, yes, of course," said Jan.

"Thank you," said Ziegler. "I expect this creature to be slaughtered and ready for collection in two days.

He paused to allow the Kommandant to speak, but he said nothing. Instead, bursting with fury, he stormed back into the house and charged straight through to the front door, leaving Ziegler alone with the Zabinskis in the courtyard.

Antonina was still standing by the pig and Stefan was clutching his father, sobbing uncontrollably. The two men looked at each other, tongue-tied. Ziegler didn't know whether to apologise for his superior officer's conduct, and Jan was unable to express his gratitude, so no words were exchanged.

But the silence was broken by the sound of pistol fire crashing into metal from the front of the villa, echoing in the morning air. The Kommandant was clearly venting his frustration on the star. The sound drew Ziegler away, leaving the Zabinski family alone in their distress.

Eventually Jan and Antonina went inside, but Stefan stayed in the courtyard. He quickly dried his eyes, took the broom that was leaning against a wall and entered the pen, eager to make his pet as comfortable as he could one final time.

SIXTY

"Do you know what I did before Otto took him away to be killed?" Stefan asked Marcus.

"What?"

"I cleaned his sty."

"That's very kind of you."

"Yeah, but that's not all. I fed him as well."

"That's good. I'm sure the Germans will be very grateful..." Marcus wasn't sure where his friend was taking the conversation but he knew he had to stay with him.

"But there was no fruit left."

"That's a pity..."

"I didn't care at first. Why should I just fatten him up for the Nazis to eat?"

"Yeah," agreed Marcus.

"But then I remembered what he did when the bombs were falling and he was left alone for days without food."

"What was that?"

"Well, he started to eat his own waste."

"Urgh! Really? That's disgusting!" said Marcus.

"Not really," replied Stefan. "Lots of animals on the zoo used to do it. My father says that it can be a good source of nutrition and it's better than dying of starvation!"

"I think I know what you're about to tell me..." said Marcus cringing, with his hands over his ears.

"Yep – that's right; all of it. Every last bit!"

"Revolting," exclaimed his friend.

"Maybe," Stefan conceded. "But it's good to know exactly what the Germans will be eating when they sit down at the banquet!"

Marcus laughed, while holding his nose in disgust.

"But there's more," said Stefan, sliding closer to his friend as if he was about to reveal the most classified of secrets. "I swept right to the back wall of his sty, which was the most revolting thing I'd smelt in my life, and guess what I found?"

"A photo of his mum…?"

"What? No."

"Ok, a special piggy telephone that he used to speak with the other animals in the zoo when he got bored…"

"Stop being silly…" said Stefan, holding up his hand, "I'm being serious; just listen."

Marcus smiled; he loved making his friend laugh.

"I found another drain cover."

"So what – that's hardly a big deal," said Marcus, leaning back in disappointment.

"But this one is different," Stefan said. "It's very old and heavy. I had to pull really hard to open it; all those years under so much muck must have sealed it…"

"You're disgusting…"

"The thing is," Stefan carried on. "It's much too old to be connected to the zoo's sewer system. I bet nobody else even knows about it. It's huge! And the water that flows through it is more like a stream – it probably goes right out into the Vistula…" Stefan's eyes were alive with excitement. "We have to explore it, Marcus."

"Why?" asked his friend.

"To see where it leads to," Stefan replied.

"But you've just told me that it flows into the Vistula. Why do you want to go there?"

"It's not that end of the sewer I'm interested in," said Stefan. "I reckon it's as old as the farmhouse. I bet if we followed it far enough we'd get to it!"

"Hold on a minute," said Marcus. "Are you suggesting that we crawl along an ancient sewer in the hope that it leads to a building full of Nazis?"

"If you put it like that," replied Stefan. "Yes!"

"You're planning something, aren't you?" said Marcus. Stefan the schemer was back! Marcus was suddenly reminded of the time his friend set the peacock trap for Pawel. Perhaps losing Hercules had changed him in some way. A few days ago Stefan insisted that it was too risky to go with him to the sewers that he already knew his way around; now he was suggesting that they explore some old tunnels they'd never seen before! It was totally crazy – but no crazier than spending the rest of his life cooped up in a cellar with his mother! And there was something irresistibly hypnotic about the look of adventure in Stefan's eyes. "When are we going then?"

"Tomorrow night," replied Stefan. "I'll have gathered all we need by then."

SIXTY-ONE

"Are you awake?" Marcus whispered to his mother in the darkness. There was no reply, but he had to be sure, so he repeated it, this time a little louder. Still no response. He slowly sat up in bed and listened intently. All he could hear was her shallow breathing from the other side of the basement room. He slid back the covers and crawled towards the door, already fully dressed, teasing it open just wide enough to squeeze through. Once outside he tiptoed up the stairs, into the hallway and through to the lounge.

"Where have you been," hissed Stefan from under the piano. "I've been waiting for ages. I thought you'd chickened out!"

"Never!" said Marcus. "What have you got there?"

"It's a flashlight," answered Stefan. "I could only find one in Otto's workshop. But I'm not sure how much power it has left." He stood up and made his way to the door that opened out onto the courtyard.

"I thought you said you could only find one," said Marcus.

"One what?"

"Flashlight."

"I did."

"So what's that in your other hand?" Marcus asked on the way to the courtyard. "What is it?" Marcus watched his friend enter the empty pig pen. "Can't you hear me?" he asked. "What else have you got?"

"It's a grenade. I took it from one of the secret weapon stores – the one in the hippo house…"

"You're crazy!" said Marcus. "What are you going to do with that?"

Stefan had both hands on the large metal handle that was moulded into the old drain cover. "What do you think?" he replied, straining his answer through gritted teeth.

"I'm not coming with you," said Marcus. "You didn't say anything about a grenade!"

"You can't go back now," said Stefan.

"Yes I can," but he didn't move. "And you should come with me."

"No way!"

"But you'll get yourself killed! What do you know about grenades?"

"Otto showed me how they work, it's dead easy."

"This is madness," Marcus said.

Stefan started to climb down the metal ladder that led down into the drain. "I'll go by myself if I have to," he said. Marcus still didn't move. He watched his friend disappear below ground level and knew he had to follow.

This old tunnel was much bigger than the zoo sewer system – there was enough room to stand up without stooping. "I knew you'd come," said Stefan.

"You do know you're crazy," said Marcus. "Don't you?"

Just as Stefan had said, the water was like a stream. As they stood on the brick walkway beside it they could see the mouth of the tunnel open out onto the Vistula. They were so close that they could see the fractured reflection of the moon on the surface of the water through the opening to the river.

"This is revenge for everyone they have killed," said Stefan. "Your grandmother, Shlomo's mother, all the creatures that lived on the zoo and Hercules – everyone!"

"But what if we get blown up as well?" asked Marcus. "We've

survived this long – it would be so stupid to end up killing ourselves."

"We won't," said Stefan. "I promise." Then he started to make his way along the old sewer and switched on the flashlight.

"That puny thing barely makes a difference," said Marcus.

"Well it's better than nothing," Stefan replied. "Just stay close to the wall, that way you won't fall in."

"Great advice!" Marcus replied.

Despite the poor light the boys made good progress and it wasn't long before they came to another ladder leading up to a drain cover.

"This must be it," said Stefan handing Marcus the flashlight. "Here goes." He slid the grenade out from inside his coat and began to climb the thin metal steps. Marcus followed behind trying to cast what little light was left onto the underside of the drain cover overhead.

"It's stuck," said Stefan straining to open the drain. "Help me." Marcus climbed up further until he was right beside his friend; together they heaved against the circle of iron above their heads. Suddenly it moved.

"Right," said Stefan, "You hold it open and I'll pull this wire and chuck the grenade through the gap. Then we'll have about five seconds to get down this ladder before it explodes."

Marcus was no longer nervous – he just followed instructions and was desperate to get it over and done with. He held his shoulder against the cover and pushed with as much force as he could to keep it open.

"Brilliant!" said Stefan poking his head through the gap. "It's the perfect place… we're in the courtyard right outside the old farmhouse… okay – I'm ready."

Stefan yanked the wire next to the handle as hard as he could and threw the metal tube towards the guard house. "Move!" he yelled. "Let's go." The two boys didn't climb down the ladder; they simply dropped on to the walkway below and crouched on the ground.

"Is that five seconds yet?" asked Marcus. Stefan didn't reply. "It should have gone off by now." He still said nothing. "It's not going to explode, is it?" Stefan slowly flopped back against the tunnel wall.

"It must have been a dud," he exclaimed. "Or the detonator was faulty, or..."

Suddenly the ground shook and an enormous low roar echoed through the tunnel. The boys looked at each other, scampered to their feet and ran along the walkway, slipping and stumbling against the wall, desperate to get as far away from the blast as possible. There was the Vistula, through the tunnel opening in the distance. They found the stairs below Hercules' pen and climbed up as quickly as they could. Then they clambered through the opening, leant against the wall of the empty sty, exploded into hysterical laughter and hugged each other.

"We did it!"

SIXTY-TWO

"Did you hear an explosion during the night?" asked Lonia, shaking Marcus' shoulder. "Or was I dreaming?" It was unusual for Lonia to have to rouse her son; he was always up first. "Hey, sleepyhead, open your eyes!" she whispered into his ear. Marcus could feel the warmth of his mother's breath, but he could barely move. She shook him harder and he turned away from her, moaning angrily. "What is wrong with you this morning?"

The answer, or course, was that he hadn't actually slept all night. When he'd finally crept back into bed he was so exhilarated that he couldn't close his eyes, and it wasn't until the first shafts of light seeped under the door that the pounding of his racing heart finally subsided.

Upstairs, sleep had swallowed Stefan the moment his head hit the pillow, and he'd woken with the same sense of elation that had coloured his dreams. He rushed to the bathroom window, which had a view of the farmhouse, desperate to revel in the success of his mission, but some trees shielded his view of the courtyard.

"How often have I told you to wash before you go to bed?" called his mother from the bathroom door. "Your sheets look like they've been dragged through a muddy puddle! Now get dressed as quickly as you can – Otto wants to see you."

Stefan was still munching his breakfast as he strode through the chilly morning air. As he made his way towards the pig field a sudden thought occurred to him – had he actually killed someone last night?

"Over here!" called Otto beside the truck. Suddenly a second wave of panic surged through his body. What if Otto had realised a grenade was missing? Maybe that's why he wanted to see him? He'd been so careful to rearrange all the others to leave no gap, but Otto could have counted them and discovered the truth.

"Get a move on, Dopey, I haven't got all morning!"

Stefan's mind started to whir… he decided his best course of action was to say nothing.

"What's the matter with you? Don't you like me calling you Dopey? You should have said…"

Stefan tried to force his mouth into a smile, but he'd lost control of his facial muscles.

"What's wrong with you this morning?"

"It's Hercules," Stefan heard himself mumble. "I miss him."

"Ah, that's it, is it? Well, let's hope Himmler chokes on him, hey?" he said, patting Stefan on the back. "Now listen very carefully, young man. You and I have a very important job to do." Otto suddenly looked very serious. He was like a favourite uncle – always ready with a laugh and a joke, so on the few occasions he looked serious, you listened. "Your father is busy this morning – *Oberscharführer* Schultz is questioning him about some incident at the farmhouse last night. It means he can't come with me to collect the pigs' food…"

Stefan was no longer listening – they were questioning his father about something that he had done. Things could not have been any worse…

"Get that frown off your face!" said Otto "I'm sure there's nothing to worry about."

"What happened last night?"

"A Nazi blew himself up. He picked up a stray grenade and it exploded in his hand. He was either very unlucky, and the weapon was faulty, or he was very stupid and set it off himself, in which case, quite frankly, it serves him right."

"Did he die?"

"Instantly," said Otto impassively. "Now wait in the truck, young man. I've got to fetch something from the villa, I won't be long."

As Stefan climbed into the cabin he caught a brief sight of his face in the wing mirror. "I am a murderer," he thought. "My father is being interrogated because of me… maybe even being tortured." He knew, at that moment, he would have to confess – he didn't have a choice.

"Got it!" said Otto on his return, putting a glass jar with a shiny red and black beetle in it on to Stefan's lap. "Don't drop this, whatever you do. It's for our friend Ziegler." He turned the ignition key and the truck growled into life.

"I've got something to tell you," said Stefan.

"Sorry?" called Otto. "You'll have to speak up."

"I have to tell you something very important," shouted Stefan. "About something I did yesterday…"

"What was that then?" said Otto, steering the truck onto the path that led to the zoo exit.

Suddenly two loud bangs on the cabin door beside Stefan made him jump…

"Careful!" called a voice. "Don't drop that beetle, lad!"

It was his father – he was okay… smiling… alive…

"How did it go with old Schultz?" called Otto, leaning across Stefan to get closer to Jan.

"It was nothing," said Stefan's father. "They're pretty sure they know what happened. They'd just taken delivery of a batch of grenades; one must have just rolled out when they were moving them. The poor guy was just unlucky – apparently it's not uncommon for those things to go off for no reason. He's not the first to die that way."

"So what did they want you for?"

"Schultz was worried that I'd mention something to Ziegler. He wants to hush the whole thing up – especially with Himmler coming soon. It was good to see the pompous old fool grovel!"

Stefan tried to appear casual and stared vacantly ahead is if he wasn't listening to the conversation – but he had never felt so relieved in his life... "I've got some work to do in my office," he said. "Are you still happy to stand in for me, Stef?"

"Of course," replied his son. "No problem!"

"Thanks. Your mother will take over your lookout duties while you're gone. Send my regards to Herr Beetle-man for me!"

Otto turned to Stefan as the truck approached the bridge that crossed the Vistula. "What were you going to tell me?"

"Sorry?"

"You were about to tell me about something you did yesterday..."

"Hercules," he replied without flinching. "I fed him all of his own muck. It's a present for Herr Himmler..." And as he described every detail of his pet's final meal, tears of laughter were streaming down Otto's face, and Stefan felt the pieces of his shattered world slowly merge back together once more.

SIXTY-THREE

Stefan started to feel nervous as the truck left the bridge; he hadn't really seen Warsaw since the Nazis had invaded, and he didn't know what sights awaited him. As he caught a glimpse of Traugutta Park, and the trees he used to climb with Marcus, he was surprised at how crowded the pavements were. Everyone seemed to be going about their business as usual, and apart from the occasional Nazi flag, the city seemed to be just as he remembered.

But things started to change as they drove on further. The German bombardment had turned so many buildings into rubble that entire blocks were propped up by huge wooden supports. They passed rows of boarded-up shops and, most distressingly for Stefan, the burnt-out shell of his favourite cinema. Ahead was the railway station where a huge swastika hung above the entrance.

But the real horrors were lurking round the next corner. As the truck slowed down, Stefan saw a sign hanging from a barrier that blocked the road: "Epidemic Quarantine Area – Only Authorised Traffic Permitted".

"What does that mean?" he asked.

"It means we're about to enter the ghetto," replied Otto. Stefan suddenly realised that the wall they'd been driving past for the last few minutes was actually the perimeter.

A German soldier approached them. Stefan could tell from his friendly demeanour that he clearly recognised Otto. "I see you have brought a new passenger with you today to stare at the Jews," he said leaning into the cabin. "Have fun!" Then he signalled to a colleague who raised the barrier to allow them through.

The first thing that Stefan noticed as they entered the ghetto was a solid mass of people standing on the pavement. "Where are they all going?" he asked.

"Nowhere," Otto replied. "They're just waiting."

"For what?"

"Food, Stef. They're waiting to be fed."

The queue was endless and barely moved. Everyone seemed be carrying a bag and at least one bowl or saucepan; some had even tied them together to wear around their necks on string. It was a bitter morning and many adults were clinging on to heavily wrapped babies.

"Why have they brought their children?" asked Stefan.

"What do you mean?"

"Wouldn't it have been better to leave them at home?"

"These people have no homes – they live in the corners of rooms," replied Otto. "They could be standing out here all morning – they really don't have very much choice."

The line seemed to snake into the distance forever. Driving past, the sea of coats merged into a blur of grey, speckled with the white of the armbands everybody wore.

"There," Stefan said eventually, "the end of the line."

At the feeding station long wooden tables spanned the street with huge vats of steaming liquid and canvas sacks of bread. "Each Jew is only allowed a bowl of soup and half a loaf of bread per day and maybe, if they're lucky, some potatoes," explained Otto.

"Are those Germans going to hand out the food?" asked Stefan as they passed a group of soldiers with dogs.

"Nazis don't serve Jews," replied Otto, "especially starving ones. They're only here to keep order."

Otto steered the truck past the scene and Stefan suddenly saw a small park where he and Marcus used to play as toddlers.

But no one was playing now; huddled beneath the broken frame where the swings once hung were clusters of small family groups, sharing out their meagre rations. Just beyond that were some market stalls. As the truck drove past, Stefan was reminded of the artists' markets that he and Marcus used to love browsing through together on Sunday afternoons with their parents. But the items on display here weren't the pictures and ornaments he was used to seeing. On sale were shoes, clothes, watches, shirts, books, plates and spoons.

"People are desperate," said Otto, sensing Stefan's confusion. "They'd sell practically anything to get money to buy a little extra food."

"But you said that they only get soup and bread. Where do they get any more from?"

"Smugglers," said Otto. "If it wasn't for the food that gets sneaked into the ghetto from the outside world there'd be even more deaths."

"Even more?!" said Stefan.

Otto nodded sadly. "Make no mistake, Stef, the Germans are creating a hell in here." And they continued on in silence towards the square where the Gestapo headquarters was.

"Good morning Mr Pigman!" said a guard who appeared to be waiting for them on the steps that led up to the entrance. "Round the back – usual place!"

"Thanks!" said Otto waving back.

"Are we going to the orphanage afterwards?" asked Stefan, hoping that he'd have a chance to see Shlomo again.

"Not this time," replied Otto, turning off the engine. "It's risky to go there too often. Any more than once a week would start to look suspicious."

"Well, well, well!" came a voice from outside, it was Ziegler holding the insect Stefan's father had loaned him last time. "Zabinski Junior has been sent to deliver my next beetle – how delightful!" Stefan was suddenly taken aback by Ziegler's effusive greeting. "I can't tell you how glad I am that you have come!" There was a look of manic excitement in his eyes and his face lit up, as if he'd just had a brilliant idea. Then he pulled opened the passenger door, took Stefan's arm and coaxed him out onto the street. "Take your time in filling your barrels today, Mr Pigman; it may be sometime before we return!" Then he placed the insect he was returning on the vacant seat and grabbed the new jar from Stefan's hands. Then, without a word of explanation, he led him away from the truck towards the main entrance of the building.

Otto was helpless as he watched Stefan glance over his shoulder in dismay and disappear round the corner.

SIXTY-FOUR

Ziegler led Stefan up the stairs without even looking at him, and steered him briskly along the dimly lit corridor. They passed a succession of identically dressed officers, some of whom acknowledged Ziegler with a rapid hail-Hitler salute, but no one seemed to question his presence. They ascended a wide sweeping staircase where a huge portrait of Hitler held Stefan's gaze with its piercing blue eyes. Daylight shone through a huge arched window at the top, which made this corridor much brighter than the one below. Ziegler released his grip and quickened his step, knowing the boy had no choice other than to follow.

"In here," ordered Ziegler and opened a heavy wooden door to reveal a pitch black windowless room. "Do not touch a thing," he warned, flicking a light switch. Then he quickly placed his new insect specimen on a desk and darted back into the corridor. Stefan slowly glanced around the room as the German's urgent footsteps raced along the marble floor outside. On the wall behind the desk was another picture of Hitler, accompanied by a series of small, framed charcoal sketches of beetles. There was a map of Warsaw, with the ghetto boundaries clearly marked in red above a sparsely populated bookcase. Stefan noticed a photo standing in the middle of the desk, in an ornate golden frame. It was of Ziegler, wearing normal everyday clothes, seated in front of two older people, probably his parents.

Stefan turned to face the picture of Hitler. This time the Fuehrer was wearing a light brown jacket with a black swastika on his left arm. "If only you were the one I killed last night," he whispered under his breath, "then the war would be over and Marcus could go home!" And as he glared at the portrait he became aware of his own reflection looking back at him in the glass.

"Come!" came Ziegler's voice from the doorway. "You are about to meet some very important people."

Stefan shadowed Ziegler along the corridor and stopped at a huge double-doorway that reminded him of the one in Zamenhof's school hall. Ziegler paused to straighten his jacket and adjust his hat before knocking, suddenly looking extremely anxious.

"Enter!" called a voice from inside.

Ziegler opened the door and Stefan instantly thought he was entering a palace. Gold trimmed chairs and sofas ringed the room, and a large colourful rug dominated the floor. At the far end two older men stooped over a massive desk, wearing light grey uniforms adorned with medals and ribbons. As they looked down at him, Stefan had to suppress a gasp as he noticed the face on the wall behind them – "not you again!" he thought to himself looking up at the gigantic familiar painting.

"Heil Hitler!" barked Ziegler raising his right arm aloft. The two men echoed the salute. "This is the boy I was telling you about." Stefan didn't know whether he was expected to say anything or stick his own arm up in the air like Ziegler did. So he decided to do nothing.

"*Obergruppenführer* Frank and *Obergruppenführer* Krüger, this is er..." then Ziegler faltered, suddenly realising that he didn't actually know Stefan's name.

"Stefan!" Stefan prompted.

"...Stefan Zabinski, the pianist I mentioned."

"Pianist?!" thought Stefan.

"I am grateful that you have agreed to spare some of your precious time to hear him..."

For a split second Stefan thought this was an elaborate joke and all three men would burst into laughter at any moment. But the stern looks on the men's faces showed that whatever it was that was going on was deadly serious.

"Very well," snapped one of the officers. "The piano is by that window."

"There's a piano in here as well?" thought Stefan. Ziegler guided Stefan towards the far end of the room. He sat on the stool and looked up at his audience, who loomed over him like a three-headed monster. "Play!" commanded a voice that could have come from any or all of their mouths.

As Stefan's fingers danced around the keyboard, he remembered the instructions his mother had given when his piano playing first became the villa's early warning system. "You're telling the world there's a Nazi nearby – make it as loud as you can!" With three Nazis literally breathing down his neck he decided to play louder than he ever had at the zoo.

"Bravo!" said one of the Germans.

"Impressive," added the second.

"A very strong player," completed the third. "You are authorised to sort out all the necessary arrangements for the performance, Herr Ziegler. Good."

Ziegler stepped backwards as if he'd suddenly been struck by lightning, stamped his foot with all the force he could muster and threw his arm up as high as he could. "Heil Hitler!" he yelled. Then he gripped Stefan's arm and deftly manoeuvred him out of the room. Whatever had just been agreed in that room definitely involved Stefan, he was sure of that much. But he had no idea what it was. Ziegler hurried the baffled boy down the stairs and towards the main entrance to the building with the broadest of smiles on his face. When they emerged into the daylight, Stefan was relieved to see Otto anxiously waiting at the bottom of the steps beside the truck.

"You will tell your master that the boy is to perform for

Reichsführer Himmler at the banquet. I will be contacting him within twenty-four hours with all the details. It is an enormous honour; I sincerely hope it is appreciated!" Then he turned and literally skipped back up the stone steps.

"What happened in there?" asked Otto.

"I... er... I... don't really know," was the best answer Stefan could give for the time being.

SIXTY-FIVE

"What were their names again?" Stefan's father slumped back into his office chair, struggling to take in the details of his son's incredible morning.

"Er… Frank and… er Cougar… I think," replied Stefan.

"Do you mean Krüger?"

"Yes, that's right – Krüger."

Jan shook his head in disbelief. "Friedrich-Wilhelm Krüger and Hans Frank are basically the Nazis who run this country now." Then he grabbed Stefan's hand. "Congratulations," he said in mock reverence. "I am so proud to have a son who mixes in such influential circles! Soon you will be taking high-tea with little-old Adolf!"

But Stefan couldn't share his father's joke. The sheer magnitude of what had been forced on him was only now sinking in and he was starting to feel sick. "Do I have to do this?" he asked nervously.

Jan dropped his smile and placed a hand on his son's shoulder. "I'm afraid so," he said. "These people don't take kindly to having their plans disrupted. They're used to getting their own way. There's really no choice."

"But what if I just refused to play? I'm the one who's playing the piano, not them…"

"I'm afraid that these men don't see things like us," said Jan. "They live in a very simple, uncomplicated world. They're a bit like toddlers – if they want to do something, they'll just do it. As long as it suits them, that's all that matters."

"So what would happen if I did refuse?"

"They would scream and shout and throw their toys about, just like a spoilt child," replied Stefan's father. "And when that child happens to be an all-powerful grown up Nazi leader, then their scream is going to be much louder and their toys a lot more dangerous!"

Stefan sighed. He felt like a pawn in somebody else's game of chess.

"What did you think of the ghetto?" asked his father. "You can see now what those poor people hiding in the zoo are escaping from."

Stefan nodded, but couldn't bring himself to talk about the dreadful sights he had witnessed. "Do you know you can still see the star from the bridge," he said, quickly changing the subject.

"What do you mean?"

"The Jewish star outside – you can still see its reflection as you cross the river. I saw it just before from the truck"

"I didn't know that the star was visible outside the zoo…"

"Well you can't actually see it's a star," said Stefan. "All you can see is the sun bouncing off the metal. Marcus pointed it out to me a long time ago. And it only lasts for a few minutes, when the sun's in just the right position, but it's really bright when it happens. Actually, today it was much brighter than ever …"

"Well I never," said Jan in genuine amazement, turning to walk towards the front door.

The sun had now moved on and the battered metallic star was shrouded in murky grey shadow. But Jan could see what Stefan had been talking about. "You don't know how happy this makes me," he said. "My heart has ached every time it has been attacked, as if the bullets were aimed at me. I would have done anything to stop them. But now I can see I was wrong."

"What do you mean?" asked Stefan.

"Look at it," he said, pointing up at the dented star, riddled with bullet holes. "They thought their guns would destroy it, but they've only made it stronger."

"How come?" asked Stefan, totally confused.

"I'm not surprised it now shines so brightly," he replied. "It used to be a perfectly smooth piece of metal. But now, thanks to its attackers, its twists and curves can reflect the sun's rays in every direction. They think they have killed it, but they've really just brought it to life!"

SIXTY-SIX

"I don't believe you!"

"Well it's true."

"When?"

"In a couple of days, I think."

"And Himmler will be there?"

"That's what they say…"

"That's crazy!"

"You're telling me!"

It was almost midnight. Marcus was playing cards with Stefan in the basement and his mother was upstairs with Antonina. They carried on in silence for a while and then, to Stefan's surprise, Marcus stood up and threw his cards onto the floor.

"What's the matter?"

"I want you to have something, Stef."

"What?"

"I've been hiding it ever since I came here."

"I don't know what you're talking about?"

Marcus went to the cupboard at the far side of room and knelt down to open the drawer at the bottom. He pulled it out completely and then slotted his arm through the gap it left.

"What are you doing?"

"My dad wanted me to give it to your father, but I kept it. I was scared. And the longer I had it the harder it was to give away. So I just hid it in here."

"I have no idea what… Oh my God – it's a gun!"

"Take it."

"Marcus! What the hell are you doing with that thing?"

"My dad got it when a Nazi was attacked by some radios. It's a long story…"

"What am I supposed to do with it?"

"Shoot Himmler!"

"What?"

"No one would suspect a kid."

"I can't, Marcus. You're being ridiculous. We should just give it to my father…" he said, backing away from his friend in shock.

"It's up to you," said Marcus throwing the gun on the mattress beside him. "But if you decide to use it, don't forget to turn the safety catch off."

SIXTY-SEVEN

Stefan hardly slept. Marcus had pleaded with him to take the gun and the huge relief on his face when he finally picked it up convinced him that it was the right decision. So now it was hidden in his room. But his mind was in a spin. Yesterday's events in the ghetto still disturbed him, and he just couldn't settle. He even neglected his look-out duties and spent most of the morning strolling around the grounds, and as Marcus and his mother were the only 'Jewish guests' he had no special deliveries to make. Eventually he ended up in the courtyard, sitting on the ground, leaning against the wall of Hercules' empty pen and flicking pebbles into Apollo's cage for his old rodent friend to chase.

"There you are, at last!" called Otto. "I've been looking for you everywhere. Have you seen my flashlight? I left it in the workshop."

"No, sorry." Stefan replied, startled.

"Okay, because I saw you rummaging about the other day and noticed you looking at it. I assumed you'd taken it for some reason. I desperately need it to check something on the truck."

"No, no… I just took some new wire to fix Apollo's cage door. He's gnawed through the old stuff again!"

"Fair enough," said Otto, walking out of the courtyard scratching his head. "But you will let me know if you happen to find it, won't you?"

"Of course!" Stefan replied calmly – but he could hardly breathe. "He probably knows I took it," Stefan whispered to

Apollo. Then he started to panic; it would only be a matter of time before Otto told his father, and then he would have to admit everything – the old sewers, the grenade, even blowing up that Nazi. There was only one thing he could do.

He had to act quickly. If he could get the flashlight back now, he could pretend he'd just found it. Yes – that'll work. As long as Otto gets it back, Stefan wouldn't have to explain anything. He remembered putting it on the floor of the sewer before climbing up the ladder beneath the old drain in Hercules' sty. It wouldn't take long to find it – a few minutes at most.

He dashed into the pen and leant over the drain that he and Marcus had used on the night of the attack.

"Stefan, can I have a word with you please?" It was his father calling him in from the house. Stefan froze. He knows! Otto must have gone straight in and told him. There was no time to get the flashlight now.

"Just a minute!" called Stefan.

"In my office, when you're ready," came the response.

Marcus has to get it – that's our only hope. It's risky, yes. But there's no one about, right now. It wouldn't take him long. Stefan rushed down to the basement room.

Marcus' mother opened the door.

"Can Marcus come up for a minute? I've got something really funny to show him."

"Are you sure it's safe?"

"Certain!" he replied. "But he's got to be quick or he'll miss it!"

"Ok," she agreed, making way for her son. "But be quick and be careful!"

As soon as they were in the hallway Stefan spat out the explanation. "Otto's asking questions – you've got to get the flashlight. I left it in the sewer," he said. "Right now! You'll be back so quickly that no one will even know you've gone. It's at the bottom of the ladder that leads up to the drain. Just leave it in Hercules' sty and I'll think up some excuse…"

Marcus knew, from the look of desperation in his friend's eyes, that there was no time to lose. He also knew that this was a very risky thing to do in daylight. But Stefan was in trouble so there was simply no choice...

"Okay," he said and dashed out to the courtyard.

"Stefan!" called his father. "How long are we going to have to wait?"

"I'm coming!" As soon as Stefan heard his father use the word "we" he was certain that Otto had told him, and was waiting in the office as well. He made his way across the hall as slowly as possible, desperately trying to concoct a convincing story that would explain why the flashlight ended up in the sty. All he had to do was stall them until Marcus had retrieved it.

"You took your time, young man," said his father as he finally entered. "We thought you were lost!"

Stefan gasped at the sight that awaited him. It was Ziegler, not Otto. And he could read the fury in his father's eyes; *'I thought you were meant to be looking out for Nazis – where was that alarm?'*

"There are a few things we need to discuss about the performance tomorrow night," said the German.

Stefan spotted an empty black car parked in the driveway, through the office window.

"You will be required to be there at six forty-five exactly. That is just before the VIPs arrive."

But at least Otto hasn't mentioned the flashlight yet – so that was okay.

"When I give the signal you will play, and then you will leave. All together you will be in the room no more than five minutes."

Stefan tried to make sense of what Ziegler was saying, but everything was a blur as a wave of relief rushed through his body at yet another close shave.

"At no point are you to speak. In fact, it would be best if you do not even look at the audience. Just focus on the piano – then play and leave..."

"*Juden! Juden!*" The harsh angry cries were coming from the courtyard. "Herr Ziegler! *Juden!*"

Chaos swept through the villa. Stefan was knocked aside as Ziegler shot out of the office like a bullet from a gun. Jan followed and both men bolted through the lounge and out of the door that led to the courtyard. Stefan arrived and looked on in horror at the turmoil outside. Marcus had been captured. Another Nazi officer was holding him by the collar with one hand and pressing a pistol into his face with the other. He must have come in that car with Ziegler…

"He came out from there!" he said, pointing towards the pig sty.

Ziegler went to inspect and quickly returned to the courtyard nodding purposefully. "The drains!" he barked. "These dirty Jews love them!" He leant down so that his mouth was right next to Marcus' ear and yelled. "You are a filthy Jewish sewer rat!"

"Shall I shoot him?" asked the officer.

Ziegler brought himself to his full height and folded his arms, clearly assessing the situation.

Don't fire! He is my friend! Let him go! Stefan knew these words would have to stay in his head. He looked across at his father. There was nothing he could do or say either. One word of protest and the whole rescue operation would unravel. The slightest suggestion that Marcus was known to either of them would be disastrous for everyone.

And clearly Marcus realised this as well. He was speaking in Yiddish, now, courageously distancing himself from the Zabinskis; risking his life to protect those who had protected him.

"Shut up!" yelled Ziegler.

Suddenly Antonina appeared in the courtyard. "What has happened?" she asked.

"They have found a Jew," said Stefan's father. "He must have swum across the Vistula!"

It was then that Stefan noticed how drenched Marcus looked.

248

He'd probably slipped into the water that flowed through the sewer. Maybe the flashlight had fallen in and Marcus had to take it from the stream? Either way, it was just as well he did; it would have been impossible to explain his appearance if he'd been wearing dry clean clothes... And the flashlight? Where was the flashlight?

"I will thank you not to kill him in front of my son!" said Antonina. "He has seen too much carnage already!"

"You are right, Mrs Zabinski," said Ziegler. "And besides, this Jew could be more useful alive. To my knowledge he is the first to have crossed the river. But I refuse to believe he swam all the way – it is much too far for a child. I suspect that he made most of the journey by boat." Then he turned to Marcus and slapped him hard across his face. "Am I right, Jewish rat?" Marcus nodded in confirmation. "I thought so! In which case, we need to find the Pole who was foolish enough to risk his life to save a Jew!"

"What will happen to him now?" asked Antonina.

"Oh, he will die eventually," answered Ziegler. "But after we have discovered who has helped him." Then he turned to the officer whose pistol was still pressed against Marcus's cheek. "We don't have time for this now. Take him to the farmhouse. I believe there is an old windmill there – it will make a perfect prison. This incident must remain hidden until *Reichsführer* Himmler has gone. Nothing must be allowed to put his visit in jeopardy!"

Stefan watched as his friend was dragged away. "I advise you to seal that drain," Ziegler said to Stefan's father as he followed behind. "It will stop any more stray Jews from invading your home."

SIXTY-EIGHT

The three Zabinskis were rooted to the ground. They'd witnessed the destruction of their zoo, and seen the city they loved pounded beyond recognition. But this was too much to bear – the disastrous consequences of Marcus' capture tore at their hearts.

Stefan's mother spoke first. "What can we possibly tell Lonia?"

"Precisely," said Jan turning to his son. "What *can* we tell her? Exactly what has happened here?" Gripped with fear Stefan couldn't lift his head to look at his father. "I am waiting for an answer." Stefan began to tremble. Unable to speak, he walked slowly to Hercules' pen and crouched down at the entrance. There, coated in the sewer's grime, was Otto's flashlight, just where Stefan had told his loyal friend to leave it.

"What's that?" asked his mother.

"I stole this from Otto's workshop," mumbled Stefan.

"Why?"

To prevent the weight of guilt from crushing him completely, Stefan spoke. And because there were no more lies to tell, he unburden himself of every last crumb of truth – from when he prised open the crate of grenades under the lion enclosure to the moment he blew up the guard.

"I am so sorry," he pleaded in tears as he concluded his confession. "And now Marcus will die and it is all my fault…"

Jan placed a hand on Stefan's shoulder "He is not dead yet," he said. Then he rushed back into the villa, leaving Antonina alone to console her son as best she could.

"You cannot take all the blame for this," she whispered, holding him closely. "You are a child. This terrible war has poisoned everything." Then she looked her son in the eye. "If there is any way your father can save Marcus, he will."

Stefan had stopped crying now, but there was a hollow pain in the pit of his stomach. "I must go to Lonia," said his mother. "She will need me now. I think it is best that you stay out of the way for a while..." With that she kissed her son on his forehead and returned to the villa.

Stefan picked up the flashlight that lay by his feet and instinctively wiped the murky lens clean with his sleeve. Almost without thinking he flicked the switch on its side and wasn't at all surprised to see there was no light at all.

As he made his way towards the staircase that led to his room, he saw Otto deep in conversation with his father through the open office door. He knew at once that they were desperately trying to work out a way of saving Marcus, and he was engulfed by a surge of guilt at being the cause of such turmoil. Saddened beyond words, he made his way upstairs and threw himself onto his bed, placing the flashlight on his bedside table.

✡ ✡ ✡

Stefan drifted in and out of sleep all day – not because he was tired, but it was the only way he could escape the pain. Much later he noticed the flashlight on the table by his head and sat up. At first he thought it was a reflection, but when he glanced out of his window he saw a densely clouded sky. It was hard to accept or believe, but there was actually a tiny speck of light shining behind the glass. Somehow the battery still had some power and the thin orange filament appeared to be doing all it could to stay alive. Stefan quickly stretched across to switch it off, anxious to save it for as long as possible.

SIXTY-NINE

The next morning Stefan was up long before his mother came in to rouse him. He was staring blankly out of the window when she entered.

"You'd better get dressed and start practicing," she said. "You've got a busy day ahead."

"Where has Otto gone?" he asked.

"I beg your pardon?"

"I saw him leave in the truck."

"You have been awake a long time, haven't you?" she said. "It was dark when he left."

"To go where?"

"To visit his parents in Glinki," she replied.

"Why?" Stefan said angrily. "I thought he was going to rescue Marcus."

"That's precisely the reason he went."

"So there is a plan!" Stefan exclaimed.

"There is. And your part is to play the piano for Himmler, tonight, like you've never played before!"

✡ ✡ ✡

Dawn was breaking as Otto approached the farm where he grew up. This was going to be the most testing day of his life and, as he drove through the orchard that had been the scene of many happy

252

childhood hours, he couldn't think of a more traumatic way of starting it.

Otto rarely returned to the family farm just outside Glinki, a tiny village on the Vistula south of Warsaw. His father was the fifth generation to own it and, as his only child, Otto was expected to become the sixth. It was a source of huge friction between father and son that he had refused to do so.

Although Otto's mother had died when he was ten, he only had the fondest of childhood memories. His world revolved around tending the herd. From an early age, he would get up at the crack of dawn to help round up the cows before school, and couldn't wait to join in with the regular chores of farm life when he returned home. As he entered his teens, he took on more responsibility for the welfare of the animals, and when he decided that he wanted to study veterinary science at university, his father greeted the news with enthusiasm. But when Otto announced that his interests in the natural world extended beyond cows, his father was devastated. Stubbornness is a family trait, and it soon became obvious that nothing would change Otto's ambitions. And the more they argued, the wider the rift between them grew. When Otto eventually left to work at the zoo, his father's heart was broken. Otto used to row down the Vistula from the zoo to visit the farm on his days off, arriving early enough to assist with the milking tasks. Although his father was glad to see him, he still harboured a deep sense of resentment and the scar of betrayal never healed. Even now, after more than ten years, it was still a source of tension, and the reason that Otto's boat was abandoned in the corner of a field – a daily reminder for his father of the son that had left.

Otto parked the truck in the farmyard and slowly made his way to the house.

Ever since his father remarried, he had come to dread re-entering his childhood home. It wasn't as if he disliked his stepmother, quite the opposite in fact. But the changes she had made unsettled him immensely. On the surface, she had merely dragged the place into the twentieth century (there was now electricity in every room) but the process had involved erasing all traces of his mother. He often pondered how different things would have been if she was still alive. If she'd been around the relationship between Franciszka and Otto's father would never have grown to be so frosty. She would have been welcomed into the heart of the family instead of seen as the person who finally stole Otto away from the farm. And, of course, his mother would have been overjoyed at the news of the Jewish baby they had adopted as their own – something that even now he hadn't told his father about.

It was only after his mother's death that Otto discovered that she was in fact Jewish and had been disowned by her family for marrying a non-Jew. A neighbouring farmer had casually mentioned it to him in passing, assuming that he'd already known. When Otto brought it up with his father it was dismissed as a historical irrelevance. "It's barely worth even thinking about," his father said. "Your mother didn't worry about such things." But as Otto grew up, he realised what a huge sacrifice she had made and regretted never being able to have spoken with her about it.

As Otto entered the house, he was determined to concentrate on why he was there – now was not the time to revisit the past.

"I have something important to ask you, father," he said once they had exchanged pleasantries. "We have a crisis at the zoo. The Nazis have..."

"Stop right there!" interjected his father. "I don't want to hear mention of the Germans or the war in this house."

Otto had expected this. Although Hitler had torn much of Europe to shreds, the devastation had bypassed places like Glinki. Rumours of what was happening in Warsaw occasionally floated down the Vistula, but nobody ever spoke about it; this infuriated Otto. "They are murdering Jews for fun up there!" he cried. "Every day they bury more bodies. For all I know they could be killing my grandparents as we speak!" His father did not reply. "Look – at this very moment a Jewish boy, who is as dear to me as a son, is in huge danger. For all I know they might have murdered him already. What's certain is that he will be dead within days."

"That has nothing to do with me…"

"But it has everything to do with me, father!" Otto shouted. "I will never be able to live with myself if I don't at least try to save him…"

"You are even crazier than I thought," said his father. "From what I hear the Germans kill anyone who helps Jews…"

"Then thank your lucky stars that my mother is no longer alive – otherwise they would be coming for you as well!"

Otto was surprised at how angry he'd become and was genuinely shocked at what he'd just said. But there was no going back and he stood in front of his father resolute and defiant.

Gita, Otto's stepmother, came into the room and laid a comforting hand on her husband's shoulder. She had clearly overheard their exchange. The three of them stood in silence for a while but eventually, to his great relief, Otto saw his father relent. "What do you want me to do?" he asked.

A few minutes later Otto's father was standing at the front door watching his son climb back into the truck. "We'll patch up your boat and carry it to the river before dark," he called out. "Good luck, son, and stay safe!"

SEVENTY

Otto's work was far from over.

"Good morning Mr Pigman!" called a voice as he approached the roadblock. "I see you're on your own today."

Otto was used to seeing the deprivation of the ghetto, but he didn't allow that to harden his heart. He was haunted by the sight of bone-thin children slouched against walls, but he was a witness. Most Poles had closed their minds to the suffering, but when the world finally woke up from this nightmare he would speak on behalf of those voices that had been silenced forever.

He found a suitably sheltered place to park and waited furtively to put the next part of the plan into action. It didn't take long for a wagon to appear. He quickly climbed down from the truck and approached the frail figure pushing it. "May I help you, sir?" he mumbled. When the man turned round Otto was surprised at how old he was. "I have a truck with me – it will make your job easier."

The wagon was covered with a thick black sheet, but Otto could see that there were already at least six bodies underneath.

"Who are you?" asked the man suspiciously.

"I am a Pole who wants to help."

"How did you get in?"

"I have a permit to work here," explained Otto. "I collect scraps of food for a pig farm."

"Ah! The zoo!" exclaimed the man. Otto was startled "Where 'Tenenbaum's runaways' go!"

"Yes… er… how did you know?"

"This is the ghetto, my friend. Everyone knows everything."

"Do you know Mr Tenenbaum?"

"We met before the war," replied the man. "He is a good man."

"Indeed," said Otto, staggered at such a coincidence. "Come, let me help you." Otto gripped the handles of the wagon and wheeled it round to the back of the truck. But he froze when he started to peel back the sheet.

"Believe me, my friend, these are the lucky ones," said the old man resting a hand on Otto's shoulder. "Their suffering in this world is over." Otto thought about Kasia's lifeless body on the floor of her enclosure. "To me, they are asleep," he continued. "I see smiles on their faces where before there was pain. What have they got to worry about now? Here, dry your eyes," he handed Otto a handkerchief. "It is good that you cry – it shows you have feelings. I promise you, I am yet to see a German tear being shed over the death of a Jew."

Slowly, they lifted the bodies onto the back of the truck – most were children. After covering them again with the sheet, Otto pushed the empty barrels to one side, to make space for the wagon. Then he opened the passenger door to let the old man in.

"I see you have gone up in the world, Abram," called a man from the road as Otto steered the truck around him. "Maybe soon you'll have a fleet of vehicles, and we can start up a business!"

Otto parked the truck by the main entrance to the cemetery. "We'll have to make two trips," said the man, "any more than three bodies and my wheels will get stuck in the mud."

"I'll stay by the truck, if it's alright with you," Otto said, after they had laid the first three bodies on the wagon.

"As you wish," he replied taking hold of the wooden handles. "I will be back in a while."

Otto waited until the man had disappeared from view and pulled back the sheet to look at the remaining bodies. There were three children – two boys and a girl. To his relief one, of the boys was exactly the right size. Checking that he was not being watched he gently lifted the chosen body into one of the barrels and quickly replaced the lid.

When the old man returned Otto was dreading having to explain why there was a body missing, but to his relief he appeared not to notice that anything was wrong, and they loaded the wagon again.

"We have met before," said the old man.

Otto didn't know how to respond. "Er… I don't think so…"

"My name is Abram Berkowicz – we danced in the street together a long time ago, outside Tenenbaum's house. I was the one with the cake…"

"Of course!" Otto exclaimed. "I remember… The man in the park that the boys rescued!"

"Precisely! And how are my heroes these days?"

Otto couldn't believe that a man he once danced with was asking about the boys for whom the entire day's plans had been devised. "They're fine," he replied, knowing it was impossible to give anything like a full answer.

"I am glad to hear it! I often think about them and their bravery!"

Then the two men shook hands. Neither knew whether to merely say goodbye or look forward to the next time they would met; anything that involved looking into the future was difficult to contemplate. So they nodded to each other in courteous silence.

SEVENTY-ONE

Stefan spent most of the time nervously practising and eavesdropping on the conversations taking place in the hall outside. If his father's daring plan was to have any chance of succeeding, then everyone needed to be totally sure about their own role in it. And ever since he'd learnt that he was going to have to keep playing for much longer than Ziegler wanted, the knot in his stomach grew tighter and tighter.

"How long for?" Stefan had asked.

"As long as it takes!" answered his father.

When it was time to get ready Stefan hardly recognised the person looking back at him in his bedroom mirror. "They've made me look like Hitler," he said to himself, feeling the grease that flattened down his hair. He glanced out of his window at the steady flow of German staff cars descending on the old farmhouse, their headlights glowing progressively brighter in the fading light. Turning away, he picked up Otto's flashlight and was shocked by the strength of its beam. Then he turned towards his wardrobe, slowly removed the drawer and shone the light on the pistol he had hidden there. "What if the plan doesn't work?" he thought. "If everything goes wrong we'll all get arrested and they'll murder Marcus for sure." He picked up the gun and located the safety catch.

"Stefan!" called a voice from downstairs. "It's time to leave."

He quickly slipped the weapon inside a sock and straightened the leg of his trousers over the handle. "If things go wrong, then Himmler will die. It's what Marcus wanted."

As he came downstairs his father was giving out final instructions. Otto was there, engulfed in a huge baggy coat. Next to him stood Feliks Cywinski with three other keepers. And beside his mother, in the doorway that led down to the basement, stood Lonia. It was the first time Stefan had seen her since Marcus' arrest and he instinctively looked away in guilt, but she stepped forward and held him in her arms. "Don't blame yourself," she said. "You weren't the one who took him away. Marcus wouldn't hold you responsible. Your friendship has kept him going through these dark times – you are his star." Then she kissed him on his forehead. "Urgh!" she exclaimed in sham-disgust, wiping her lips with the back of her hand. "Who covered your lovely curls in engine oil?"

"Come on maestro," called Stefan's father. "Your audience awaits!"

Antonina added her kiss to Lonia's. They were both heavily wrapped up against the cold of the night and Marcus' mother was carrying a suitcase.

As Stefan climbed into the truck, Feliks and the keepers drove away from the villa in a jeep.

"Right," said Otto turning the ignition key. "Let's give those Nazis a night they'll never forget!"

SEVENTY-TWO

The old farmhouse courtyard was lined by a meticulously neat row of vehicles, and there were clusters of men wearing uniforms, heavily adorned with medals, sharing jokes and smoking cigars.

"Every important Nazi in Warsaw must be here tonight," said Jan. "Security is going to be very tight."

"The drain cover must be under one of those cars," added Otto. "It'll take some time to locate."

"Halt! State your purpose!"

"We have brought the boy who will be playing the piano tonight," replied Jan. "Herr Ziegler has arranged for him to perform at the banquet tonight."

"Who is Ziegler?"

"He is stationed in Warsaw..."

"Lies!" snapped the officer. "Tonight's entertainers are currently preparing themselves in that building over there." He pointed at the disused windmill beyond the main building. Then he barked an order at a nearby group of soldiers: "Search this vehicle, now!"

Jan's heart sank – his plan seemed to be unravelling before it had even started. Maybe Stefan's performance had been cancelled at the last minute? And who were these other entertainers? If they are in the windmill, where is Marcus? And what will happen if they find the body in the back of the truck?

"It is okay, officer. I will deal with this." It was Ziegler; Jan had never been so relieved to see a Nazi. "These are authorised visitors." Then the two officers embarked on a heated exchange as the sound of the back of the truck being yanked open echoed through the cabin.

"Herr Ziegler," called Jan. "Stefan is desperate to use the bathroom. I think the nerves are starting to get to him!" Then with all the urgent desperation he could muster he added, "I really must insist!"

Ziegler briskly turned away from the officer he'd been arguing with and bellowed for the men to get down from the back of the truck. "You and the boy get out and wait by the main entrance," he ordered, opening the passenger door. "Driver, park as far away from the building as possible. And stay in the vehicle at all times!"

"Herr Ziegler, a quick word, if you please" said Otto leaning towards him conspiratorially.

"What is it, man? I am in a hurry..."

"Let me ask you, have you killed that dirty Jew yet?"

"I beg your pardon?"

"The vermin you caught at the zoo, is he dead yet?"

Ziegler looked at Otto with an expression of surprise on his face, as if to say 'I didn't know you were one of us!' "No, not yet – he is locked in that windmill. We still need to question him. But don't worry; one way or another he'll be dead by tomorrow."

"I'm glad to hear it," he replied to the Nazi with a wink.

It was freezing in the old sewers and even colder where it opened out onto the Vistula.

"What if he doesn't come?" asked Lonia.

"He will," Antonina said, calming her friend.

"What makes you so sure?"

"Because I have no other choice."

✿✿✿

Otto parked beside the old windmill, under the branches of an overhanging tree. Inside he could see a group of young women, probably dancers, helping each other with their costumes and make up. After a while they emerged into the night and dashed across the courtyard towards the farmhouse, struggling to keep their balance on their thin, high heels. They must be frozen, he thought.

✡✡✡

Stefan and his father followed Ziegler into the farmhouse through the throng of guests in the entrance hall and up a grand wooden staircase that led to the banqueting suite. Inside lines of tables were laid out in a huge "E" shape and the wall was adorned with two full length red Nazi flags, between which hung a gigantic portrait of Hitler.

"The bathroom facilities are in here," said Ziegler pushing open a door. "Remain inside until you are called."

"Where's the piano?" asked Stefan.

"It is over there," replied Ziegler, pointing in the general direction of Hitler's head. "All the entertainment will take place in front of the guest of honour – it is crucial that *Reichsführer* Himmler has the perfect view."

✡✡✡

Otto completed his scan of the area and was ready to make his move. He'd located the drain cover – it was next to a Mercedes, but still quite accessible. All of the guests had now gone into the farmhouse, leaving a dozen or so guards on patrol outside who soon retreated to the guardhouse at the far side of the courtyard, lighting up cigarettes. Convinced it was safe, Otto darted to the back of the truck, felt in the dark for the lock and reached inside for the barrel that contained the grisly cargo. Taking a deep breath, he removed the lid and clasped the dead boy's body, resting it over his shoulder, the way he held his own baby. Then he ghosted out of the shadows and dashed into the windmill, stepping over the discarded day-clothes of the dancers. Ahead was a flimsy wooden staircase that led to a trap door – this had to be it, he thought.

"Marcus, are you in there?" he whispered as loudly as he thought was safe. There was no reply. "Marcus! It's me Otto – are you there?" Again there was no response, but he was sure he could hear a faint knocking sound, like stone being tapped against wood. "Marcus?" There it was again, although this time much stronger and quicker. Otto pushed at the door – it was locked. Then, carefully resting the body on the steps, he pushed his shoulder hard into the wood. It started to weaken and with a sharp crack it snapped off its hinges. Sliding the door to one side, Otto retrieved the body and climbed up into the darkness. A muffled sound came from the far side of the room and he raced into the shadows – there was Marcus, bound and gagged.

"You came!" Marcus croaked as the cloth was removed from his mouth.

"Of course!" replied Otto.

"Who's that?" he asked, pointing to body.

"I'll explain later. But we've got to move fast now. Just get your clothes off as quickly as you can...."

SEVENTY-THREE

Everyone who visited the washroom where Stefan and his father were waiting totally ignored them. "They probably think we work here!" said Jan as another Nazi washed his hands and checked his uniform in the mirror.

Outside, in the hall, the excitement was mounting. Himmler's name was being chanted to the thud of feet stamping on the floor.

"Nervous?" asked Jan.

"A little," replied his son. "But once I start playing I'll be fine."

"That's not what we're going to tell Ziegler. I want him to think that you're nervous as hell and need me out there with you for moral support."

"Okay," replied Stefan.

Suddenly a huge cheer erupted in the hall. "That's him," whispered Jan gently opening the door. "The little guy with the glasses."

"He's got a moustache just like Hitler," said Stefan. "Is it part of their uniform?"

"You'll be able to ask him yourself soon enough!" joked his father.

Himmler floated impassively past his admirers, as the room shook with the fervour of the faithful, eventually reaching his seat at the centre of the top table. It was much grander than everyone else's and looked more like a throne.

Stefan was mesmerised; he suddenly realised just how

dangerous and powerful these people were. When the noise abated, everyone sat down except Himmler. Placing his black military cap on the table, he slowly surveyed his audience and began to speak. Although Stefan's knowledge of German was excellent for a Polish child of his age, he needed his father to translate everything that was being said. And the more he listened the more terrified he became…

"*…we are on a mission to create a future fit for our Aryan children to grow up in…*"

"'Aryan'?" whispered Stefan.

"In this case it means 'non-Jew,'" replied his father.

"*…And our main obstacle is The Jew. The Jew is a cancer on the face of the earth – it needs to be removed to prevent its disease from spreading! And I urge you not listen to those who speak up against us. I assure you, they will be the first to thank us when the Jewish problem has been solved once and for all! Heil Hitler!*"

✡ ✡ ✡

"Who was he?" asked Marcus.

"I don't know," replied Otto helping him put on the dead boy's jacket.

"Must I wear the arm band with the blue star as well?"

"Probably not," said Otto. "Just put it in your pocket."

"Now what?"

"We've got to dress him up in your clothes."

"Why?"

"You'll see soon enough…"

✡ ✡ ✡

"It is time," said Ziegler, popping his head round the door.

"We have a problem," said Jan.

"Not now – the boy must come out. Everyone is waiting."

"That is the problem," Jan persisted. "I think his nerves have finally got the better of him."

Ziegler stepped into the room to see Stefan hunched over the basin appearing to be sick. "I am sure he will be fine once he's out there…"

"Don't want to…" stuttered Stefan.

"You're going to have to give it a go, Stef," said his father.

"Can't…" snapped his son.

"Look, what if I came out with you. Would that help?"

"Er, maybe…" said Stefan.

"Fine, that's settled," said Ziegler, who was clearly far more nervous than Stefan was pretending to be. "But now. Hurry!"

Jan coaxed his son towards the door and out into the hushed hall. Ziegler led them towards the performance area and Stefan realised just how close to Himmler he was going to be. He suddenly became aware of the cold metal of the pistol in his sock. "Well at least I won't miss if I have to shoot him," he thought.

"Remember, five minutes, no more," whispered Ziegler to Jan. "Then the boy goes."

Stefan sat on the piano stool. "Don't play yet," whispered his father as Ziegler stepped away from the stage. "Honoured guests!" he bellowed. "It gives me great pleasure to present my son, who has the privilege of entertaining you this evening." Instantly Ziegler's face was contorted in horror. "In honour of our esteemed guest, *Reichsführer* Himmler, he has chosen something from the magnificent cultural contribution that your nation has given the world!" Gradually, throughout the hall, heads began to nod and harsh expressions started to melt. Even Ziegler seemed to be slightly less alarmed. "He sincerely hopes that you enjoy his rendition of Beethoven's *Moonlight Sonata*." The soft gasps of approval and gentle ripple of applause showed that the audience had been won round. There was even a smile on Himmler's face.

As Stefan's hands hovered above the keyboard he felt his back stiffen and a surge of confidence sweep through his body. This was going to be the performance of his life – but he was not going to play for the crowd, now perched in silence on the edges of their seats. This was for Marcus, who he prayed was outside by now, and poor Hercules, who was looking up at him from a huge platter in the centre of the room.

So he began, and the room was entranced from the very first note.

✡✡✡

Otto and Marcus scrambled out of the old windmill towards the truck.

"Why did we need to swap clothes?"

"The Nazis need to think that he is you," said Otto pulling Marcus into the shadows.

"But they'll know it's not me just by looking!"

"Don't worry," said Otto. "That's being dealt with…"

Marcus was confused. "And why did you replace the trap door so carefully? The boy is dead. He's not going to try to escape, is he?"

"If the Germans find out it was forced open, they'd immediately get suspicious. Getting you out is just one part of the plan – covering our tracks is the other!"

"Listen," said Marcus. "I can hear the piano. It's Stef, isn't it? He's playing for Himmler!"

"He's playing for you!" corrected Otto, which only confused Marcus further.

✡✡✡

Jan Zabinski looked out at the audience and thought about the customers in The Café Sztuka. Just like them, these Nazis were lost in the music. He was suddenly overwhelmed by how beauty could touch even the hardest of hearts.

But such thoughts were a million miles away from Stefan. As the frenetic final section of the sonata approached, he was thinking of the time he once played this piece for Marcus with Apollo on the piano lid. The faster Stefan played the more desperately the rat spun round, trying to keep up with the music. Eventually he fell off the piano and onto the floor; Marcus laughed so much that he cried.

✡✡✡

"Shall I just get into one of those barrels in the back of the truck, then?" asked Marcus.

"It's not as easy as that," Otto replied. "Remember what I said about covering our tracks?" Then he unbuttoned his heavy coat to reveal the stolen German uniform he'd been wearing underneath.

"What are you wearing that for?" asked Marcus.

"It's all part of the plan," said Otto, reaching under the driver's seat and pulling out a long metal tube. Marcus recognised its shape immediately – he last saw one of those in Stefan's hands on their previous visit to the old farmhouse.

"Your job is to find that drain cover and slip into the sewer unnoticed."

"But I can't even see it," said Marcus. "There are so many cars over there."

"See that van with the ripped canvas canopy?"

"Yes."

"Count three vehicles along from its right. There's an open-top Mercedes… huge thing. See it?"

"Yes."

"Well the drain is just in front of that. And don't forget to replace the cover once you're through…"

"Covering my tracks?"

"Precisely! And when you're down there, go right to the end of the tunnel," said Otto. "Don't stop at the zoo – go straight to the river."

"If you say so…" Marcus replied.

"I do!"

Stefan's playing filled the night air. Even the guards had drifted towards the farmhouse to listen more closely. "It's time to make a run for it," said Otto.

"Not yet," said Marcus.

"Why?"

"Do you know this piece?" he asked.

"Er… yes… why…?"

"There's a really brilliant fast bit coming up soon – that'll be the best time to go!"

SEVENTY-FOUR

As Stefan's fingers raced over the keys, the audience gasped at the speed of his playing. He could see Himmler's inane grin out of the corner of his eye.

I know that you're out there, Marcus. Get ready to ride on my notes...

Marcus set himself ready to charge at the drain as the guards gathered beneath the open window, transfixed at the marvellous music floating out into the cold night air.

I can hear you, my friend, I can hear you...

His fingers were a blur now; he'd never played it faster...

Fly, Marcus fly! As fast as the wind...

Like a coiled spring, Marcus was ready to pounce...

I'm ready to go... nearly there...

And still he played faster – the power kept building...

This is the place where it happened, remember?

Marcus took one long last deep breath... put his head down, ready to charge...

yes – when Apollo spun out of control!

NOW, MARCUS, RUN!

I'M FLYING, STEF – I'M FLYING!

Otto knew that as long as he lived, he would never forget the sight of Marcus charging at the drain and disappearing into the ground, or the huge sense of relief he felt as he saw the cover slide back into place. He was safe...

…but the job was only half done. Otto had to make it safe for everyone else. Clutching the grenade in his hand he scurried back to the windmill. It's practically made of wood, he thought; it'll be one massive bonfire. Then, pulling out the detonation wire, he hurled the explosive into the windmill and charged towards the guards.

"Help! Attack! Come quickly" he screamed in his broadest German accent, tripping and stumbling. "A car stopped – a man ran out – something has been thrown into the compound from the road beyond the…"

Then thunder struck! The ground shuddered! The force of the blast blew Otto clean off his feet as the other guards ran past him in panic to where he'd been pointing. Then, right on cue, Feliks Cywinski, who had been waiting in place for this moment all evening, revved up the engine of his decoy jeep as loudly as possible and sped off into the night, easily outrunning the volley of bullets being fired at him in vain by the guards.

By the time Otto had staggered to his feet and retreated back to his truck to hide, the old windmill was a crackling ball of flames. His work had been done – when they recover the body it'll be unrecognisable. Every track had now been covered…

Soon a crowd of people were rushing out of the farmhouse to see what had happened. To Otto's delight most of them were drawn to where the guards had been firing – the final confirmation that the plan had worked.

"Are you alright, old friend?" Otto turned to see Jan and Stefan peering through the door of the truck behind him. "Are you hurt? Did they get you?"

"I'm fine," said Otto frantically buttoning up his coat to hide his disguise. "I was lucky." Then with a wink and a smile he lifted all the weight of the world from Stefan's shoulders. "But I can assure you, it was quite an escape!"

As Stefan climbed into the truck he saw Himmler being bundled into a car and whisked away from the compound, presumably in case there was a second attack. As the windmill continued to burn behind them, he reached down into his sock and quickly removed the gun. Then, making sure that neither Otto nor his father were watching, he held it out of the open window and dropped it onto the stony courtyard floor.

✡ ✡ ✡

"I think he is coming," said Antonina. "I can hear footsteps."

Lonia moved forward. She too could hear running, but it was too dark to see...

"Is that him?" came a gruff voice from the boat in the river behind them.

"I think so," said Antonina.

"It is! It is!" cried Lonia. "They have saved him. Thank God!"

As Marcus melted into his mother's arms Antonina handed the suitcase to Otto's father. "Hurry," she said. "The Germans will be all over the zoo soon. They're bound to want to search the villa – I've got to be there when they come."

Lonia hugged her friend. "How can I ever thank you?"

"By staying alive, that's how!" she replied.

"Can you give this to Stefan for me?" Marcus handed his friend's mother what appeared to be a piece of white rag – it was a torn half of the dead boy's Star of David armband that he'd put in his pocket earlier. "Tell him I will always keep the other half."

Part Seven

November 2011

SEVENTY-FIVE

The Warsaw Zoo – November 2011

"Please put that phone away, Annie."

"But I can't understand a word of it. Why don't they do it in English?"

"Shush."

"...and it is a pleasure to be able to pay tribute to the memory of Jan Zabinski, who was the director of the Warsaw Zoo before, during and after the war, and his wife Antonina. It is impossible to say exactly how many Jews they helped to save, but some estimates put the number at around 300, many of whom were sheltered in the villa behind me. I would like to thank everyone who enabled us to renovate the building, which was severely damaged towards the end of the war, making it possible for us to house this permanent memorial that tells the story of their extraordinary courage. I am particularly pleased that members of the Zabinski family are here with us today, and we are honoured that some of those who were helped by them are here as well. Thank you for listening, and may I now invite you all to follow me into the villa as the very first visitors to this exhibition."

Polite applause rippled over the small gathering of people.

"Can we go now?"

"Hold on a minute, I think I can see him..."

The woman edged her way through the crowd towards the handful of smartly dressed guests that had been standing behind the person who was making the speech. She was surprised at how nervous she felt as she approached the elderly man at the back.

"Excuse me… hello…" she mumbled. This was so awkward – why hadn't she planned what she was going to say? "Er… are you Stefan?"

The old man smiled and nodded. "Yes, I am Stefan" he responded. "I am sorry, my English is very bad…"

"I am Marcus' daughter," she said pointing vigorously at herself. "Margaret." She held out her hand, embarrassed at how much it was shaking.

"Marcus' daughter? You?" replied the man.

"Yes." She suddenly felt so inadequate. She had dreamt about this moment for so long and now she didn't have the words to express herself. How could she tell him how important he was, how her father had always spoken about him and that, although they had never met, he had been her hero since she was a child? If only she'd written what she wanted to say and had it translated into Polish – at least she wouldn't have ended up, like this, standing here blubbing like a fool.

Then she was engulfed in an embrace. At first she thought the poor man was merely taking pity on this pathetic English woman, but then she realised that he was crying as well, so she held him too. Time stopped – she had no idea how long they were holding each other, but in a way it felt like seventy years.

When they withdrew Margaret realised that a small crowd had gathered around them, confused and concerned.

"*Marcus' córka!*" Stefan announced. "The daughter of my Marcus!" he repeated in English. Soon Margaret was engulfed in an octopus of hugs.

"Come," she said holding out her hand. Stefan took it and allowed himself to be led towards a sheepish eighteen year old girl… "Annie, my daughter, Marcus' granddaughter."

Stefan shook Annie's hand "*Panią poznać*," he said. "Nice to meet you!" came a translation from an excited bystander.

"Nice to meet you too," Annie replied.

Margaret was still holding Stefan's hand, and gave it a gentle tug. As they walked along the path, shadowed by a handful of followers, she struggled to stop her tears returning. This was so unreal – she could hardly feel the ground, it was like floating on air. Then she stopped – they had reached the lion house. She let go of Stefan's hand and withdrew to join the small crowd of onlookers. Annie stepped forward and greeted her with a hug.

Stefan stood alone, unable to move, waiting for the man who was looking up at the lions to turn around. He had long since given up hope that this moment would ever arrive. So much had happened; so much time had been lost. Over the years he had come to see their shattered lives as two tiny leaves amongst millions, wrenched from their branch and scattered by the winds of war. He had learnt to be content with his memories. The fact that the end to a lifetime of longing was now only a few steps away was almost too much to bear.

The other man was no longer looking up at the lions. He slowly released his grip on the rails in front of him and turned.

When there is too much to say, nothing needs to be said.

Stefan pulled a thin silver box from inside his jacket and flipped it open. Marcus unclenched his fist and held his palm out flat. And finally their star was complete again.

FROM THE AUTHOR

Writers of historical fiction lay their creations as gently as possible onto the truth, desperately trying to honour the facts while they play with them. I have strived to create an authentic account of life in Warsaw at the time. Most of the events you have just read about actually happened: the bombardment of Warsaw that ignited World War II, the creation of the Jewish Ghetto, the rescue operation at the zoo, the establishment of a pig farm and even the 1939 football match between Poland and Hungary. Most of the characters are real, including: Jan and Antonina Zabinski, Simon and Lonia Tenenbaum, Lutz Heck, Janusz Korczak and Ziegler, the German soldier. I have tried to depict them as accurately as possible, but they inevitably do and say some things in this book that they didn't in real life.

It is estimated that the Zabinskis sheltered about 300 Jews in the basement of their villa and the empty cages of their zoo. The operation was code-named "The House under a Crazy Star" – which was the inspiration for the idea of inventing the Star of David on the outside wall of the villa (the image of a battered bullet-peppered metal star reflecting the sunlight ever stronger has stayed with me from the moment I first read that phrase). Although the characters of Marcus and Stefan are also my own creation, they symbolise the many real examples of friendship that spanned the Jewish and non-Jewish communities of Warsaw.

It is true that at the time, the vast majority of people didn't endanger themselves like the Zabinskis by acting to save Jewish lives, but it has always been the case that dictators can only succeed when the silent majority are too afraid to protest. Before we pass judgement on those that looked the other way we need to consider what we would have done in such circumstances. I have asked myself this question many times and I honestly doubt that I would have had Jan and Antonina's courage. They, alongside over 6000 other fellow Poles, have been honoured by Yad Vashem (the Holocaust Martyrs' and Heroes' Remembrance Authority in Jerusalem) as "Righteous Among the Nations" – and it is certain that many more anonymous heroes performed deeds that history has never recorded. This book has been written in their honour as well.

Writers of fiction travel singlehandedly, spending countless hours with their thoughts searching for new worlds to put into words. But authors of historical fiction are never alone. We tell the stories of others; often those who no longer have a voice. I am privileged to have met many who survived the terrible days depicted in this book, as well as those whose valour and self-sacrifice ensured that the evil of Nazism was defeated – specifically Margaret Kaldor and Major Ellis Koder, whose dignity, humility and pure zest for life humbles all who know them.

THANKS
&
ACKNOWLEDGEMENTS

I wish to thank the many people whose help has been so invaluable. Ewa Zbonikowska, Andrzej Kruszewicz and Agata Borucka at the Warsaw Zoo, the custodians of the Zabinskis' memory, for their expertise and vision. To Ryszard Burek and the other staff at the Jewish Historical Institute in Warsaw and Helise Lieberman from the Taube Foundation, for their generosity and guidance. Rabbi Shoshana Gelfand and Amy Braier at the Pears Foundation, and Louise Heilbron for their encouragement and advice. Agnieszka Witkowska at the Korczakianum Centre in Warsaw, Alicja Szulc and Piotr Kowalik at the Museum of the History of Jews in Poland and Rabbi Mati Pawlak for their knowledge and inspiration. To Jadwiga Weralska for her support and friendship. Thanks to Alice Williams and Laura West at David Highams and Leila and Ali Dewji at Acorn for their textual insight and professional belief. Thanks as well to the lovely Benji Lanyado for his perfectionism, Monika Chandler for her empathy, Charles Barry for his probing questions and the phenomenal Kate Goldberg for her insight, enthusiasm and shared love of bagels. Also to the many friends who have had to tolerate my obsession with this story, especially Simon Gallant and Andrew Cohen, the world's best sounding boards and to Jens Hukelmann for capitalising my German nouns! Thanks, as well, to Natalia and Sebastian Dąbrowska for helping to capture those Warsaw moments.

And finally, most importantly, to Deborah, Emily, Sam and Jessica who have had to live with this story for as long as I have (according to the file date on my computer, over eight years), thank you.